KINGPIN

A COURT UNIVERSITY NOVEL

EDEN O'NEILL

KINGPIN: Court University Book 2

Copyright © 2020 by Eden O'Neill

This book is a work of fiction and any resemblance to any person, living or dead, any place, events or occurrences, is purely coincidental and not intended by the author.

Cover Art: RBA Designs
Editing: Straight on till Morningside

Table of Contents

Chapter One

Billie

The elegant writing blurred beneath my fingertips, two names.

"You are cordially invited to…"

My teeth gnashed together reading over the calligraphy. All I could do not to shred the wedding invitation in my hands. He'd done it. My dad, a once respected man in our law-abiding community, had finally done it. He was getting married.

And he was doing it with a woman half his age.

Clarise could very well be my sister at her age, and here Dad was embarrassing himself, embarrassing me.

I slammed the mailbox closed, wanting to get out of the slush and ice of the Midwest. I'd just hopped outside to put the trash out, my legs beading in goosebump pimples as I hadn't even thought to put a coat on. My boots soaked, I stepped delicately over the salted walk, then back into my new house. I'd barely been here three days, and there were still boxes stacked around.

I warmed myself, tossing that invite on the kitchen counter before kicking off my snow boots. The weather had been gratefully clear outside when I moved in, but it was still cold enough where the snow wouldn't be melting anytime soon. At least my landlord had thought to shovel and salt the walk before I moved in, one of his good tidings in hopes

I'd actually buy the place and not just rent. This was a possibility if I liked it, but I hadn't wanted to make any permanent decisions since I was just a grad student. I'd just needed to get out of my apartment and was totally over roommates this term, too old for it and no patience.

I pushed back my frizzy red hair and made it into the living room, my boyfriend Sinclair on the couch watching some sport. He'd been pretty much a permanent fixture on the red leather love seat all day, how he got when he watched sports. Seeing me, he smiled with his beer in his hand, reaching a hand out and securing my hip. He guided me over to sit with him, and though I wasn't interested—I *loathed* any kind of sport—I was happy for the attention. He got really lovey when comfortable, and I liked that, squeezing up beside him under his muscular arm. He hadn't brought clothes tonight, but I hoped he'd stay. I needed to get off something fierce. It might loosen me up and get me out of my head a little.

Hoping for some of that ease now, I took Sinclair's beer, chugging the yeasty liquid down in a big gulp. He chuckled, watching me before taking it back, and shaking his head, he got back into his game. His hand gripped my hip again, rubbing it. "You just go outside?"

"Mmhmm," I said, stealing a swig of his beer again. I charged it down, then gave it back, and after eyeing the empty bottle, Sinclair slid it on my coffee table.

He lounged back. "I could have gotten you your own, you know?" He jostled, dashing his well-trimmed eyebrows at me. Dark hair and smoldering features, he was a partner now at Huntington,

Huntington, and Brewer, his family's law firm. He'd worked hard to get there too, not much older than me at twenty-eight. Of course, it helped that it was his family's firm. My boyfriend was legacy. He pinched at my hip. "And since when do you drink anything other than margaritas?"

"Since my dad decided to marry a woman half his age. Excuse me." I got up to get my own beer, getting another one for him too. I came back with the invite, tossing it on the coffee table, and Sinclair extended his long reach to study it.

"I see," he said, flicking the thing back where it was before settling himself back into the couch. I returned under his arm after he cracked opened both beers. He drew off his. "You're still going, though, right?"

I was sure he expected me to, the two of us always two minds about the issue. After all, how many men in his family had trophy wives like my dad? The whole thing was commonplace and not unusual to him at all.

But it was for me, and it wasn't just the fact that my dad decided to marry one of his colleagues, the woman *working at his office* when they met. It was the fact that he'd lied about it, cheated on my mom and threw away an over-twenty-year marriage to do it. That's what grated me about the whole thing, not Clarise's age.

Annoyed by how much Sinclair wasn't bothered about the whole thing, I started to get up, but he dragged me back, bigger than me and far more muscular. Sinclair wasn't a huge man. He had more of a runner's physique and had done cross country when he went to Woodcreek University. That was his

3

alma mater and where I currently went for my graduate degree. He frowned. "Don't be upset."

"But why should I go?" I pouted. "*He* left Mom and me."

"It's not about who left who." He warmed my arm. "It's about you being the bigger person in the situation. Not to mention people would *talk* and you don't want them talking."

Ah, the Coventry family image. He was right, of course, people did talk and in both our circles. The Huntingtons tried to avoid scandal just as much as we did, but since my mom and me were already in the thick of it with my dad's crap, what did I care. And why should I be the bigger person? Dad hurt me, not the other way around. True, he had tried to reach out in the past, but I hadn't made it easy. Eventually, he realized it was a losing game. Especially after I went to college on the West Coast and put distance between us. Coming home to the Midwest for graduate school hadn't changed much even though I was back. I imagined it wouldn't until I was ready to make that happen.

Sinclair folded a hand over my shoulder before bowing my head to kiss the top. We'd dated all throughout his time in law school, our essential meeting at a bar during one of my holiday breaks back home. I didn't think things would last after that considering we were long distance for a time, but we had. He smiled at me. "I know it sucks. You know my dad left my mom too."

This was true, but I also knew it ended up working out in the end. His dad had come back. My dad... no, he wasn't coming back. That wasn't his way. I thought at first he had just gone for some hot, young tail, but that wasn't the case when I saw the two of them together. It was like he couldn't see beyond her.

Like he loved her.

"You know I'll be there by your side, right? At the wedding and supporting you?" Sinclair assured, and when he flashed that handsome grin of his at me, it was hard to stay mad for too long. He shook me. "You'll get through this, and like said, I'll be with you."

I appreciated that, appreciated him. My body warming, I crawled from the couch and into his lap, my boyfriend chuckling as he was forced to put his arms around me to keep me from falling off the couch.

I kissed his neck, his hand playing with my T-shirt. I wasn't wearing a bra so my nipples were on fire against the hard panes of his chest.

"Billie…" he husked, a gravelly sigh in his voice. I reached down, going for the remote. I started to turn off his sports, but that's when he grabbed my hand. He eyed me. "What do you think you're doing?"

"I thought it was obvious." And sucking on his neck, I straddled him. "I'm clearly trying to have sex with my boyfriend."

"Mmhmm." He chuckled again, but my kisses should not be eliciting chuckles. They should be turning him the hell on, but for whatever reason, he was trying to watch the game over my shoulder. Undeterred, I kissed his neck harder, rolling my hips against him, but he pulled me back. He frowned. "You know I'm too old to be coming into work with a hickey on my neck."

I frowned now. "No, you're not, and if anything, that'll just tell your colleagues you got game and please your girlfriend."

"Or," he stated, sliding me off his lap entirely. "My brothers will never let me live it down, and my father and uncles will give me shit the entire day. They might not even let me deal with clients, and I wouldn't blame them. It's not professional."

"So having *private* sex with your girlfriend at her house is not professional?"

"You know that's not what I meant. I just mean there's a time and place."

If at home with just him and me wasn't that place, then I didn't know what was. Scoffing, I got up from the couch, deciding to go to bed.

A heavy sigh instantly could be heard from behind me. "Where are you going?"

"Bed," I called from my bedroom. "I got stuff to do tomorrow too. Classes?" In fact, my first day back. On top of being a student, I was a teaching assistant. I'd have classes as well, priorities just like him.

The less than dulcet sounds of a sports announcer coming from my living room could be heard again before another sigh. "You're going to be funny about this, right? There's not much longer on the game. I can come in after? Stay the night?"

Since he didn't really do that, always pulling an early night to go to work the next day, I sat with the decision. Literally sitting on my bed.

"You're thinking about it," came in from the next room, a clear smile in his voice. He had me, and he knew it. "I'll make it worth your while."

"You better," I cut, only a little pout before

getting changed into a bed shirt and shorts and climbing into bed. His deep chuckle could be heard from the living room as I did, and shaking my head, I lay on the pillow. I waited, my thoughts lulling over my day tomorrow. I tried not to think about the whole situation with my dad and I did well, the soft sounds of the television gently playing in the next room drowning my thoughts out. I closed my eyes but decided to do so only for a moment. Sinclair said he'd be in soon, and he wasn't getting out of his promise.

Chapter Two

Billie

My house vibrating basically blasted me awake later that night, the room pitch black and a body next to mine.

Groaning, I realized I had slept a lot longer than I meant to, and turning, I noticed Sinclair, hugged up on the opposite side of my bed. He'd fallen asleep too, shirtless and on the *other side* of my queen bed.

I growled. Had he even tried to wake me up? Shaking my head but too annoyed to do anything about it, I rolled over and curled back up on my end. House music charged through my bedroom like I was in the actual club, and gnashing my teeth, I tossed the blankets off my body. My nearest neighbor was across the street, but apparently that wasn't far enough away to keep their music out of my bedroom.

I shot up, immediately pressing myself up against the blinds and peering through the window. The nicest property on the block stared back at me, a multi-level, modern style with pewter brick walls and crystal-clear windows. The entire structure had them, a looking glass of colorful lights that strobed across the street and the snow-covered lawn. People were out there too, young people smoking and bearing the cold to do it, and I rolled my eyes. These people would have a party in the middle of January like the day before classes began. Never too soon for undergrads apparently. At least, I assumed that's who they were.

I hopped back on the bed, nudging Sinclair,

and all I got was a pillow coming over his head. He'd obviously heard the music too but was attempting to ignore it. I nudged him again. "Sinclair?"

"What?"

"You don't hear that?"

"Of course, I hear it." His voice muffled, he ripped the pillow off. "Try to ignore it and go back to sleep."

Ignore that? I could feel that base in my heart. I nudged him again and he groaned.

"Billie. *Stop*. I gotta work in the morning."

He'd made that clear when I'd asked, quite reasonably, to be fucked before bed and he'd decided to simply stay the night and ignore me. Frowning, I hopped off the bed, grabbing a pair of socks.

Sinclair growled. "What are you doing?"

I jumped into my socks, basically half awake. By then, Sinclair sat up on his elbows. I cut him a look. "About to go do something about my neighbors since you won't."

If he wanted to try to sleep through that racket, fine, but I wasn't a heavy sleeper nor did I feel I should try. We were both living in this neighborhood and some respect needed to be had. Especially on my neighbor's end, since outside of my own graduate classes, I was a teaching assistant. I couldn't afford to lose out on valuable sleep, and upon getting on my socks, I stormed out of the bedroom. By the door, I got my snow boots on. I was so angry I didn't even bother to backtrack and put a bra on or anything. I simply grabbed my white fleece off the coat rack and opened the door. The chill hit my limbs like a son of a bitch, but I worked the fleece on, then shot out into it. At least, I would have if not for Sinclair.

Tugging me back in, he had nothing but his boxers on, what I assumed he'd chosen to sleep in since he hadn't brought any clothes to stay over. I assumed eventually, he'd keep some stuff here, but since he didn't have anything now, that's what he was wearing. He had his clothes in his arms, giving me a look of death as he pulled me back inside and closed the door.

"I'm going. Fuck," he cursed, completely disheveled. He wasn't one to lose his temper but being pulled out of his sleep to wrangle me, he wasn't too happy. He jumped into his jeans like I did into my socks, working a shirt over of his chiseled frame before grabbing his coat. He shot arms through it before opening the door, and before he could stop me, I followed behind him. I only had on my fleece, a T-shirt underneath, and a pair of sleep shorts so I was damn cold as I sprinted after him. With the heavy music, Sinclair didn't notice my trailing strides, but the moment I sidled up to him across the street on my neighbor's big ole lawn, his eyes widened.

He got me by the arm again, tugging me a little too hard to the point where it hurt. "What the *hell* are you doing? I told you I was going to handle this."

I jerked my arm away, letting him have that one since he was angry and clearly irritated by the situation at hand. I shrugged. "I figured you could use backup."

Eyes lifted toward the heavens, his fingers shoved into his hair before he shot a finger across the street. "Go back in the house. I got this."

"You're right. You do. But you're going to

have me too." My teeth chattering, I really wasn't trying to continue this debate, and I think the only reason he did raise his hands at me was because I was half naked in the snow. Clearly washing his hands of me, he left, and I stalked him all the way past the folks puffing weed on the lawn up the steps to the house. Truth be told, I would have rented this property myself had it been available. It was sleek and beautiful, but I signed a lease late and it'd already been taken.

Hands shoved into his jacket pockets, Sinclair faced me. "If you're here, you keep quiet. I told you I have this handled."

His warning unusual, I stood there as he rapped against the door. I thought it weird he was knocking. Clearly, these people were having a party, but I guessed formality and all that. There were enough people smoking on the lawn for us to blend in, but I supposed I wouldn't just want people waltzing into my house. The door breezed open and a wash of alcohol and more weed cut right over me, as well as the guy's scent who opened the door. A fragrance, woodsy and nature-esque, breezed right over me, a guy who could only be described as a demigod filling the entirety of the door frame.

"Can I help you?" he asked, flicking a toothpick to the side of his mouth. Dark hair and even darker eyes, he pulled his gaze over the two of us, wearing nothing but a pair of jeans that housed thighs the size of tree trunks and a shirt he left open for all to see. He had a freakin' twelve pack. This guy was huge, and he clearly, had no idea why Sinclair and I were standing on his front stoop.

Sinclair wet his lips. "Yes, um. Across the

street. Um…" He must have been frazzled like me because he waved his hands a little. He pointed at me. "She lives across the street."

"Okay." Ebony dark eyes flicked over to me. He took his toothpick out. "What do you want?"

I started to say something, but apparently Sinclair got his wits back. He dampened his lips again at the guy before staring at me. "She, Billie, my girlfriend, is your new neighbor."

Apparently curious now, the demigod lounged against the door. He tossed the toothpick outside, then tipped his chin at me. "You here to say hi or…"

"Not exactly." Sinclair held me back again, and I didn't understand why. His hand cuffed my arm. "There's a little bit of a noise issue here."

"A noise issue?"

Sinclair nodded, but I noticed he did swallow after. It was like this guy was seriously bothering the shit out of him for some reason. Sinclair rubbed my arm, and when my teeth started clacking, Demigod pushed off the door frame.

"Why don't, uh, y'all come inside?" he requested, scrubbing into his lengthy, dark hair. It was like waxy blades. His gaze circulating over my naked legs and furry UGG boots, the guy grinned a little. "Get out of the cold or whatever. Name's Niko, and as you can see, we're having a little party inside. The least I can do for the noise."

That sounding actually really good right now considering the cold, I started to walk in, but Sinclair tugged me back a little. I removed my arm. "What's your deal?"

But Sinclair was only looking at Niko, his gaze traveling over to me while the demigod waited.

He eyed me. "We should just go. We already said what we had to say—"

"In or out, folks?" Niko widened the door, and though he appeared abrasive when he first opened it, he obviously was having a good time here watching us. His smirk was more than wide, and whatever challenge I saw there, I decided to take.

"Just for a few moments," I told Sinclair, sliding past him before cutting in front of Niko. He smelled *good* and so obviously knew that, the delight in his eyes as peered over me and to my boyfriend.

Niko put his hand out. "And you're..."

"Sinclair," he said, his shake hard and smile more than stiff. He hadn't even graced Niko with the look he reserved for clients before coming inside, rubbing his arms. "Sinclair Huntington."

"Well, Sinclair Huntington..." Niko flicked a finger at me. "Billie, my new neighbor. Welcome to Never Never Land."

And never have I ever seen such a display, people, college students I assumed, bumping and grinding in little to no clothing. Many were just as half naked as Niko, women letting men pour booze into their mouths while colorful lights flickered and glistened off the crystal chandeliers and walls. I felt like I was in some bachelor pad off the beach, not in a college neighborhood in the Midwest.

"Nice place," I stated. Though a bit uncivilized. I sneered as some guy drank shots off a girls tits who lay on the middle of a table like a buffet. She literally *was* the buffet. Covered completely in body paint, she had tropical fruit and sushi decorating her body, people pulling California rolls off her like *that* was normal.

Niko smirked. "Thanks. Appreciate it." Then he pointed over to Sinclair. "Sinclair, bro. Drink for you and your girl?"

"Sure." Though something of a grumble left Sinclair's lips as Niko guided us through the circus and circus it was. There were people everywhere and basically falling out the windows there were so many. I couldn't believe all this was going on across the street from my rental, a modest cottage-style. We followed Niko's wide frame through and while he stalked, Sinclair grabbed me. "I asked you to let me do the talking outside."

He never asked. He told me. I shook my head. "I know, but it's not a big deal."

"Actually, it is a big deal. You don't *know* these people—"

A collision, red wine completely covering my white fleece. A girl had dropped it, a beautiful girl with dark hair in a red dress, and the guy across from her joined the party too with his beer. Surprised, he sloshed the contents of the mug all over me, completely drenching me through to my T-shirt underneath. I knew because I felt immediately sticky, freaking out.

Both parties involved stopped dancing around me.

"Oh, my gosh I'm so sorry!" The girl with the now *empty* wine glass waved her arms wildly. Beside her, the guy with the empty mug just stared. She hit him. "Knight! Get her a towel or something."

"Right. Towel." He looked around, a blond girl under his arm. "Okay. Don't have a towel." He frowned at the girl with the wine glass. "You got a towel, December? You should look too. *You* dropped the wine on her."

"I don't have a towel. Fuck!" She flailed again and beside her was another guy, a blond one who was beautiful as fuck like basically the rest of them. *He* had his arm around December's waist, and when she looked at him, he simply shrugged.

He shook his head. "I don't have anything," he said, then looked at me. He put a hand out, patting the air. "We'll figure this out."

"What's to figure out? She's covered in wine and booze." The girl with platinum blond hair under Knight's arm tugged his shirt. "Knight?"

He groaned. "I said I didn't have anything."

"Eh. What's the hold up?" Niko swung back around, and at this point, Sinclair had stripped *his coat* off and was attempting to pat me dry with that. Niko's eyebrows dashed up, a chuckle curling his lips up. He shot a thumb back. "We got towels in the kitchen."

At least someone had something, and groaning, I left Sinclair and stalked away from the crew freaking out on me. The girls were completely out of sorts while the two guys just stood there. Meanwhile, my boyfriend was trailing after me, *still* trying to pat me down with his coat, and chuckling, Niko led us on.

"I feel so bad. I didn't even see her."

The dark-haired girl had said that, December as I recognized her voice. I was more so focusing on getting dry and saving my fleece at this point, and getting to the kitchen, Niko redirected Sinclair and me to the bar there. He had an array of booze set up on the counter and taking some club soda, he lifted it. "For the wine stain?"

"Good idea," Sinclair said, waving for my fleece, and though I took it off, I exchanged it for his coat. I pressed it up to my beer-soaked tits. Since I wasn't wearing a bra on under my oversized shirt on, I looked like I was going for a wet t-shirt contest. My shirt was even white to boot.

Trying not to call attention to myself, I waited as Niko grabbed a bunch of kitchen towels across the kitchen. He handed them off to me, and with a muffled thanks, I took them before tucking Sinclair's coat between my legs and attempting to get some of the beer off my shirt. The thing was soaked through so I immediately went for the sink to at least try to get some of the beer out. They had a sprayer there. I turned on the water, then grabbed for it, but Niko launched for me.

"Wait. That doesn't work—"

Soaked when the sprayer lost its complete mind and covered my shirt. I fought with it, screaming while Niko took the initiative and turned the thing off. If I was wet before I was submerged now, my pink nipples basically on display, and Sinclair's eyes widening, he took my fleece and covered me.

"Okay. We need to go now," he said, and at this point, Niko was completely howling. He'd fought it before with stiff cheeks but burst through with the nozzle in his hand.

"Don't make her go, bro," he chuckled, basically crying in laughter. He slapped his leg before returning the sprayer to the sink. "We're, uh, working on getting that fixed. And your girl is completely soaked, and it's cold outside. I'll get her something to wear before you guys go back."

"Please."

Niko waved at him, and when I moved, Sinclair grabbed at me. "You're staying."

"Uh, no way am I getting dressed in this kitchen." I snatched the fleece, using it to cover myself before jerking my chin at Niko. "I'm assuming you have a bathroom."

"A few." He smirked again before dashing his well-trimmed eyebrows over at Sinclair. "You going to be good by yourself or do you need to help her dress too?"

The jab had pissed me off but shot so much color into Sinclair's cheeks his nostrils actually flared. Growling, he stared. "No, she doesn't need me."

And since I didn't, I pulled his coat from between my legs and handed it to him. He looked like he wanted to do anything but stand there, but with what Niko said, I think we both were trying to prove a point here. I told him I'd be okay before following Niko through his Never Never Land and scaling up the stairs to the second level. There was less foot traffic up here, a guy or girl or two making out on the stairwell, but Niko stalked passed them like it wasn't an issue. It clearly wasn't for him and heading down the hall, he stopped in front of the first door.

"Just let me get a shirt out of my room real quick," he started, widened the door, but the moment he had, my eyes twitched wide. There were three people already there on his bed, but the thing was, I couldn't see where any of them started or began.

Grunting, a guy fucked a girl on her knees while he himself got impaled from behind by another guy. *That guy* had the other by his hair and not only had none of them stopped upon Niko opening the door, they grinned at him. The one fucking the guy jerked his chin at him, and shaking his head, Niko closed the door.

"Suppose that room's taken then," he said, unfazed by the orgy happening on his bed. Either that was very commonplace or he was already well aware of it. I supposed he had answered the door with his shirt open, and I idly wondered if he'd been a part of the orgy before coming downstairs.

None of that any of my business, I strode on as the demigod let go of his bedroom door and eased long strides down the hall. Every casual step displayed his ripped back muscles through his dress shirt and when he caught me looking, he winked at me.

"See something you like?" he teased, stopping in front of a door with his hand on the doorknob. "I mean, if your boyfriend doesn't mind…."

"In your dreams." My arms hugging tight across my chest, I got another one of his throaty chuckles as his head dropped back, and he let so much smoke into the hallway I thought the room he'd opened was on fire. As it turned out, the elegant array of scent was distinctly weed, and I nearly choked on it as he waved me in.

"We'll borrow one of Jay's shirts," he said, leaving me at the door, and though I did follow him, I lost him in the cloud. I assumed he went for a closet or something.

The room was *thick* with cannabis, and hugging my body more, I waited for Niko inside only to find others already in the room. I supposed the smoke had to come from somewhere, two people on the couch rubbing on each other. They passed a joint between them, the source of the apparent smoke. The guy also had his shirt open while the girl rubbed on his chest, their high obviously making them very friendly.

When they weren't smoking they were breathing kisses on each other's throats, and I peered away, waiting for Niko while dulcet sounds of hip hop beats thumped gently into the room. No lyrics at all, the music weaved through the room like easy jazz, and I took in the display, this room extravagant just like every other one in the house so far.

Niko's room had been pretty nice, but this one was about twice the size, a king bed with silk sheets and a fireplace over in the corner by the "friendly" couple. They barely looked at me as they rolled smoke through the room, and I was about to backtrack and wait for Niko outside when my arm was grabbed.

"About time," rolled a deep voice. The owner tugged me, and I was in his hands, the fleece instantly dropping from my fingers.

Half naked, this guy's bronzed frame glistened from his lounge pants up, the guy blond and husky in physique. He wore a chrome ring, a chunky one right below one of his thick knuckles. He was also all broad shoulders but narrow at the waist and tall to the point where his hands at my shoulders had me staring straight at his chest. His smile coy, he had a square-cut jaw with just a bit of blond stubble, his eyes blue and his blond hair trimmed short on the sides. In fact, one side was actually shorter than the other, like at one point he'd buzzed one of the sides and was growing it out. Now, the longer side sat just above his ear, the majority of his length curling over his eyes and rubbing my shoulders, he wet his lips at me. "Now, let me get a look at you."

And look he did, my nipples incredibly hard and piercing through my drenched top. I started to cover them when he wrapped those lengthy digits around my arms.

"Nah, don't do that," hummed deep from within his wide chest. A breath and he tongued his mouth, his eyes flaring. "Don't want to waste that."

"Excuse me?"

Ignoring me, he let go, causing me to sway and inadvertently check out his ass as he walked away. This guy had a great ass and one only made better-looking due to the fact that he clearly wasn't wearing anything on under his lounge pants. The waistband sat right below two prominent back dimples, a curve to his firm ass I was almost jealous of.

I wet my lips and immediately felt guilty for even looking, but what the guy said next instantly pulled me out of my rogue thoughts and caused me to stiffen.

He frowned once he turned around, probably because I hadn't done anything after what he'd said. I couldn't have heard him right, but then he came over to me. He touched my chin. "I said take off your clothes, love."

What. The. Hell.

By then, Niko had returned, a shirt in his beefy hands, but stopped next to the blond staring over me. "What's going on, bro?"

"Um, I'm thinking your girl is shy," he said, tucking hands under his chiseled arms. It only made his chest look that much more defined, a smattering of blond hairs trailing across his muscled pecs. I peered my way back up to his eyes, but the blond noticed my more than wandering gaze. He grinned a little. "Or maybe I was wrong. What's the problem then, beautiful? You going to work that ass for us tonight or what?"

My eyebrows had to have jumped the height of my forehead, and by then, the *friendly* couple had given the blond their weed. He smoked it, his perfect cheekbones hallowing before passing it to Niko, and Niko, though he smoked the gift given to him, was clearly at a loss for words.

"My girl, Jay?" he asked him, but then looked at me. "Are you my girl?"

Okay, so I wasn't *anyone's* girl, but for whatever reason glee took on a new form as Niko bumped his fist with the blond, Jay, then retreated over to the coffee table. Niko quickly moved it out the way before sinking himself down in a lounge chair near the friendly couple. He tipped his chin back, getting all settled in, and I about said something about that before hands came to my arms again.

"Now, just relax," Blond, *Jay*, said, rubbing on me and fogging my brain like a hot car's windows in the middle of a snowstorm. I didn't know what it was about this guy's touch, but for whatever reason, it knocked me stupid at a mere feel of his rough palms. He smiled his beautiful lips. "We just want a little show. We won't touch you. Not unless you want that too."

A curled finger beneath my chin and he was letting me go. He took a seat on the arm of Niko's chair, but when I *still* didn't do anything, Jay shook his head. "I'm paying you by the hour, lovely," he said, then displayed the space in front of the couch. "Now, give my friends and me my money's worth." A look and he peered at Niko. "What's with this stripper you hired?"

Holy shit.

"Stripper?" I asked, but then it all came together, them sitting back for a show, this room filled with so much weed I thought I'd choke where I stood. Then there was the smooth music and the touchy-feely couple. What the hell? I frowned. "I'm not a stripper."

"Right." Blond chuckled, instantly grating me. Especially when his friends joined in for a round. Taking the weed back from Niko, he pointed it toward me. "Now, please. If you would take off your clothes. I'm starting to lose my buzz."

On fire now, I growled in his direction. "I said I'm *not* a stripper, asshole. You take off your clothes."

Up in an instant, *in my face* in an instant and all humor in the room left. His friends and everything stopped. Like a record had been scratched except for the fact the hip hop beats still played. It bumped with the heat in my chest, my body *chest to chest* with this guy, Jay's, muscled abdomen. Blond eyebrows narrowed hard. "You're not a stripper?"

"No."

He stepped back, a smoke trail wafting as he waved a *S* shape in front of me. "Dressed like that? Your wet tits all pink and popping out and you're not a stripper?"

Fire *hot* as I reared back. I had every intention of slapping this asshole right in his goddamn face. If anything, to teach him some manners, but he stopped the assault full stop when he caught my hand and tugged me hard to his firm body…

And kissed me right on the mouth.

His lips fell down on mine with heat, aggression as if to prove a point, and rendered speechless, my limbs submitted to his strong hands. He gathered me up, the growl low in his throat as he tasted my tongue and altered my senses. He tasted like weed, sin and sex, and every other mind-dizzying thing. My nipples dragging down the hard panes of his chest, it took me a second to get my thoughts back, but the moment I had, I gut checked him so hard in his abs, he growled.

I backed away, falling into another set of hands. Turned out, they'd been my boyfriend's because when I looked up, I saw nothing but shock in Sinclair's eyes. He had his coat on, obviously ready to go and looking for me, and swiping up my fleece from the floor, I covered myself. "Sinclair—"

"What's going on?" So much tension in his eyes, the majority of it on this guy Jay. Sinclair forced my arms through my fleece even though it was wet with wine and beer. "You kiss my girl?"

Jay just stood there, and all humor, once again, had left the room. It was like he commanded it, his hands shoved in his lounge pants. "I guess I did." He shrugged. "Though I will say, I thought she was the stripper."

More chuckles and clearly at Sinclair's and my expense. My fleece on, Sinclair's hands stayed at my shoulders. "So a misunderstanding then?"

"Yes, and apologies." Jay put out a hand. "I'm Lance. Friends call me LJ since the last name is

Johnson."

"I know who you are," Sinclair stated, surprising the hell out of me. His expression deadpan, he tucked his own hands under his arms. "I went to undergrad, then law school at the university. Heard about you around campus during my law program. I guess your reputation precedes you."

So they went to the same school, *my school* as of last fall. But still, the campus was big enough where Sinclair knowing about this guy might be unusual. But then again, maybe not. They might travel in the same circles.

But judging by LJ's sex and party den, I found that hard to believe. Sinclair and I both traveled in a bit higher circles, ones with *class* and not all this.

All LJ did was chuckle upon being presented with his past. He cuffed his thick arms. "I guess so."

At this point, I thought the guys would start clubbing each other with the looks exchanged, but by then, Niko had stood and appeared at LJ's side. He rested an arm on his shoulder. "They came over tonight talking about the noise. I invited them in to apologize. They said they're our new neighbors. At least, she is. I got kind of confused at the whole stripper thing when that happened."

Obviously, but he ran with it. A tried and true *guy*, and sneering, I hugged my wet fleece.

LJ nodded at what Niko said with a smile. "Wish you'd told us sooner…"

"Billie," I cut, but he grinned.

"Billie. Could have avoided some confusion there," he said to me despite the fact I totally *had* told him. His smile hiked. "Apologies to you and double about the noise. My roommate and I had no idea you'd already moved in. We would have thought about that."

"Would you have?" I eyed him, my mouth still burning annoyingly from his kiss. I hated it and even more so at the jump in my throat when he canceled all the space between us.

He peered down at me with that stupid grin. "Of course. I'm nothing if not mindful. You gotta give respect to get it."

"And I agree." Sinclair put space between us both. He squeezed my arm. "And now that everybody knows who everybody is, there's no problems here."

He'd said that like it was some kind of negotiation, like he was in the boardroom dealing with clients and not my boyfriend standing across from a complete and utter asshole.

LJ wet his lips in response but, in the end, nodded. "No problems from me."

Rubbing my arm, Sinclair looked at me. "You ready to go?"

More than, hugging into my boyfriend as he guided me toward the door.

"Sorry for the misunderstanding, new neighbor," LJ said behind my back, a noticeable lightness dancing in his voice. "And welcome to the neighborhood."

Chapter Three

Billie

I basically shot out of Starbucks like a horse out of the gate, running late that morning and lacking sleep. I'd finally fallen into it around three-ish, but still woke up pissed and cranky. Sinclair had gratefully had an early morning meeting so we hadn't had to juggle over shower time and working our way around my room. I hadn't much to say to him at all that morning anyway, more than annoyed by how quite a few things were handled last night.

Visions of my cocky, arrogant as hell neighbor swarmed my brain, but I had no time to think about it since I had to get my professor coffee. He'd assigned me the task that morning via email, and though I hadn't worked with him before, only my second semester as a teaching assistant, I had a feeling I was in for the workload of my life. His syllabus was jam-packed, and though I was one of three TAs for his film class, it was a sizable class. Almost one hundred. Combined with how many students I had in my individual recitation class, I'd be grading a lot of course work. That would be in addition to anything Professor Douglas wanted his TAs to do—coffee runs included. His other TAs, Davey and Griffin, sent me their orders too on our group email since today's coffee run was my day, so I juggled about three coffees outside of my own. I peeled into campus about fifteen minutes prior to the start of Professor Douglas' class, and groaning, I got the coffees, my bag, and purse before closing my SUV with my hip.

Shuffling onto campus, I balanced the drink orders and my stuff, trying not to slip and slide on the salted paths. I wore a skirt today with my UGG boots, my red hair pinned up, and a nice sweater on under my wool coat, and I wasn't trying to flash anyone on the slippery walks.

Woodcreek University itself was a moderately sized campus, and it was my first year here as a graduate student. I'd done undergrad on the coast, which was pretty much a party school, and about twice the size. I'd blended in there and hadn't really enjoyed the whole getting lost amongst the numbers thing, hence my choice to go to the Midwestern Ivy League today. The school also happened to be closer to my mom, which wasn't a bad thing. I'd decided to be around for her more considering my parents' divorce, and she'd been overjoyed when I decided to come home.

I slid into Gretchen Hall with the coffees, cursing under my breath that the halls were quieter than they should be. I knew I was running late, but still had a couple minutes considering what my car's dash said. Even still, I was a teaching assistant and was supposed to be early to class, not on time like the students.

I forced the door open with my hip, the auditorium wide and filled with students. They were all talking amongst themselves, and since there were so many, no one noticed when I came in.

At least no one that mattered.

Professor Douglas was off to the side of the podium with the other TAs. I'd met Davey and Griffin for coffee over holiday break. We thought it best we meet each other before term started, the pair friendly enough but the typical uppity film students if I'd ever seen them. Most would go on to teach like myself, film always a huge thing in my life. I had busy parents, and I loved wrapping myself up in a good comedy or romance. It was just my thing, always had been, so when I'd decided to go to school to become a professor, the first thing I'd decided to do was head for the film track. Again, it was just my thing.

"I'm so sorry," I whispered, despite the room being full of chatty undergrads. I handed Griffin his coffee, black, and Davey her iced mocha latte. I found this choice odd considering how cold it was outside, but hey, to each their own. Quickly, I handed Professor Douglas his espresso, and though he'd taken it, he frowned at me.

"I don't have to tell you you're late," he said, clearly going over things with the others. Hands in his pockets, he towered over them while they held stacks of syllabi. A buzz in his pocket, and he pulled out his cell phone, scratching his neck with a finger as he read the front. "In any case, I just missed an important phone call. I'm going to go take it quickly, and while I'm gone, I need you three to hand out the syllabi. Let the students know I'll return shortly."

He was away with a huff after that, so very dramatic like film and movie buffs could be. I dealt with a lot of them in undergrad, my same major then.

Davey and Griffin both handed me some of their stack once I discarded my coat and personal items, and after Davey let the class know we were coming around, I informed them Professor Douglas would be back in a few moments. I didn't use the mic though it was set up, and considering how all the students dove into the syllabus the moment they were handed it, I figured they all knew what was up. I was fairly good at projecting, and I took the back of the class while Davey stayed up front and Griffin took one of the sides. We figured we'd meet up in the middle eventually.

Right away, the class silenced, serious since this was college and an Ivy League at that. Woodcreek University was one of the best in the state and people got their money's worth for that tuition. Myself and the other TAs didn't have to do much in regards to keeping people silent. The students got right into reading over everything, but some whispering in the back where I was did get my attention. Everyone else was focused in on their task, but *I* was paying attention to very soft but clear *moans* coming from the back of the room. There was a girl up there with bright pink hair, a guy basically on top of her, and she had a hand basically between his legs. She rubbed on his junk, the girl doing the moaning as he kissed on her neck. I couldn't see the guy much since he had his face buried in her neck, and everyone else around either seemed to just be trying to ignore them or didn't care.

Enraged, I stalked the last several feet up the steps to the, err, um, *couple*, and tapping my foot, I crossed my arms. "Excuse me?"

"You're excused." The guy hadn't missed a beat as he folded long fingers around the girl's neck, and it'd been the ring to give me pause, that chrome ring with some type of animal forged into the metal.

It'd been that same ring to touch *my flesh*, burn across my cheek and body as he kissed me just last night. He'd made me submit to him just like this girl, and upon clearing my throat *loudly*, the blond asshole with a smart mouth and the body of a Grecian god finally peeled away from his latest conquest to look up at me.

He looked like he'd basically just got done fucking, his tight, baby tee disheveled and revealing a sliver of his golden abs. This girl had gotten her work in all right, his spools of honey blond locks all over the place and making an entirely too good-looking guy look even more good-looking. The worst part was he knew it, lounging his big body back in his stadium seat to see what all the hubbub was about. The moment he saw me, those golden eyebrows twitched up, and the second that arrogant smile of his returned, I knew he definitely remembered me. His grin angled right. "You're... erm, um, Billie, right?"

He pointed a finger and everything, a real Einstein here, as he managed to recall my name through the fog of weed and sex I was sure he'd partaken in after I left. I had to say I was impressed, but at the present way too pissed off to give him props. He took me in from my boots to my short skirt, wearing black tights this time since it was cold. I wore a sweater set today, trying to be professional on my first day, but the way he looked at me, one would have thought I'd all out dressed for the club.

Appraising my entire body, he lounged back even deeper in his chair and stamped out those big legs like he actually was about to get a show, and I couldn't believe this asshole.

"Right," I cut, my tone more than gritted. Again, everyone around was paying attention to their own little piece of the classroom, and if someone did look, they made sure to cut right back to their syllabus in front of them. I mean, that was good, I guessed, but kind of weird. I shrugged. "And you and your, um, friend…"

"Cherry," he said, making her giggle. She pulled a manicured finger down his chest and I thought for a moment there he might have actually hired a stripper to come make out with him in his class today. He dropped a thick arm across her shoulders. "I take it you're a TA."

So he noticed the stack of syllabi in my hands, a real genius this one. "Correct and it's neither the time nor place for you both to be doing that. This is a classroom. Not a brothel."

My back straight, I felt a little empowered telling this guy off. Especially considering how he'd embarrassed me and Sinclair last night. My boyfriend wasn't one to just be put in his place, and for whatever reason, he let this asswipe talk to both of us the way he had, even after LJ had kissed me. The whole thing was terrible, and even worse once I recalled what Sinclair did say to me before finally going to bed last night.

"Stay away from that guy if you know what's good for you," he'd said, not offering much more after that. He'd shaken his head. *"He's trouble, and believe me, you don't want any more of that. I mean, considering all that with your dad."*

He'd been right, of course. My dad completely betraying my mom and me and making our whole family basically a laughing stock amongst our friends. People didn't get divorced in our circles, and if they did, everyone knew and talked about it. People were well aware of the Coventrys and their dirty laundry.

Again, Sinclair hadn't offered many more words after that and the thing with LJ I was going to let go. I figured he was a problem nothing but some good earplugs couldn't correct, but if he was in this class, I figured better to nip this disrespect right in the bud.

He didn't say anything after what I said, eerily silent with his arm around his girl, but I figured he'd gotten the point since he had ears and appeared to have more than two brain cells. I tossed two syllabi his way, one for him and one for his friend on their lap desks. I turned but shifted back following a throat clear.

"You gonna pick that up?" LJ asked, removing his arm from his Cherry. Blue eyes shifted down and I noticed the syllabi I placed on his desk was now on the carpeted floor.

My eyes narrowed. "You dropped that."

"I didn't." And then he lifted a hand. "And I got about a dozen witnesses that saw you throw it at me. It fell to the ground..."

And suddenly, we did have witnesses, all suddenly completely aware of LJ, me, and this situation. He had the whole top row looking at us, like a conductor with an orchestra and though I found that unusual I didn't step down. I shook my head. "You pick it up. You dropped it—"

"Is there a problem here?"

I turned to find Professor Douglas, his hands in his pockets. All students had resumed their attention back to their syllabi. All but LJ and Cherry, of course. Relief that Professor Douglas was here and could put this guy in his place I looked at him. "Professor..."

"She threw your syllabus at me, Professor," LJ cut in, his blond eyebrows dashing up at me once before facing Professor Douglas. He grinned a little. "Have no idea why. I was just sitting back here."

The audacity of it all made me want to slap him across his face again. Though I obviously couldn't this time in our new environment. It wouldn't be appropriate. My heart charging, I opened my mouth to plead my case. "That's not exactly true. He…"

"Just pick it up, Ms. Coventry," Professor Douglas said to *me*, though he was looking right at LJ. Quickly, the man scratched his neck, making eye contact in my direction. "And do it quickly. I have a class to begin."

And with that, he was going and stalking back down the steps. I stood there, frozen until a giggle behind made me look. There had been a few there, Cherry and a couple other girls surrounding LJ as they watched me pick up his syllabus and slam it on his desk.

"Thanks, gorgeous," he said, winking at me before throwing his lengthy wingspan across two girls this time. Not just Cherry. The pair of us were in a stare off, but not long as the professor took the mic, and I was forced to retreat. I got up front, and Professor Douglas proceeded on as if nothing had happened. He spoke as if one of his students wasn't back there with his mitts all over the girls he hugged between his biceps, and I got to watch as LJ exchanged kisses between both his conquests all period. All the while, he made more than one notice of me. Something I was well aware of…

My sight caught *his on me* often.

Chapter Four

LJ

I kept an eye up as Niko made his way over to me
from across the student union, my hand ready and
waiting for the cash when he delivered it. I pocketed
it quick, lounging back into the couches. My buddy
was gone for a long time, and when I asked him about
that, he smirked.

"People aren't too happy about how much
cash they gotta part with these days," he said, and by
people he meant drug dealers.

I'd be the first to say it wasn't cheap to sell on
campus, *my campus*, and if these dealers wanted any
piece of the action at all, they'd keep their mouth shut
and keep that money flowing mine and Niko's way. I
was the middleman between them and the product,
and though I wasn't a greedy motherfucker, I took
what was mine. I earned it. Niko and I both did as he
helped.

I filtered through the cash in my pocket before
shrugging and throwing my arms back behind the
couch.

"Well, they don't have much of a choice now,
do they?" I had people to pay too, making sure these
bright-eyed and promising collegiates had access to
all the drugs of their heart's desires. Nothing came
through this campus unless I knew about it,
pharmaceuticals like Adderall and the like a hot
commodity around here. The forbidden fruit didn't
come without a cost though, and my supplier also got
what was theirs. If they were happy, everybody was
happy, especially Niko and me since we could set the

terms after that.

Things hadn't always started this way for me. Fuck, I'd arrived on campus a bright-eyed student just like everyone else. Unlike a lot of these Ivy Leaguers, though, I'd been a scholarship kid and hadn't had daddy's personal pocketbook to pull from wherever I liked. I was used to that shit, though, considering where I came from. I always hung with the rich kids from my small town Maywood Heights but never actually could call any of those spoils my own.

When I came to college, I knew I had to be scrappy, and even though my degree in architecture would help my single-parent household and siblings after I graduated, I needed a way to provide for them while I was in school. I was pretty much my mom and sisters' everything back in high school. Sometimes working up to three jobs just to help, and the only way I was even okay with going away to school was knowing I had a means to provide while away. That means started as small stuff, promoting parties and shit, but quickly, I found my way in with the real moneymakers. The hustlers and guys and women who knew what they were doing. Through those contacts, I gained access to where I needed to go, and I brought Niko in along the way. We started as roommates freshman year but quickly came up to rise together. He shared a similar story to me, smart but on the bottom of this place.

Needless to say, we didn't stay there long.

Niko grinned his big-ass teeth, everything about this guy huge. He split out his shirts like my high school buddy Knight with the way he lifted and dropped weights in the gym. He took up like two cushions for my one, and with him hanging out with me, one might mistake him for a flunky. We were partners in this game, though. We rose from those depths together, took over the motherfucking campus, and nothing happened around here without either one of us knowing about it. He tapped my fist, watching me as I pulled out my phone and scrolled my social media.

"Shit, is that Dasha?" Fucker almost fell out of his seat peering over my shoulder, his smile slow. "You sure she's in high school?"

"Um, yeah," I grumbled not too excited my friend was perving over my eighteen-year-old sister. Those shorts she wore on her feed were a little short, though, and I might have to shoot a text to her real quick.

Me: Take the photo down.
Dasha: What photo?
Me: The one of you basically naked in booty shorts. Do it or Mom's getting a call.

Mom didn't stalk Dasha or my other sisters Gwen and Lia's profiles like I did. She worked too goddamn much at the department store in Maywood Heights and didn't have time. I supposed that was my job being away.

I got nothing but a swift flip off emoji in response, but after refreshing the hell out of Instagram, I noticed she'd taken the photo down. She could be mad at me all she wanted as long as she listened to me.

Seeing what I just did, Niko shook his head. He tipped his chin. "An iron fist even from here, yeah?"

And fuck it'd stay that way. My sisters knew who the boss was. First it was Mom, but then me.

Always.

Grinning like a son of a bitch, I tapped Niko's fist before checking up on my other sisters and that grin widened by what I saw. Gwen and Lia were in middle school and it made me happy like a proud papa just to see where they were at in their lives. Their feeds were filled with nothing but after-school activities and sports like Dasha too. Dasha was captain of the tennis team while Gwen and Lia were in Mathletes and track respectively. I'd helped my mom raise some fucking kickass girls, and it brought me lots of joy to see both Gwen and Lia showing off the new kicks I'd sent them in their photos. I tried to send them things whenever I could, well aware that kids could be bullies when they wanted to be. You were either the one bullying or the one being bullied most of the time in school, and hell, if I'd let my sisters be on the wrong end.

I swiped and swiped and swiped before a whistle from Niko sent my gaze in the other direction. Angling his neck, he pointed out not only who turned out to be my neighbor but the teaching assistant in my film gen-ed class. I took that shit just to graduate, simply delighted by the reappearance of a pair of soft tits and lips crafted by the gods for giving head. That was all my cloudier-than-fuck mind could go upon meeting my neighbor Billie, a fire cracker with deep red hair the tone of her perfectly fuckable lips and anger. The girl had actually talked back to me, more than once, which I found cute.

Smiling now, I found it even more so that she tried to hide those delicious tits of hers under a sweater set. The girl was basically a walking porno, one of those where the school teacher wore a sweater to cover her gorgeous tits and rocked a skirt so tight it barely covered her ass. Billie's came to the midpoint of her thighs, and though she housed those shapely legs of hers in stockings, there was no hiding the goods. The whole display of her was a goddamn Greek tragedy since the girl was so high-strung, and smirking, I watched Niko basically salivating over her. She came in with the other TAs from my class today, Davey and Griffin. They sat at the bar, ordering food, and upon turning around, Niko jabbed me.

"Still can't believe you called that chick the stripper," he said, a sure as fuck disappointment when the stripper actually did come around that night. The brunette hadn't been nearly as hot. A damn letdown. Niko chuckled. "What a waste, man."

He was right about that, my own whistling sounded. The girl was basically the chick from *Clueless* in those skintight stockings and visions of me pushing that skirt up, ripping those stockings off while I drove my dick inside her had me more than uncomfortable in my jeans. That girl was high maintenance as fuck and not something I wanted to deal with. I could smell snobbery from a mile away, my radar strong with that considering I'd been surrounded by it a lot coming up. With the exception of my close buddies back home, the elite could really be something else, and I got that off Billie. In *bounds*.

"You find out anything about Billie?" I asked Niko now. I'd sent him on a little errand after she'd stormed my house like a hurricane last night, and though I wasn't trying to fuck with her, I did want to know everything I could. This was my campus, and I needed to know.

"Oh, a fucking lot. Did you know she was a beauty queen?"

My gaze shot right. "Fucking really?"

A sea of chuckles as Niko threw his arms back. "Miss Sweet Apple Ridge," he singsonged. "Wasn't hard to find out about her. I guess she and her family are from around the area. A local girl. We're talking captain of the cheerleading squad, homecoming queen," he ticked one by one.

"Naturally." I dashed my eyebrows up. "What else?"

"Eh, uh. I suppose there's her name. It's Coventry, and her dad, I guess, is some big-time lawyer, the DA actually."

"Really?" I looked at her again. She and the crew were still waiting at the bar, chatting amongst each other.

Niko nodded. "Dad ain't in the picture, though, from what I understand. Ran off with some young thing while she was in college on the coast. Billie just moved back. Her mom's here, so I guess that makes sense. Might even why she's going to school here now."

I rubbed my king ring, a symbol of a history from my small town. Many of the guys from Maywood Heights had them, a gorilla mouth on the front, and our way to throw our weight around. It proved very helpful for me since I grew up on the wrong side of the privilege for many years.

I didn't know how I felt about hearing Miss Sweet Apple Ridge's history, a similar story there with our absent fathers. Truth be told, I hadn't even gotten to know mine. The asshole had walked out on our entire family when my sisters had been basically still in diapers.

"And her boy?" I questioned, cutting back over to Niko. "The one who talked to me."

The one who thought he could talk, the whole thing funny really. He obviously knew who I was and tread lightly because of it.

Niko smirked. "Sinclair Huntington the third," he emphasized. "Comes from a long line of Huntingtons, also lawyers and pretty prominent in this town."

I rubbed the ring below my knuckle again. He'd been quick to throw that shit around, his education or whatever bullshit. I smirked this time and especially when I peered over to Billie's backside propped like a sweet peach on her barstool. I took a good long look, maybe reconsidering my previous position about not fucking with her.

"Uh oh."

"What?"

"I know that look."

I swung it back to Niko, catching his grin again.

He jerked his chin. "You want to fuck with the beauty queen."

Did my friend know me or did he know me? And smirking, I tapped his fist. Getting up, I passed him, and my friend followed me. I had a few minutes before my next class.

Might as well fill it.

Billie

A blond titan and his dark-eyed demigod stalked my way, Lance Johnson easily believing he was sex on legs. He carried himself with a swagger reserved for one who felt they ran supreme—clearly, with his plastered on grin and blond locks tousled with product. Still slightly too long on one side, it swayed over his eyes, making him more dashing than I was willing to admit in an open forum. He'd embarrassed me today *again* and made me a fool in front of the entire class as well as suddenly making both Davey *and* Griffin nervous now. They noticed him coming over and immediately hunkered down in my direction. Griffin's jaw worked. "What the hell did you do, Coventry?" he asked before tipping his head back. "Pissing that guy off…"

"You do know they call him the kingpin, right?" Davey asked, basically gnawing on her lip as she turned back. "As in, *he is* the ins and outs of everything around here? You need drugs? He knows a guy. Test answers? Again, he knows a guy. Fuck, even if you want sex—"

"Let me guess." I propped an elbow on the counter, resting my chin on my hand. "He knows a guy."

"I was going to say prostitutes, but yeah, same thing. The guy is a legend around here. Has been since he was a freshman." Davey cupped her mouth. "I even heard Professor Douglas gets his weed through him."

Well, I supposed that explained this morning. *Just my damn luck.*

Wondering if that'd been Sinclair's deal last night as well with his warning about the pair, I watched as Niko arrived first and threw his long wingspan around my fellow TAs. We'd all been trying to enjoy some lunch after this morning's disaster zone class, the hell I guess never-ending. Niko jerked his chin at me. "What's up, Queen B?" he asked, then faced Griff and Davey. "The royal court, I presume?"

"Queen B?" I stole LJ's personal attention with the question, arriving last when he sidled his hard body up against me.

And he was *hard*, chiseled from his jean-clad thighs to that baby tee that stretched just a little too tight across his broad chest. He grinned. "Miss Sweet Apple Ridge." He bowed. "Had no idea we were in the presence of royalty."

I rolled my eyes, my history in beauty pageants nothing secret. Everyone did them around here. Not just me. It was like you really weren't from the Midwest unless your pushy mother forced you in one or *five*. Though, I supposed, maybe that was just my experience with my own. I angled my body back to the counter. "Can we help you with something, Mr. Johnson?"

"Ooh, Mr. Johnson." And then he was close, real close when his breath ghosted the shell of my ear. "Be careful with that, beauty queen. You just might get me hard."

What the fuck...

Jaw slacked and more than uncomfortable, I actually attempted to cover myself a little with my sweater. The nudge of the material brushed over my nipples and I forced in a curse that all the sudden they were way more sensitive than they should be. Growling, I crossed my legs, elbowing LJ until he got off me with a chuckle. I sneered. "And you're inappropriate."

And definitely a student in a class I was a

teaching assistant for. I huffed, pushing hair out of my face. "You're a student in Professor Douglas's class, a class I TA for, so I'd appreciate you treating our relationship as such."

Suddenly hard biceps hugged around me when he gripped the bar, his mouth to my ear again. "Last night you were quivering something a little different."

If he meant that kiss he stole, that hadn't been my choice at all and something he had no right to do. I had a boyfriend, and he'd been a jackass.

I didn't move despite his arms around me, not intimidated in the slightest, and I noticed Griffin and Davey incredibly silent beside me. Niko still had his arms around them, watching the show, and Davey and Griff, well, I wasn't getting any help from them. They stared forward during this whole thing. Like any sudden movements may hurt them. I had no idea if it would, but I had a feeling these would-be "gangsters" might just be all bark and no bite. They pushed drugs and sex to college students. Big whoop.

"You're nothing but a rapey asshole," I said to LJ, right in his face when I made eye contact. He was just as beautiful as he'd been last night, his eyes like crystals in a stark ocean-toned sea. It was only a shame such beauty was wasted on a complete D-Bag. My eyebrows narrowed. "That's all last night told me."

His eyes heated to a lustrous blaze, my tongue drying, but even still, I didn't back down. I stayed until he made the first move, and he eventually did when he spun fingers in my hair.

The red curled around his lengthy digits, escaping from my updo. Letting go, he pushed off the bar. "I'd watch your step around here, beauty queen. I can make life pretty difficult for you."

"Can you now?"

Blue fire now in his irises. "Just fucking try me." He waved Niko to come on but not before stealing one of my fries. He popped one his mouth, sauntering his firm ass away and letting go of Griffin and Davey, Niko trailed after him.

"So long, Queen B," he stated, bowing. He saluted Griffin and Davey. "Royal court."

Catching up, Niko dropped an arm around LJ who didn't once turn back around. He'd made his point and was now leaving, his bodyguard going after him.

"Do yourself a favor and don't make an enemy out of those guys, Billie." Apparently all lunched out, Griffin slid off his chair, Davey doing the same when she grabbed her bag. Griff frowned. "Davey's right. They run this place and I knew that in undergrad."

"Me too." Davey shrugged. "Grad school is already hard enough. Pick your battles, huh?"

And let assholes treat me like crap? No way. Guys like him? Beautiful guys with swagger and a smile for days only needed to be tugged down a peg. Especially when they had money, which this guy obviously did. I knew money. I knew creeps, and if you let them throw their weight around, you were basically at the mercy of them.

I was over powerful men and their god complexes. I got to stare one in the face as he ripped my family apart. My dad used to be my superhero once upon a time.

Now, he was just the guy who raised me.

Chapter Five

Billie

I found my mom at home passed out on her couch that following weekend, day drinking, and how did I know? Because the margarita in her hands still held the slush.

Sighing, I bent beside her, tapping her face on the white leather sofa. "Mom?"

A groan as she shifted in her feathery bathrobe, her house and my childhood home a complete sty. Honestly, it looked like her closest exploded in the living room, her dresses all over the place, and considering our housekeepers came once a week, she'd done this all since the last time I'd seen her. I had no idea if she'd decided to entertain a little fashion show or what, but half her closest was downstairs and lining the furniture.

Getting up, I gathered some of it, and she moaned the moment I tossed opened the curtains and let some light into the place. She lived like a freaking vampire sometimes. I swear. Seeing me clean and get her things, she waved me off, getting up. "Don't mess with that, sweetie. You know the cleaners are coming."

So goes my mom's life, reliant on other people to take care of her as always. I supposed I was here trying to do that for her. She'd just gotten worse since Daddy left.

I shook my head. "You need to get up. Eat something?"

It was just shy of eleven, which meant mom got an early start on her drinking. Or a late start depending on how one looked at it. She very well could have gone to bed after dawn, but considering half of her margarita was still intact, something told me she hit her Margaritaville Maker well after the sun had risen. She pressed a palm to her eyes. "What time is it, darling?"

"Eleven," I let her know, not even checking. That's when I usually came to check on her to make sure she was alive every few weekends since I'd moved back. She wasn't always good about texting when I used to check that way, or returning my calls. I bunched up her laundry. "Want me to start you a bath?"

"A shower if you could, sweets?" But then she smiled at me, that scathingly beautiful smile that reminded me of my mom and not this shell of a person she'd become. She barely did anything these days besides drink, pamper, and party. A typical affluent housewife without the wife part. She pushed some of her blond extensions back. "I never meant to get such a late start."

"You never do, Mom." Leaving her and finding the laundry shoot, I tossed it all down to the basement for when the cleaners came. I tossed my head back to yell into the other room. "Want me to reschedule with Dr. Clayton?"

He was her therapist, and I knew she had an appointment with him this morning because I had access to her date calendar. She could see my calendar as well, but I had a feeling she never looked at mine. I ignored the nail and spa appointments, mostly just concentrating on when she was supposed to be going to therapy.

Stretching, she came into the hallway,

shrugging before going into the kitchen. This too was dark, and when I opened the blinds, she cringed. "Don't bother with the reschedule. I'll do it."

"Will you?"

"Of course, my darling. I told you I would." She popped her little tush out when she dipped into the fridge, grabbing orange juice, so I gratefully hadn't had to take anything away from her. Giving the bottle a shake of delight, she faced me. "How was your first week of classes?"

"Good, Mom. Good," I said, knowing that was true after the first hiccup. The bright side had been when LJ hadn't shown up to recitation this week. Of course he'd been assigned to my class, but since he hadn't shown, I could focus on teaching and going over the course material instead of thinking about him. The bonus I got was the sick thrill of marking him absent. Attendance wasn't taken into consideration during lecture, but in recitation, it was worth over a quarter of the grade.

Just call me Petty Betty.

The guy was basically a prick and a half, so yes, I'd been happy to deduct points from his grade. I'd also decided someone was looking out for me because his pal Niko wasn't in the film class period. I'd checked the class roster myself just to make sure. Having to deal with *the pair of them* would most certainly send me to my grave.

Mom kissed my cheek as she passed me. "Good. Good. So proud of you."

She smacked my bottom, getting some of her energy back. Growing up, all my guy friends would call my mom a MILF, and being on the other side of all that, I could see it. She looked more like my sister than my actual mother, long flowing hair and tight little body. The only difference was she was a blonde and I was a redhead, and in addition, Mom never took life seriously in the way I did. I took more after my workaholic father in that way, which was perhaps what might have attracted Daddy to her. Mom was a free spirit. She enjoyed pretty things and making the world lovely, hence why there were always fresh-cut flowers sprinkled all around the house.

The old, colonial-style home with white brick and cream-colored lattice was simply filled with flowers, my childhood home smelling like a meadow and the blooms in Mom's garden outside matched. Mom took great joy in tending to her flowers as well as sewing pretty things. She made all my pageant gowns growing up and even my prom and homecoming dresses. I wished she'd do something more with that than just spend Daddy's money. He was forced to pay her alimony after the divorce and probably would be until he was dead and gone as long as Mom outlived him.

It was the least he could do.

Stifling the growl about all that, I composed myself. I promised my mom a shower so I decided to run it for her, getting it nice and warm before picking up more scattered clothing in the hallways. Mom had clothes literally everywhere and passed me in a towel on the way to the bathroom. She nudged her little button nose against mine before hopping into the steaming room and closing the door.

"And stop cleaning this house," she demanded on the other side. She cracked the bathroom open, steam billowing into the hallway. "Otherwise, I won't make your favorite chocolate chip pancakes."

Another reason I came home on the weekends sometimes, Mom's cooking and baking supreme. I also knew she liked to take care of me too, and I rolled my eyes, promising I'd put what I had in my arms away, then go downstairs. She had a few clothes sprinkled outside her door so I decided to grab those too, pushing open her bedroom door to gather a discarded shirt. There were a pair of jeans as well, and those, along with the boxers next to them, gave me pause. The jeans didn't look like my mothers, and she obviously didn't wear boxers. It was rare she wore underwear at all under her silk dresses and designer threads.

Despite that, I reached for them too, getting up, but the sight of a male backside halted all movements. Swallowing, I followed the curve of the most firm ass I'd possibly ever seen to a guy's back, a pillow over his head, while well over six feet of chiseled male stretched long across my mom's circular bed. The guy didn't even fit on it, the back of his feet and ankles hanging off the mattress, and I stifled a gasp, nearly barking out in laughter when I realized what I was looking at.

Oh, my God. My mom's got game...

This guy was beautiful—at least the back of him was. Completely naked, he was totally sprawled out on my mom's bed, belly down with his muscular arms tucked beneath him. Groaning, he pulled those arms out, removing the pillow off his head and tossing it in sleep. A sea of blond remained, and though I couldn't see his face at this angle, that wasn't needed at all. This guy was gorgeous, and though I obviously knew my mom partook in a few dates here and there since the divorce, I had no idea she was bringing guys home on the weekends.

Okay, Mom.

Nodding my head in satisfaction, I could admire a gorgeous backside despite having a boyfriend. I had eyes, didn't I? Snickering a little, I started to back away when my name drifted into the room from the hallway.

"Darling," Mom followed up with, basically screaming and making this guy twitch. "Can you get me my terry cloth bathrobe out of the bedroom!"

Okay, so she instantly woke this guy up, and upon him turning, I got full view of his entire cock when he eased that big body around to face the direction of the noise. In fact, I was so distracted by his length and how it clearly curved up and hit the first section of some seriously toned abs that I missed his face completely. It wasn't until I heard my name again, a husky and curious "Billie?," that my gaze shot up, and I instantly dropped all the clothing in my hands.

I dropped *his* clothing, my eyes twitching wide as I stared at a pair of baby blues.

LJ's smile was coy as he looked at me, and when my mom called my name again, asking what the hold up was, his gaze veered in the direction of the open door only moments before finding me again. Something of a wicked gleam hit his sleep-laced eyes as he stared at me and tucking one of those big arms under his head, he winked.

"So beauty queen is the daughter," he said, and like that, realization flashed. He bounced thick eyebrows beneath his bedhead. "Unexpected but a nice little surprise. You come to join us, or…"

He actually spread out his legs, his junk on

full display, and jerking, I screamed my mom's name so loud that they had to have heard me on the other side of the world. I stormed out of her room, slamming the door, and by the time I came down the hall, she had the door open again, poking her head outside.

"Oh my God, honey. What's wrong?"

"There is a guy. *That* guy." Literally freaking out, I was shaking. I shot a finger in the direction of her room. "Why is that guy in your room?"

This had to be a trick, a sick joke in front of my eyes but when my mom smiled just as devilish as LJ had I thought I'd be sick to my damn stomach.

She pulled wet hair out of her face. "Really, honey. I don't need to explain how all this works to you, do I?" she asked, giggling a little before poking her head out more. "And isn't he cute? I met him at a friend's party last night. He's a little on the youngish side, but..."

"Young!" I nearly growled, working my hair through my hands. "Mom, he's what? Twenty?" He was too young *for me*, let alone her. At least, maturity wise. I groaned. "Mom—"

"I'm twenty-one actually." LJ came sauntering down the hall like the sex god he believed he was in nothing but a pair of jeans and a wicked grin, his arms stretched above his head before he dropped his hands in his perfect hair. It literally looked like he styled it that way on purpose, working a few fingers threw it before propping his muscular arm on the wall. He had his T-shirt in his hands and winked at me before angling forward and pressing a kiss to my mom's cheek. "Morning, gorgeous. You sleep well?"

The whole thing had me about to throw up in my mouth, and I got a look from Mom who obviously couldn't understand what all the freak-out was about. After the kiss, he grabbed her hand, and I actually did cover my mouth to hold back the chunks. I whisper-shrieked. "Mom, you need to get tested. *Now.* You have no idea where that's been."

This guy was *everywhere* and probably had sex in the classroom the other day with those two women he had in the back.

LJ gave no reaction at all to what I said, but the audacity of the statement clearly bothered my mother. She smacked me right on the arm. "Apologize to Lance."

"It's cool, Gen," he said, already on a short named basis with my mom. The only person who called my mom anything other than Genevieve had been my dad, and they'd been married for over twenty years.

Oh, God. Thoughts of LJ somehow becoming my stepdad serious made me ill, and I dizzied, actually holding on to the wall. Mom hit me again out of my stupor.

"Now, you stop it," she said, before taking LJ's hand again. Once in his mitts, he gave a kiss on the back that worked that flush up in her cheeks about ten dials and did nothing short of heat an inferno in me. "You gonna stay for breakfast? I'm making my rude daughter and I chocolate chip pancakes."

Good God now she was feeding us like we *both* were her kids. Ugh! I was going to lose it. I was going to fucking *lose my shit*, but gratefully, he turned her down.

"Can't, babe," he said, truly gagging me. He

brushed a finger under her chin, their fingers still laced. "Already got classwork for this week. Probably better get to it. I have a feeling one of my TAs is going to be riding my ass all term."

He dashed perfect eyebrows up at me after that, and Mom frowned.

"Ah, a shame," she whined. "Why are they always so hard on you guys?"

"No idea. But don't want to give her a reason to hate me all semester."

I already did, the fiery flames of Hades only hotter than what I felt brewing inside me right now. I wanted to kill him, ruin his entire world where he stood, and after he pulled her in, giving her a little hug from where she stood behind the door, I thought I would.

"We had a good time, though?" he questioned to her, and she nodded only too quick. He grinned again. "Good. Hope to see you around at another event."

He was letting my mom down easy clearly, and I only didn't fight that because *he was* letting my mom down. The whole thing was disgusting, and after letting her go and a quick nod at me, he took his leave. Mom angled her head out a little, watching him stride down the hallway. She waved a hand. "Go make sure he gets out okay."

Oh, I definitely would, stalking down the hallway and right after him down the stairs. LJ's legs were longer than mine, so it took me almost getting to the front door before I could grab him. He was working on his shirt when I tugged him around, and chuckling, he dropped his arms. He'd only gotten the shirt partially on at this point, half his chiseled frame hanging out of it. He lifted his hands. "I mean, we *could* do this in the hall," he said, stalking when he backed me up against the wall. He pressed arms on either side of my head. "But I'd have preferred to have you in my bed, beauty queen."

Completely mortified, I shoved at his body, and he barked another chuckle, smirking at me before pulling his shirt all the way down. I sneered. "Seriously, you have no boundaries. Screwing my mom?"

"I didn't know she was your mom," he said, and his shoes by the door, he sat on the wooden hall bench, putting them on one by one with his socks. He danced blond eyebrows. "Like I said, that was just a nice little surprise and funny as fuck."

He reached for his last shoe, but I picked it up, opened the front door, and threw it outside. He watched me, unfazed as probably a two-hundred-dollar sneaker went flying out into the snow-covered lawn. He scratched his neck. "You gonna go get that?"

"No." I strode right up to him, and he angled up from his seat. He was sitting down, but our eyesight was nearly level considering how tall he was. I hugged my chest. "This isn't the classroom. You may have Professor Douglas in your back pocket, but you don't have me. You're in *my house*, and you're going to stay away from my mom."

"Your mom and I had a good time." He stretched his arms back. "We met at party. I don't promote anymore, but I do for a few close friends. We met during one of my events, and like I said, *we had a good time*. Probably won't even see each other again. It was casual, an understanding between both of us."

"That better be the case."

He tugged me close after that, a hand under each ass cheek, and I stiffened, my hands easily curling into fists as he bit down on his bottom lip. He squeezed my thighs. "*Fuck,* what a waste this is. Why are you so uptight? You should relax more."

He massaged the back of my thighs to the point where I almost did, my body buzzing, but when his finger traced the seam of my ass through my leggings I reared a fist back.

He grabbed it, a full hand like a baseball in a catcher's mitt, and grinning, he brought my heated fist to his mouth and sunk his teeth slightly into it.

"I'm going to enjoy this game," he said, and I wiggled out of his hands, bracing my fist that pulsed and burned from his teeth. He hadn't bit me hard, not at all really, but I still felt him.

Body shaking, I shot a finger out the door. "Get out of my house."

He stood, growing like a Redwood and about nearly as tall as one. He pressed a hand to the side of my head against the wall. "See you back on *my* block."

And with that, he left me swaying, *simmering,* as he grabbed his coat off the coat hook, then headed outside. He pretended to not even let the snow bother him, sliding on his shoe before headed over to the garage. He just waltzed inside from the side door, and before I knew it, the garage door was opening and he was pulling a car out of *my daddy's* old parking spot. An electric blue luxury vehicle charged the air, the ass winking at me through the window as he pulled out. I slammed the door before he could see my reaction to that.

And I did my best not to feel the sensation of his teeth still in my flesh.

Chapter Six

LJ

Term passed quickly for the most part over the next two months, the days starting to warm up and the snow completely melted despite it being mid-March. Before I knew it, midterm grades were rolling in, and for the most part, nothing was a surprise. I kept up on my shit. Took school seriously but then my gaze scanned my computer down to my film 110 class.

I don't fucking believe it.

A sixty-eight percent average stared back at me. Roughly a D when I'd gotten nothing short of A minus average my entire academic career. Grade school included. I'd put priority on grades. Something I could control despite my parents failed relationship and a dad who walked out on his entire family. It was something I could hold tight onto when my friends cruised around in their fancy rides and invited me out to stuff when I barely had two nickels to rub together in my pocket. School had never come easy to me despite what I led my friends to believe when coming up, but what did was work ethic and grit. *That* I could control, and the thing that ultimately gave me the edge over many of my affluent friends. It also got me a full ride to one of the best schools in the country, so this grade I was staring at right now? Complete bullshit.

Seems the beauty queen came out to play.

She obviously was still a bit sore about what happened between her mom and me at the beginning of term, and shit, had it been a delight to see her that weekend. It'd come as a huge surprise to me, of course. I didn't particularly go looking for people's moms to screw, but it'd been a bonus finding out Gen was hers. Billie's mom had been nice, and though I hadn't seen her since, a good time. I thought the feeling was mutual that day.

My teeth gnashed at my current situation, all this grade business was Billie's doing. I hadn't really spoken to her since that weekend, easily blending into a sizable class, and in recitation, I didn't care much to participate—when I showed. I had other more important classes and activities I actually cared about, but apparently that meant something to her. True, I knew participation and attendance came into affect with my film grade. I had read the syllabus after all, but I figured I could make all that shit up when midterm exams happened.

A big and obnoxious C stared at me in that department, hence my D average. Billie had marked me an F in regards to participation, and yeah, I could go to class a bit more, but that C definitely hadn't been warranted. I hadn't given a shit about film class all term, but I had done better than that. I showed up to every lecture outside of recitation, watched the films and absorbed what I could. I didn't necessarily "get" all of it, but I absorbed it. I fluffed my essays up a bit, something I was good at, but obviously not good enough for Professor Douglas's TA. This C on my written midterm examination had her name all over it, despite the fact we took the exam in lecture. The TAs were known for doing the grading.

Niko whistled over my shoulder, coming into the living room in a pair of sweats that sat at his hips and cut across his calves in a way *I knew* they were mine. I may have been taller, but if this dude didn't stop stretching the shit out of my clothes, I would very well kill him.

Seeing my eyes on *my clothes* he wore, Niko chuckled before guzzling his bottle of water. He'd obviously just got done working out in our basement gym. He recapped his water. "D average? Shit, bro. You lose your IQ or something?" He whistled again. "That definitely ain't you."

And *not* my fault. Billie Coventry definitely had it out for me, my shrug subtle before I picked up a pillow and lodged it at him from the couch. He side-swiped it, but I hit him with my second round of launches. I'd played every sport imaginable under the sun when I'd gone to high school, my aim pretty damn good. I growled. "I told you not to fucking wear my clothes."

This dude was bougie as fuck, had a closet full of his own expensive threads, but still had the nerve to work his way into my walk-in. Clothes were just the guy's thing, I guess, and I'd even dated girls with less interest.

Tossing his big body on the couch, our sectional beneath him labored at the seams. Bottle of water pinched to the side of his teeth, Niko grabbed one of the Xbox controllers on the ottoman. He let the bottle fall to cradle in his arm. "I like your stuff. Gives me more options."

"You mean other than the five T-shirts you have for every one of mine." I snorted, then shot a finger. "Keep your ass literally out of my stuff."

"Okay, okay." His big shoulders bumping in laughter, Niko pulled up some basketball video game.

From what I understood, he'd played that at high school. He angled his head of sweaty hair back. "What's seriously going on with that grade, though? Thought you took shit seriously."

"I fucking do," I growled. "It's the beauty queen. She has it out for me."

"Yeah?" More chuckles, his tongue sticking out. He shook his head. "Poor Queen B."

Poor indeed, as I clicked to my college email for a quick draft. After plugging Professor Douglas's name and the subject line in, I got right to work. I typed a while before Niko angled his gaze over to me again.

"You emailing your professor?" he asked me.

"Yep." My grin was strong, thinking it was funny she thought she could fuck me over. Professor Douglas got weed… amongst other things from people who worked for and *paid* me. The whole thing was laughable really. I had him and several other educators and professionals literally by their junk. A few of the deans of Woodcreek University included. I was the first they came to for "entertainment" for their parties.

I'd even been invited to brunch at more than one of their houses.

Saying I held an iron fist on this campus was an understatement, and the people I didn't have influence over were smart enough to stay the hell away. Apparently, not the beauty queen and her lip, and after hitting send, I relaxed back. I took the other game controller, playing with Niko one on one. After a few moments of me kicking his ass, he made up some sorry excuse about needing sustenance. I joined him in the kitchen for some Doritos and pizza bagels, lounging a hip against the kitchen island as I dumped the chips out into a bowl.

"Really funny about the beauty queen, though," he said, sliding the pizza bagels into the oven.

I growled again. "Yeah, she thinks she's fucking God's gift. Little miss perfect."

I saw how she carried herself around in lecture and recitation when I actually went. She had an air of uppityness I'd seen more than once before in my life, and it never ceased to grate me. She definitely thought herself better, but we all had skeletons. We all had demons, and maybe it was time to look into hers a little bit more. She'd already made the mistake of giving me a little something when she most certainly kissed me back that night at the house. I had the beauty queen quivering under my mouth that night, and she'd done that despite having a boyfriend. She couldn't get enough of me that night, and when I mentioned that, Niko chuckled by the oven.

"Did I mention I saw Mr. Sinclair Huntington the third at the strip club the other night?" he asked, and I popped up.

"Hell no. Really?"

"Mmmhmm." So much satisfaction in my buddy's voice as he pulled the pizza bagels out the oven. "Little Miss Perfect nowhere in sight. Wonder if she ain't doing it for him?"

To which I say, the guy was either batting for another team or crazy, Billie with fucking curves for days and a mouth on her that would look real good around my cock. The fact her mother was a straight MILF was only a bonus, a snapshot of what the beauty queen would look like when she was older.

Despite her sweater sets and Sperry loafers, Billie Coventry had the most supple and suckable looking tits I'd ever seen, *had* seen through that see-through-ass top she'd worn that night to our party. Niko later told me a couple of my friends had spilled alcohol all over her, accidentally but it happened, and I'd have to thank my friends. She'd stood out to me that night, made me want to kiss her despite wanting to strangle her for giving me lip.

My cock clearly thinking about that now, I adjusted myself before lacing my fingers on the counter. I jerked my chin at Niko. "Invite her guy to one of our parties. Let him have his good time here."

If he was looking for a visual feast outside the beauty queen we could definitely help him out. Celebrities came to my parties, video girls and the like despite us being in the Midwest. People heard about my and Niko's parties all over this country, obviously needing to see what the fuss was about, and we always delivered. Every time.

Niko's gleam in his eyes so obviously matched mine, his brow jumping as he got a spatula and plates for the pizza bagels. "I swear, you are a new kind of evil."

"Eh," I told him, then grinned. "I mean, you're not wrong."

Niko smirked. "And only too proud too. You sick fuck."

Grabbing a handful of chips, I threw them at him, and the dude lost his fucking mind by tossing a pizza bagel at me. I dodged it, launching off the barstool like a samurai. And with our height difference, I easily got him under my arm. "Take that shit back."

"Okay. Okay. Shit!" He raised hands in surrender, the guy messing with his hair like he wasn't already a sweaty fucking mess from his workout, and I chuckled, tossing him a wink before propping up on a barstool at the island.

"And what you doing at the strip club anyway?" I asked him, curious now when I got serious. I crunched a chip. "You know all the strip clubs in town are Marvelli territory."

Aka the mafia, the real live mafia like something out of *The Sopranos*. Niko and I dealt with the Marvellis. Obviously the drugs supplied to the hungry market at Woodcreek University had to come from somewhere. The Marvellis took care of that, and after they got their cut, they were out of the picture as far as Niko and I were concerned. Neither of us were dumb enough to get any deeper than that, an understanding between us. All this shit, drugs, parties, and women, were a means to an end for us both. I didn't intend to be doing this shit forever, and Niko didn't either. Both of us came to Woodcreek-U for actual educations, ones we intended to use upon getting out of here.

Niko's shrug was casual when he came around the island. He set the pizza bagels between us. "Just doing a cash drop. You know, for our stuff."

He popped a pizza bagel in his mouth, like the whole fucking thing, which showed how big this guy's mouth actually was.

"Yeah, but you don't have to do it there." Usually, the Marvellis came to us, part of our deal. We didn't cross their territory unless we had to, smarter and easier that way when it was on our turf. I frowned. "That's all you were doing?"

"That's all I was doing, Jay. Jesus." His statement made it seem like what I said was obvious, but it never was. A guy could be real fucking tempted sometimes. Especially when other men in positions of power dangled all kinds of shit in front of him. It'd been done to both Niko and me, a life even finer than the ones we already lived presented to us on a silver platter. The Marvellis had a lot of power in this town. Fuck, this whole region. But anything that tended to come from them usually turned out to be rotten fruit and wound a guy even tighter to them than he wanted to be. That was a big reason why I personally was getting out of the game as soon as I felt secure enough to let go. Niko shrugged. "I'm not stupid."

He wasn't, but the best of us could be tempted, easily him. I jerked my chin. "How's your mom doing?"

A sensitive topic, and though he passed it off with humor most days, the stress in the guy's eyes couldn't be ignored. His mom was sick, breast cancer, and where I sent money back home for my sisters and an easier life for my mom, *his* went toward his mother's medical bills. He took up a barstool. "Latest clinical trial is doing well for her. She seems stronger."

In the short time I'd known the guy, I knew the woman had been through the ringer. When we were originally assigned as roommates our freshman year, he'd had to miss a lot of school to go back home just to take care of her. He had a younger sister too, just the three of them, and because Kate was older now, she was able to step in while he was here. The guy barely made up what he missed over the summer just to be a junior now like me.

Reaching over, I gripped his arm. "Just stay strong with it. I got a buddy whose mom woke up from a coma after like twelve years. She's not only awake but doing real well." Though my friend Knight's situation was a little more complicated than that, the fact of the matter was, his mom was okay. "Don't give up. You do, and it's even harder for her."

"You're right. You're right." And standing up, he stretched his long body. "Now, enough with this serious shit. I'm about to fucking own you on *the real* court."

A real funny guy, but after eating, he really thought he could challenge me on our basketball court. We played well into the afternoon, even missing our final classes of the day, but I had no problem doing that. This guy had become my closest friend outside of the ones from my hometown, and anything I could do to take his mind off his current situation with his mom I would.

I knew he'd do the same for me.

Chapter Seven

Billie

A tap at my door, and my stomach twisted, but I shut that crap down. "Come in."

The door creaked open, and LJ actually had to dip his head to come into my office, the TA office door frames sized to accommodate most people.

Lance Johnson wasn't most people.

He sauntered in during my office hours, black jeans sagging low and university hoodie pulled up over his head. He tugged the hood down, a wash of restless blond hair he fingered through. "Sup? You wanted to see me?"

Not really, but considering I didn't have a choice, I approached him with a paper in my hand. It had his extra credit assignment on it.

An assignment I'd been forced to give him.

Honestly, I thought Professor Douglas had been joking this morning when he'd approached me about needing to come up with a way to allow LJ to make up for his, quite frankly, piss-poor job on his midterm examination. It'd been like he hadn't attended class at all, let alone watched the films there. I'd seen him in lecture, but since he hadn't really come to recitation all term, aka *my class*, he hadn't been able to expand on any of the conceptions. He couldn't answer why the class was watching the films assigned, so therefore, that bled into the performance on his midterm examination. A C grade had been generous and add to the fact that he basically wasn't coming to a third of his classes by not attending mine, his grade had tanked. This was of no fault but his own, but for whatever reason, I got to hear about it this morning.

LJ turned the paper around. "What's this?"

"Your extra credit assignment." Saying the words physically boiled my blood, the crow I was eating able to feed a small village. I folded my arms. "Though, you shouldn't be surprised, right? You have spoken to Professor Douglas, haven't you? A way to make up for your term grade thus far?"

Professor Douglas had been unreasonably livid at me, the distinguished professional basically two seconds away from losing his shit. He couldn't fathom how LJ's grade could have possibly happened.

"You must not be following my direction in regards to the students."

He'd actually said that to me, and I'd seriously looked around to see if I was being Punk'd. This guy standing in front of me now had literally dug his own grave with his grade, and I'd been punished for it. I bunched my arms. "So now you have to give me a ten-page essay on the film we watched this week in class."

LJ analyzed it long and hard before dragging those his eyes up at me. "When's it due?"

"Two weeks. That sound like enough time for you?"

A smirk touched those pretty lips, but he did tuck the assignment into his back pocket.

"So if we're done then—"

Apparently not with me, LJ's fingers wrapped around my arm, tugging me back, and the audacity floored me. I ripped my arm away, immediately putting space between us. "I'm going to pretend you didn't touch me just now. Let you walk away?"

The threat in my voice was clear, but for whatever reason, his fingers came to find my sweater. A bunch and he had me smacked hard against his chest, another and he backed me to the wall. Before I knew it, he had his lengthy arms positioned on either side of my head.

"How about this?" he asked, running his nose along my cheek. I twitched, and he smiled. "We going to pretend I'm not doing this either?"

I swallowed, but I didn't relent, immediately recognizing his challenge. "What in fuck's name do you think you're doing?"

"Trying to figure something out."

"What?"

His mouth hovered over mine, my whole body quivering as I couldn't figure out whether to sock him in his face or knee him in his balls. I chose neither as he honed in, silky blond lashes fanning above his crystal blue eyes.

"How far you'll let me take this," he stated, his voice gruff as he encased nearly my entire waist with his hands. He wet his lips. "Tell me something, beauty queen. Did you push me off you that night at my house because you felt you had to or because you wanted to?"

His hand massaged my waist and my tummy quivered, my mouth burning as I recalled that night. Frankly, I'd tried a lot not to think about that night and that kiss he had no right to take. It had taken effort not to think about it but I did it. I refused to give in to him.

"I have a boyfriend." My throat constricted as my jaw trembled. His hands still on me. My eyebrows narrowed. "And you're an asshole."

A husky chuckle as he passed cool breath over my mouth. Mouthwash and something spicy, cinnamon and orange zest. An aftershave or something. Hands left my waist as he bit his lip, palms on either side of my head again. "I noticed you didn't answer the question."

"And I noticed." I paused, throwing hands at his chest. He barely moved, the guy a mountain. "You can't take a hint. Not to mention you slept with my mom, you dick."

I still got shivers thinking about that, and though Mom hadn't mentioned seeing him again, that didn't mean he hadn't. The whole thing was a complete violation and...

Like stated, I had a boyfriend.

Thoughts of Sinclair took my brain, and I tried to keep them there, LJ's smile wide. He tucked his hands under his arms, still way too close for my liking. He leaned in. "I haven't seen your mom *in that way* since that morning. We had a fun time, and that was it. She's moved on. I've seen her at other parties. It's cool, and *you* are talking about everything else but what I asked you."

His hand encased my throat, and I jabbed at him. "Stop."

"I want you to admit it," he hummed, my windpipe jumping in his hand. His eyes burned like blue fire. "I want you to quit dancing around it and tell the truth. *Admit* that you didn't want that kiss to stop that night. *Admit* that you don't want *this* to stop now."

His hand ensnared my wrist, and he jerked me up against him, my legs shaking as I grappled his hoodie just to hold on. He was hard *everywhere*, and I could feel every inch of him. Even through his thick hoodie.

"You'll be holding your breath," I cut, working my wrist away, but he handled me again, my fist in his hand.

"I'm going to have fun breaking you, beauty queen," he threatened, dragging my knuckles across his lips. Heat seeped directly into my digits, the peek of his tongue hardening my nipples. I wanted him to stop. I wanted to knee him right in his balls and tell him to get the fuck out of my office.

"What's going on here?"

But for some reason, I only forced him away at the sound of a voice, my boyfriend's voice.

Sinclair, in his suit for a day at the office, stood in my door frame, his hands in his pockets. He'd texted that morning saying he'd be meeting me for lunch. His morning meetings were going to be wrapping up early, and he wanted to see me.

I just hadn't thought it'd be this early.

It couldn't even be eleven yet, but still. He was here. He frowned, and I realized how much space LJ and I *didn't* have in proximity to each other. He was still all up on me, hadn't even moved despite me pushing him away.

I backed up, moving to my desk. I put a hand out to LJ. "He came by for some extra credit."

Sinclair knew LJ was in one of the classes I TA for. In fact, I was sure he knew to the point where it was ad nauseam. Especially in those first few weeks of classes. I'd bitched about my situation more than once after that day LJ had embarrassed me in front of the whole class and even more so that LJ was arrogant enough to think he didn't have to show up to recitation. Sinclair *had heard* it, a running joke at the dinner table between us.

But no one was laughing now, LJ's hands sliding into his pockets as he watched this tension back and forth. He looked about two seconds away from grabbing a tub of popcorn, wetting his lips a little. "Yeah, extra credit."

Sinclair rocked back on his patent leather shoes. "Interesting way to do it."

LJ did almost laugh then and mortified, I raised my hands. "I was giving him an assignment."

"Yeah, looked like it." His gaze transferred over to me. "Anyway. You done now, or can we go to lunch?"

A lot sat underneath that tone and more than I wanted to deal with in front of LJ. I cut him a look. "Get it done and on time."

"Sure thing." He took it out of his back pocket for emphasis, but upon passing a simmering Sinclair, he stopped. "Good seeing you at the party the other night, bro. You coming again soon?"

Since I didn't know *what the hell* that was about I shifted my gaze to Sinclair, the guy suddenly averting his eyes.

Ignoring LJ, he squeezed them before looking at me. "I may have stopped by the other night."

"Other night? Where? His house across the street?"

Grumbling a little, Sinclair nodded. "Uh, yeah. One of the partners wanted to stop by. Got an invite out of the blue." He panned to LJ, eyes cold. "Wasn't there long. Came to your house after actually."

"Which night?" Because he hadn't mentioned a damn thing, and the last time he'd been to *my house* was last week. He said he'd been busy, working.

A sigh before Sinclair worked his jaw. "Last Monday. Like I said, it was quick."

"And you were supposed to be working."

"I was, babe. I went after." He lifted and dropped his hands. "Like I said, a partner wanted to go so I took him. I felt obligated. It *wasn't* a big deal and definitely nothing to be getting excited over. I told you. I came to your house after."

If it wasn't a big deal why hadn't he mentioned it? I didn't understand, nor why he seemed to not be able to find my eyes now. A sight of clear and distinct red crushed this guy's cheeks, frustration causing him to scrub into his hair. He appeared terse and agitated; meanwhile, I'd been the one who was lied to. I stayed silent since we were still in the presence of LJ, the guy standing in front of us like he actually might pull out that popcorn tub. In the end, he decided not to, stating he'd catch me later.

LJ bowed to Sinclair along the way, and the look my boyfriend tossed back was nothing but cold. He faced me after LJ closed the door, his arms folded.

"I think we need to talk," he said, again not looking at my eyes, and all I could do was lean back against the desk. Usually when anybody said that, it wasn't good.

At least whenever I'd used the words in the past.

Chapter Eight

Billie

I stamped the shot glass down on the bar, receiving curious looks from both Griffin and Davey. I'd been drowning my sorrows for the past two hours in vodka tonics so I supposed I couldn't blame them.

"I'm sorry, Bill. I think we're just headed in different places."

Laughing hysterically at my own tortured thoughts, I waved the bartender over, nearly falling off my barstool, and both Davey and Griff shielded their faces. We always went to the bar once during the week. It was a nice way to mellow out. They had their own graduate classes outside of our TA work, as did I, but most evenings didn't consist of me getting piss-ass drunk in front of them.

Well, when a girl's boyfriend broke up with her, I guessed she couldn't help herself.

Sinclair's words still played in my head. How he thought we were two different people and he was confused about some stuff and needed time to hammer it out. All of it had been a complete brush-off if I'd ever heard it. Especially considering the crap he walked in on upon coming to my office. He'd seen me with LJ, and that had obviously bothered him.

"Bill... I'm just so sorry."

"Sorry!" I cried, lifting and dropping my hand on the bar. I faced Davey and Griff. "He said he was sorry. Can you believe that? I was going to freaking marry the guy!"

At least, I thought I might have had it gotten that far. We'd talked about marriage more than once.

All of that, I was sure, was way more information than my fellow TAs probably wanted to know tonight during our weekly drink outing. I told them about my somehow failed relationship and how my boyfriend broke up with me. I didn't go heavy into details, and definitely, didn't surrounding that stuff that happened before with LJ. The whole breakup itself had been some weird-ass shit and still hadn't made sense to me. *I* should have been the one mad at Sinclair. *I* should have been the one dumping his ass and not the other way around. He'd lied to me today. *He lied to me*, but not just that, he'd gone over to my arch nemesis's house.

And how smug Lance Johnson had been.

The bartender slid me another vodka tonic, but it was Davey to put her hand out. She covered me. "I think she's done. Thank you."

"She's done when she tells you she's done, missy," I slurred, slapping her hand away. I basically downed the thing, rubbing my mouth with my hand before wagging my finger at her. "I'm tired of people telling me what to do."

Sinclair had all kinds of rules, always having to look a certain way when his colleagues or family were around. I couldn't leave the house showing my shoulders half the time, and I liked my shoulders.

I sighed. "Lance Johnson just thinks he's the shit. Smug bastard."

Okay, so LJ had made it into the conversation a little. Again, no details about the Sinclair, him, and me drama, but I had bitched to Griffin and Davey about him. Hell, I felt I griped about him to everyone I could get to listen. The guy had completely worked his way into my life, a manipulative little prick, and how the fuck would he know what I wanted? How could he ever know that I…

I pointed, shaking my head at Griff and Davey. "I don't want to kiss him. I don't care what he says. I don't want to…"

At least not much, and groaning, I reached for my glass again. Griffin and Davey couldn't look more confused, and considering how much I was talking in circles, I supposed that wasn't surprising.

Griffin got off his barstool. "It's probably time to call this a night, yeah?" he asked, lifting his hand for his tab. He frowned. "And you should probably get home. Sleep this off?"

He was probably right, both of them, as Davey too asked for her tab. They both got their coats after paying, but I didn't move with them.

I shrugged. "You guys go. I'll send for a ride-share or something."

We'd all driven separately over here, and no way should I be driving. I supposed I was sober enough to know that, and though the two didn't look too keen on leaving me by myself, I was an adult and they couldn't force me to do anything I didn't want to do.

"Just take it easy on this then," Davey said, pushing my glass away. "Maybe soda the rest of the night?"

Soda at a bar didn't sound fun, but I told them what they wanted so they'd lay off. I didn't need their reasoning. I needed more drinks, and after they left, I had a few more that made things triple when I eventually pulled my phone out of my pocket at the end of the night. I meant to use an app for a ride-share but ended up in my university email account. A few touches, and I hit the subject line.

"You're an asshole," I grumbled out, typing the very phrase. I was bumped in the crowded bar, but still managed to find LJ's email address to put into the recipient line. The address auto populated with just his L since I'd recently sent him an email to come to my office hours about the extra credit.

Snorting at how easy it was, I thumbed down to the text area, my fingers moving in rapid fire.

"Dear Mr. Asshole, congratulations. Your assholery—" I backspaced, trying to figure out if that was a word or not. I shrugged, typing on. *"Your assholery won you this round. Congratu-fucking-lations. You may think because you're sexy as fuck you can walk around this place like a damn god, but you can't. You know why? Because I see you for who you truly are. You're a big, stupid turd you TURD and I may not be able to fail you but I'll be watching you and you better watch out! I'm CC-ing Professor Douglas on this email and now he'll know what an asshole you are too. Haha. HA! I win this round you dick. And you think you're going to break me? Well, I'm going to break you, you... DICK."*

I didn't even type my name at the end. He'd know who this came from since I sent it. Instead, I popped Professor Douglas's email address in the CC line and jovially hit send.

Laughing at how much trouble he'd get into now that the professor knew the truth, I thumbed through my contacts. I had been going to send for a ride-share, but suddenly tears filled my eyes. I was a sloppy drunk. I knew I was, and suddenly I didn't want to be alone.

I needed my mom.

Chapter Nine

Billie

I woke up with the most epic hangover and truly no idea why my mom was shaking me. It took me a moment to realize I was back home, *in my mom's house*, and splayed out on her couch like I'd collapsed there. I had my clothes on and everything, blankets wrapped around my legs while my mom nudged me with a frown on her face. I groaned, lifting my head. "How did I get here?"

I really didn't remember, the pounding inside my noggin telling me why. Last thoughts I recalled, I'd been at the bar with Davey and Griffin. I'd been drinking… well, a lot because my boyfriend broke up with me.

Emotion immediately heated my throat, my eyes welling at the memory. He'd said he wanted a break, but this had come only after he found LJ basically all over me. I told him nothing went on there, but even still, Sinclair said he needed space. He said he had his own shit to work out or something…

His excuse was complete crap, and I felt on the brink of tears again. Hugging a pillow in my arms, my mom pulled one of those numbers I usually did when she left my sorry butt on the couch and jerked the curtains open.

I hissed like a vampire from the sun, cowering like a wounded animal. This scene was terribly familiar as I'd just done that with Mom at the beginning of term. Well, she was sober now, her hands on her trim hips and disappointment twisting her brow. She was also fully dressed, in her pumps and cute dress. She pouted. "You don't remember me coming to get you last night? Well, basically this morning? I actually came away from a party sober to get you."

I didn't remember any of that. Not calling her or even seeing her last night. I palmed my eyes from the bright sun. "I don't remember. What time is it?"

"Um, almost nine o'clock. Don't you have classes today?"

Fuck, not my class this early, but I did have my recitation for Professor Douglas.

My head sagged forward as I attempted to even think about doing anything today, my mom's smoke filling the room. She had a cigarette, the end red from her lipstick.

"Honestly, what's gotten into you, my love?" She sighed. Something else she hadn't done until after her and my father's divorce—smoke. She puffed a cloud. "And you get at me for drinking too much."

I totally did because *she did* drink too much. Gripping the couch, I stood, shaking my head, and Mom joined me in her cute, little dress. She frowned. "Is this a cry for help?"

I didn't think so, but then again, maybe it was. I'd gotten drunk, basically wasted with colleagues, and then called my mom like a little baby to pick me up. If that didn't scream cry for help, I didn't know what did, but sighing, my mom put her arm around me.

"I don't want to rush you out, but I'm having a gathering later, a brunch," she said, hence why she was actually put together before noon. "I have some help coming over to get the house together, but I'll cancel the whole thing if you need me to."

No, she was so not pulling a me right now. Trying to be the shoulder to lean on when the other was falling apart. And I definitely wasn't her, a sad woman moaning over the sad loss of her man. I loved my mother, but that's exactly what she did, and still did, after Daddy left. My mother, God love her, pissed her days away to social events, alcohol, and at least a fair amount of the opposite sex. That was if her tryst with LJ was any indicator.

"I'm fine." I wavered a bit, ignoring her hands. I patted the air. "I swear just… let me go. I got it."

She said nothing, sighing again. I supposed she didn't have a choice.

I guessed she knew what it felt like now to watch someone broken.

*

Professor Douglas caught me on the way to recitation. His and the TA offices were on the way to my classroom and what a fine time for the educator to see me. I'd showered at Mom's house, but I was still hung the hell over. I also hadn't had any clothes over at my mom's house and had to wear some of hers, the yellow sundress and heeled pumps the best I could do at trying to appear at all professional. It was the longest dress she had, the belled skirt stopping mid-calf. I would have went for some of her pants, but unfortunately, everything I tried on in her closet basically looked painted on my ass. I'd like to say Mom's sultry personal tastes came after my dad and her divorce, but my mom had always been that way. She knew she looked good and wanted to flaunt it.

Unfortunately for me, that left me with very little options when trying to come to essentially my job and look like I didn't step out of a beach catalog. I was even wearing sunglasses, my head still pounding from last night.

"Yes, Professor?" Even saying the words killed my head, and I did take the sunglasses off so he didn't think I was making some kind of weird statement. Gratefully, he seemed to not notice my change of style or the fact I'd worn sunglasses in the middle of the hallway. Messenger bag on his arm, he was probably headed to teach a class himself in this building.

"I don't want to keep you, but I have a question," he said, tugging that bag further up his arm. "And actually, I can walk with you for a bit. I'm headed in that same direction for a class."

He obviously knew where my instruction room was, and taking him up on that walk out of merely obligation, I did go with him. All the film and art classes were in this building, so I shouldn't be surprised to run into him. He looked at me. "I was just wondering what that message was about you recalled?"

"Recalled, sir?"

He nodded, his look curious. "The, um, email? It came in pretty late last night. Around eleven or so? Anyway, I saw it come in last night, but since I was headed to bed, I didn't check it. Woke up this morning and it was gone, so I assumed you recalled it." He frowned. "You don't remember?"

And then the visions clouded by vodka and tonics came rushing back to me—*me* sending an email to him about my student who'd been terrorizing me. Also me, sending that very same email to the one who'd been terrorizing me, and actually, the whole thing had been for him. I'd CC'd Professor Douglas only so he'd know what an absolute jerk LJ was.

The panic chased its way in a charged heat through my chest, my swallow hard. "Recall? As in…"

"You took it back?" Really curious now, Professor Douglas lifted his head. He pushed hands inside his pockets. "What did it say, Ms. Coventry?"

"What did it say?" A nervous laugh as I didn't exactly remember, but even if I did, I wouldn't be rehashing that now. I recalled it being pretty vulgar and very sophomoric. Something about a turd? I shook my head. "You know what, I did send you an email."

"You did?"

"Yep, but the thing was, I wasn't done with it. It was about some classwork I wanted to go over with you. Classwork." I sounded as about believable to myself as a sinner in church, but Professor Douglas had no reason to doubt me. I mean, why would I lie to him?

His head tilted. "All right. Well, what was it about?"

We'd gotten in front of my classroom at this point, and thank God for that. I had a reason to go. I put my hand on the knob. "You know what? I'm almost done with it, and as soon as I am I'll send it right over. Got class now, but I'll send it as soon as I can."

I pointed to the door for emphasis, the need to go, and he nodded.

"Of course. I'll let you get to it, and I'll be

expecting that email later then."

I was sure he was, but gratefully, the issue wasn't something that required my immediate attention. He started to go, but then raised his hand. "One more thing. Were you able to take care of that issue with Mr. Johnson? I'd like to think he's been taken care of in regards to an option to make up for his midterm."

My eye definitely ticked, my smile forced. "I did take care of it, Professor. I assigned him a suitable extra credit assignment."

"As well as ample time to complete it, of course?"

Eye ticked once more. "Yes, sir, and he did agree to the terms. I assumed the conditions were manageable for him."

The man visibly sighed when I said that, completely pathetic and a new kind of crazy I couldn't believe I was seeing. LJ held a tight fist over this man. Well, at least when it came to how he most assuredly smoked up his evenings, judging by what Davey and Griffin said. That was none of my business, but him asking me to do the things I was doing when it came to LJ did. It was completely unethical, and as far as I knew, no one else was getting special treatment but him. Professor Douglas flattened his tie. "Very well. You can proceed and have a good class. Also, don't forget to send me that email when you get a chance. I'm quite curious about it now."

Knowing I'd have to make something up, I waved only too casually, another forced smile, before pushing my sunglasses over my eyes and dodging into my classroom.

Only after I had the blinds closed did I take the things off, tossing my bag on the podium before palming my face. I had maybe three minutes before students would start arriving, and I started to prepare when I noticed a body sitting in the back of the classroom.

I jumped literally out of my pumps, stumbling off one when a set of lustrous eyes and a coy smile stared back at me.

LJ was actually here today, *here first*, and sitting in the back of the room with one of his kicks propped up on the chair in front of him. He had a backwards cap on, his fingers to his lips as he jerked his chin in my direction. "Beauty queen."

I sighed as I realized I dropped all my crap too. My bag and all my papers for class were scattered across the table below the podium.

Shaking my head, I bent to pick it all up. "You scared the crap out of me."

"Clearly," he said, unmoved in my periphery. I had no idea why he'd showed up today, obviously to continue torturing me. First, he pretty much gets Sinclair to break up with me. I didn't know how exactly the breakup was his fault, but there'd been no talks of "breaking up" before the incident in my office, and now this with him showing up out of the blue.

I tapped my papers together on the table, ignoring LJ before setting the papers off to the side and logging in to the computer. It was set up to the room's audiovisual system, and I might play some clips today from the film reviewed this week. I say might because really the concept of lesson plans at all hurt my head. I was going to do what my body allowed.

Clearly seeing me fumble around stuff, I heard a chuckle from the back of the room. LJ still hadn't moved when I glanced that way, but he was laughing at me, a pencil behind his ear. I growled. "What's so funny?"

He lifted his mighty wingspan, seemingly stretching as he propped his arms behind his head. This room was set up to play video like a lot of the lecture halls in this building, stadium seating like a little movie theater despite only having about thirty or so seats. As stated, LJ sat at the back row, and his smile couldn't be denied. "Just find it funny you're here today."

"Why's that?" Logged in, I checked my email before looking at him again.

His smile grew. "I don't know. Because you look a little hung over."

Fingers froze immediately over the keys, my heart charging and working its way up into my throat. I literally choked on it, unable to breathe. Especially when LJ stood, his seat snapping back into place as he sauntered over in his royal blue kicks.

I backed up from the podium as he approached, then loomed over me. He stretched out his arm and propped it on the wall, cornering me in and looking directly at me. He tapped my chin. "So here's what's going to happen. *You're* going to play a movie for everyone today," he said, my throat jumping. "And after, you're going to join me in the back of the room. We're going to have a nice little talk."

"A talk about what?"

"I don't know. Whatever I want." A reach and

a lengthy digit twirled around a lock of my hair. I'd worn it down today. He smirked. "About emails and the damage they can do to TAs."

And just like that, he threw out his trump card. He'd obviously gotten the email that had been mysteriously recalled from Professor Douglas's email account. He got it, and now he was going to do something about it.

The door opened behind him, and completely cool, LJ backed off, a warning in his eyes as he returned to his seat in the back of the room. His classmates filtered in but avoided the back row with LJ. Actually, that had been all my doing, the twenty or so students taking seats only in the first couple rows so they couldn't hide from participation.

It was almost like he knew.

My throat constricted as I got behind the podium, quickly greeting the class before telling them there was a change in today's lesson plan.

"I'll be replaying the last thirty minutes of the film we watched this week, class," I said, queuing it up. "This will give you some extra time to soak up the material again, and we'll go over it at the back of the hour."

Classes were only fifty minutes, so that gave us plenty of time for it. It also wouldn't let LJ take up the whole hour, and after I got the film going, then dimmed the lights, I headed toward the back of the room, completely ignoring the fact that I knew I had a certain set of eyes on me.

LJ's lingering gaze continued as I took my seat beside him, a couple of spaces between us. I did that on purpose because if I did sit directly next to him, I'd be pressed up on him, his massive size and extended limbs out of the ordinary in these tiny seats. I'd just eased myself in when LJ put a hand out. He gave the cushy chair beside him a small tap, and I rolled my eyes.

Forcing myself to get up, I held my dress, taking that chair. Immediately, I felt his heat pulse into my side, his reach long when he extended it behind my chair.

"What do you want?" I gritted, looking at the film and not him. I played a classic black and white film called *Nosferatu*, the ancient vampire on the screen while I stared at the back of the heads of LJ's classmates. The film was intriguing, even for a second viewing, and since most film majors were into it, I knew no one would be looking back here until it was over.

I think LJ did too, that firm body of his hugging mine as he got adjusted in my direction. He had all his attention on me, a stark heat I felt despite not looking directly at him.

I swallowed. "You obviously know about the email."

"Obviously." His finger dragged down my naked arm and I forced myself from lashing out and force feeding the digit to him. But one thing I couldn't stop was that undying warmth, a trail of lava flowing down my arm.

My body buzzing, I hugged my arms. "How did you get it and not Professor Douglas? He told me it was recalled."

Our muted whispers went unnoticed by the other students and much to my dismay. A part of me wanted someone to see, to find this odd, LJ, *a student*, with his arm around me. The other part wanted no one to find out at all. I had no idea what looks I was giving or what my body was doing. I just knew what I was feeling, discomfort, yes, but also the slowest of burns. I absolutely hated myself for it. I should be reacting completely in the opposite way with him touching me.

But the thing was, the casual touch wasn't normal for me. Obviously, my boyfriend touched me. Obviously, we'd been intimate, but it'd always been so routine for Sinclair and almost like a chore. Sex was something timed between football games and bed time and nothing out in the open. There was no touching in public. No intimacy.

There was no finger tracing lazily along my naked shoulder, no tugging of my dress strap. Feeling weird about it, I worked my arm away, and LJ leaned inward.

His lips parted. "Let's just say I know someone who can take care of things like that."

"Oh, a guy," I said, thinking about what Davey had said. I faced him and basically jumped. He was so close to my actual face I could taste him, study every angle on his handsome face and chiseled jawline. He'd shaved that morning, no stubble, and his orange zest aftershave pretty much assaulted my senses he smelled so good.

He wet his lips. "Actually, a good friend." His hand folded behind my neck, his lazy touch in my hair when he played with it. "He's into computer stuff. More so in high school. He can hack his way into anything."

My thighs simmering, I crossed my legs. "And in this case, my email account."

"Exactly." His grin as lazy as his fingers, he

looked at me. "And I'm glad you think I'm sexy."

Shooting off the chair, I tugged my hair away from him. "I so didn't say you were sexy." At least, I didn't *think* I had. My mouth came together. "I didn't type that because I don't think you are."

Much.

My discomfort making him chuckle, he held it in, a fist to his mouth. When no one looked back at us, he leaned in again. "Oh, I got proof, beauty queen. Solid proof, and it's all sitting right there in my campus email account. Also, something about turds…"

I covered his mouth before I thought better of it, but by the time I attempted to remove the mistake, he had my hand.

His lips dragged against my palm, sending waves of hot fire through my skin.

"What do you want?" I quivered as his hand found my thigh, pushing my skirt up. His hand was so big it basically ate my entire leg.

"I told you what I want." His teeth skidded down my ear, a tortured ache I had to mute. Especially when he tugged. "I want you to admit the truth. That you don't want me to stop…"

My fingers bunched my skirt as his hand ventured inside my dress. No one was looking at us. No one could see. My breath hiked. "Stop."

"Stop?" A question in his voice. "Or make you come, beauty queen?"

As if to emphasize he pushed my legs apart, a digit playing at my lower lips through my panties, and I hugged my thighs together, needing the friction.

He jerked my legs apart. "No. No, you don't get to make yourself come. You don't because you want me to do it. Say it."

Shadows from the film played across his face, his eyes wild. He could do anything he wanted to me back here, something he knew and something he needed.

"Say it, Billie," he mouthed my ear, forcing my eyes to close. "Say you don't want me to stop. Say you want my fingers inside you. Say you want me to *fuck* you."

"I want you to fuck me."

A breath and a hand cradled my pussy, squeezing before a finger jerked my panties to the side. LJ immediately made good on his promise when his thumb dragged between my pussy lips and two lengthy digits entered me without volition.

I gripped his biceps. "LJ…"

I wriggled on his hand, biting my wrist just to quiet myself, and LJ chuckled, nothing if not light and quiet like myself. He wasn't trying to draw any attention, his thumb flicking my clit like a drum while my body worked on his hand.

"That's it, beauty queen," he gritted, seemingly getting off on my muted pants as he grinned. His other hand gripping my scalp, he forced me to look at him. "Let me fuck you."

His fingers curled, causing my body to rise as he stroked with vigor. I nearly cried out as he dug deeper, pushing my face into his neck the only thing holding me back. This rolled a deep laugh from his chest, one he kept in only because he had to. We couldn't get caught, another one of his games. He obviously wanted to get away with this, his power play and intention clear. He was showing his hand here, showing what he could do to me with everyone else in the room, and I was not only letting him do it. I wanted him to do it.

And I didn't want him to stop.

He looked me harshly in the eyes as I fucked his hand, not letting up for even a moment. A couple of times I thought he'd actually kiss me, but when he'd come close he'd only force me away by the hair, pulling me back. He was in control here, *showing it*, and no mercy was given to me.

A quieted grunt and his fingers turned piston-like, his eyes wild as he probed me over the edge.

I lifted my hips, coming apart and his hand moved over my mouth this time. I bit and the heat in his eyes sizzled to electric blue, his fingers digging inside me as I called out behind his hand.

I gushed completely around his digits, a never-ending river as I bathed his fingers in my essence. He only let my bottom return to my seat when he was done, and smiling, he tugged my panties back over.

His two digits glistened with my arousal in the room's dim lighting, the film's shadows spotlighting the sticky heat. Pinching his fingers together, he guided them toward my mouth. "Suck."

I did and without much probing, wanting to, as I took his fingers deep into my mouth.

A muffled groan, and his muscled frame tightened, eyes especially wild when he pulled his fingers out of my mouth, then pressed his lips against mine.

It all happened so quickly the kiss, mind dizzying as LJ closed his eyes and he wrapped his hand behind my neck. He drank me in, his tongue dueling with mine, but when I started to grab his shirt, kiss him back, he pulled me away.

He had a confusion there, deep in his lustrous eyes. All too quickly he jerked my hand away from his shirt. He gripped my wrist. "Just in case you forget."

Before I knew it, he was kissing me again. Kissing me hot, but different than it'd been before. He was commanding this time, rushed as he pinched my lips between his. His hand moved between my legs, and next thing I knew, he was grabbing my pussy again.

I gasped.

"I own this," he growled, squeezing and making me pulse. "*Mine* and you wanted me to have it. You understand?"

He let go, his chair snapping up when he stood.

That instantly broke the calm in the room, and everyone looked back. LJ didn't seem to care as he grabbed his stuff, then crossed over me. The door on my other side, he shot right through it, everyone looking at each other while I adjusted my skirt. He was right, of course. I did want him to have it.

I let him do whatever he wanted.

Chapter Ten

LJ

My right hook sent one of my best friends flying, Jax hitting the canvas of the boxing ring like a box of rocks.

Eyes wide, my other best friends, Knight and Royal immediately crawled into the ring, and I rushed too to see if the dude was still alive. We got by his side, and with a grunt, Jax was up on his elbows. He frowned, rubbing his reddened cheek with his boxing glove. "What the fuck, bro?"

Cringing, I immediately took my glove off, offering a hand. "Guess I got a little too into it."

"Ya think?" The chide came from Royal who was helping Jax up to his feet too, Knight on the other side. Between the three of us, we got our buddy steady, but he looked dazed to hell and definitely not ready for another round in the ring with me. We'd been sparing for only a few seconds, and I'd already clocked him cold.

Jax rubbed his cheek again, pulling off his glove. "What did I do to you?"

Absolutely nothing, all this in my head. I apologized again, and he worked himself out of the ring, getting his bottle of water off to the side.

The four of us tried to hit up the local boxing gym in our hometown, Maywood Heights, at least once a term. We'd met up over the holidays, of course, but today's date stayed. Working out and hitting each other was generally a way to bond since the majority of us went to different colleges after high school. The exception was Knight and Royal, and this was actually probably the last time we'd all get to meet up like this during the academic year. Jax was planning on transferring to a school down in Florida soon. His dad was down there, a dad he rarely saw, and the move was supposed to be a way for them to connect again, his dad's idea. Jax had wanted anything but, but he'd decided to go. This, of course, was to much disappointment of his moms. His mom remarried after his parents' divorce when Jax had been a kid, and the woman she married pretty much raised him as if he were her own. As far as Jax would tell anyone, he had a bio dad and two moms and he wouldn't let anyone tell him otherwise.

Feeling terrible, I apologized to him again, and cracking his fist, Knight told me to take on someone his own size before putting on his own set of boxing gloves. Tapping them together, he hunkered low, and I smirked at the size comment. I may have been taller but this dude was a big-ass motherfucker, bigger than all of this.

"Oh, I gotta see this." Royal grinned, quickly getting out of the ring to join Jax. The traitorous fuckers pounded fists before hanging on the ropes like they were waiting for a prize fight. Boxing used to be pretty big in Maywood Heights, and as kids, we used to go to all the matches. We hung out outside the ring, peering on while idiots clocked each other.

It was the time of our lives.

My spar with Knight was reminiscent of that, and he did let me get a few good hits in before turning on his strength and tacking my ass. I didn't make the fight easy, blocking every shot when he climbed on top of me with pummeling hits, and after punching the shit out of each other for a while, we took a break a bit and let some more of the locals take the ring. We wouldn't be able to stay real long today. Jax and I had to travel across states just to get back to our campuses. We all went to school in the Midwest but varying parts.

"So was there a reason you were kicking my ass?" Jax asked me, his eyebrows bouncing. He smiled. "We should do that to you for what you keep doing to your hair."

The three ragged on me good when I decided to lob it off my freshman year at Woodcreek. I'd had hair down past my shoulders for as long as I could remember, but once in college, I hadn't had the time. Such a shame since it got me laid even more than my cut now. Don't get me wrong. I was still *getting it in*, but the girls went fucking apeshit whenever they got a hand of the gold. I grinned. "Nothing. Just had a weird week."

Billie Coventry weird, and since I had the boys with me today, I actually had some questions. I tipped my chin. "Any of y'all know anything about the name Coventry?"

My friends all were, and still are, in that high society shit, something I'd distanced myself from since going away to college. Those circles had never been mine, felt foreign since I'd been dirt poor growing up, so where I'd put space, they might be able to fill in some blanks. My buddy Niko had found out some stuff about Billie since she'd been local back in Indiana, but these guys may know even more. Surprisingly enough, the name actually got a reaction out of my buddy Knight. He threw his fingers through his dark hair, looking a little unsettled.

"Why you asking about Coventrys?" he asked,

squirting water into his mouth, and Royal tapped his arm.

Royal frowned his way. "Isn't that the guy that like offed himself in front of you?"

My eyes twitched wide, recalling the story Knight had told us all last term. Some guy had actually killed himself in front of him, and Knight had told us the whole thing over the holidays. It'd been a fucking long-ass story too, all of us drinking into the night about the evening Knight ended up finding his girlfriend Greer. The pair of them already had a history, but she was reintroduced into his life again upon the incident of that guy's suicide.

Knight rubbed his head. "Yeah, man," he said to Royal. "Fucking crazy." Then Knight looked at me. "Why you asking about him?"

"Not him, *the name* Coventry. There's this girl on campus, has the same surname."

"What's her first name?"

"Billie," I said, my dick actually hardening. The stupid fuck kept imagining her little mouth as I drove my fingers inside her, a mouth perfect for my cock itself. The only thing keeping me from doing anything about it that day in class was the fact there'd been others around. I wouldn't have been able to hold back with her mouth around me, making her gag and enjoying the sounds.

It was some kind of sick shit, the joy I got in breaking her. I'd made her admit the truth, that she wanted me, and that made me so damn hard that day my cock could have cut glass. It was some new kind of evil like Niko said, but I couldn't even feel bad. It just felt too good.

Knight considered the name I said, and it kind

of worried me there may be a connection there between Billie and that guy Bryce who killed himself. From what I understood, that dude and the situation hadn't been a good one for Knight, and I wasn't trying to work up shit that didn't need to be worked up. He eyed me. "Her mom Genevieve?"

Because he was surprisingly right, I nodded and Knight visibly relaxed against the ring when I did.

"Yeah, there's a relation there, but not much," he said. "Distant cousins, and from what I understand, Bryce's lot and the rest of the Coventrys don't really talk to Billie and her mom anymore. Not since her parents' divorce anyway. Her dad was a Coventry. *Billie born in*, so when the marriage ended…"

"Wait. How the fuck do you know all this?"

His eyebrows wagged, a cocky shit as he shrugged. "I know all, bro. Especially when it comes to that asshole Bryce. I had to do my due diligence after what he did. Found out all about him, who his people are, *where his money comes from*." He paused, then arched an eyebrow. "Why you asking about them anyway? Billie?"

I passed off the question with a shrug. "Just wondering. She's giving me problems."

"What kind?" Knight moved in, my other buddies too in the wolf pack fashion we were known for. One of us got fucked with we made sure to fuck that person up—together. This obviously wasn't the case here, but I did feel I needed to know more. According to Niko, Billie did have money, some ties, and I wanted to know what I was dealing with if I continued to mess with her.

Or she messed with me…

My jaw working, I passed that off too. "Just tell me about the Coventrys. Who they are and where their money comes from?"

Knight braced his big arms. "Newer money, stocks or some shit. Made out like bandits, I guess, in the eighties. The younger generation is in tech. Making millions on apps and shit. Though they're mostly on the West Coast…"

"And Billie and her family?"

Knight looked at me. "Like I said, estranged. Still loaded but the black sheep for not keeping their house together. Rich people can be fickle like that."

Knowing that well considering the type of elitism I'd been around with the exception of my friends, I nodded, but then Knight's eyes twitched wide.

He tapped my leg. "Her dad Dean is like this super high-powered lawyer."

I eyed him, basically knowing that part because of Niko. I mean, I knew he was a lawyer, the DA. "Okay…"

"Well, what he's known for is taking down members of that crime family I think you're working with. The Marvellis?" My eyes twitched now, and Knight whistled. He shook his head. "I'd stay the fuck away from her. Her dad's like a district attorney or some shit, got one of those hero complexes. Might make trouble for you with the Marvellis."

I did work with the Marvellis, hard not to, but I wasn't in deep with them. I could walk away at anytime, and of course, my friends knew all about what I did to earn my money. They also knew my ties to the Marvellis were a means to an end for me, which was probably a big reason they didn't give me too much shit about essentially getting in with the mob.

"Why you asking about this girl anyway, bro?" Royal asked me, sliding a ball cap on backwards over his blond hair. He grinned. "You sweet on this girl or something?"

"Sweet on her?" Rolling my goddamn eyes, I chuckled. "Who even talks like that?"

"Fucking these two." Jax dropped his arms around both Royal and Knight, getting grunts from them both. Jax laughed. "So in *love* the both of them."

Jax puckered his lips at them, and when I did too, Knight tackled my ass clear off my folding chair. Royal got Jax, and both Jax and I couldn't keep our shit together, roaring in laughter.

It was well-known in our crew how fucking right Jax was. Since our buddies Knight and Royal had girls, they'd been nothing but doe-eyed and fucking whipped.

Of course, Jax and I loved the girls they chose. Knight's girl, Greer, was awesome. At least what I knew about her since I just met her over break, and Royal's girl, December, was basically a part of the family. She *was* family, and we all adored her. Having girls around, though, did make it hard for us guys to even schedule boxing days, let alone have them. That was saying something considering we only met up once a term, and I barely saw Knight's ass at all over the holidays. Between his mom's recovery and his new girlfriend, our boy was basically absent.

The four of us wrestled around until the owner of the gym gave us looks, and after, Knight ended up being the one to pull me to my feet. Royal got Jax, and as a unit, we decided on an early lunch before we all had to head back on the road for school.

"I can handle Billie Coventry," I told the guys once we got outside. "She's just a thorn in my side. She's my TA this term, and she seems hellbent on failing my ass."

This had Royal and Knight exchanging glances, and when they howled back in laughter outside of our cars both Jax and I frowned.

"What?" I asked, Jax clearly confused too. Knight dropped his arms around us both, and Royal tapped Knight's chest.

"We've just heard *that* before. Haven't we, Knight?" Royal chuckled. He seriously couldn't get his shit together, holding his stomach even.

Knight barked his laugh. "Sure have. Good luck with that one, eh, buddy?" He nudged me. "And try not to let her get you *killed*. I wouldn't be fucking with no mob. Bold even for me. But I guess if that pussy's good…"

I growled, but all my friends did was laugh, Jax too. I wasn't fucking with Billie, at least not like that. Besides, I'd already done the job I'd set out to do. Billie Coventry was dripping hot pussy, pussy *I'd owned*, and now that I'd gotten what I wanted, there was no reason to fuck with her anymore.

No matter how much I kept thinking about her.

I swallowed, my friends' laughter dying around me. I shifted the conversation to food, and Knight gratefully moved on. The guy could eat an entire restaurant, and after all this shit, I was ready for a damn beer to go with it too.

Chapter Eleven

Billie

Professor Douglas drowned me in course work for his classes over the next few weeks. Between grading exams and essays for him and my own school work, I was basically buried, but I didn't complain because all the work kept my mind busy. I didn't have to think about anything else, LJ and what happened in particular. Funny enough, I didn't even think I'd ever see any recourse for what happened between him and me. At least, when it came to Professor Douglas. LJ obviously had the guy by the balls in some way, none of my business. What truly bothered me was not only that *his touches* had happened, but that I had let them happen.

I'd begged for it.

I'd sat in the back of that classroom, quivering in my seat, and asked him to fuck me with his fingers. The whole thing was horrifying, and I could only blame myself. I rationalized perhaps the breakup with Sinclair had been harder on me than I'd believed. I'd been freshly coming off it and given in to a need to feel good. That had been my excuse, but LJ hadn't had one at all. He didn't know I'd broken up with Sinclair and definitely hadn't cared that I had a boyfriend. He'd just wanted to win. He'd wanted to break me, and I'd basically handed that triumph to him on a silver platter.

My only saving grace as the term continued on was that LJ didn't show up for recitation at all after that, clearly forfeiting that part of his grade. Honestly, it didn't matter considering how much his extra credit assignment bumped his scores up. He'd surprisingly aced the paper, and I wondered why he'd crashed and burned so badly on his initial exam in the first place. He clearly understood the material once he actually put some effort into it. I didn't think long about that since I just wanted to rid my thoughts of him and everything that surrounded him. I rarely saw him in lecture either, outside of test and quiz days that is. But each time he showed up and his examination managed to make it into my hands, his scores were always on the up. I assumed he was renting the films at home and watching them outside of class. Whatever he was doing, it was working for him and him not being in class at all was working for me. It kept my nose in the books and reaching toward the end of my first year as a graduate student, which was what was most important to me anyway.

I visited with my mom a lot after the "incident in question" with LJ, and oddly enough, she asked about him on occasion. I guessed he'd told her we went to the same school at some point, and eventually, I did admit to her that he was in one of my classes. I passed it off, of course. That I hadn't realized he'd been the one I caught her with that day. She only asked about him in passing because like he said, they'd just had a good time together, and at least, I didn't have to worry about coming home over the weekends and finding him naked in her bed again. I wanted my mom to have a social life but definitely not with the guy who finger-fucked me in the back of my classroom.

Obviously, I left that bit out during my visits with mom.

There were a few things I had to tiptoe

around. Obviously, my drunken night was one of embarrassment and had totally confused my mom until I explained what happened with Sinclair. She let me hear it for that since she always loved him, and I rolled my eyes because I think she liked *the idea* of him more than actually adoring him. She liked his upbringing, who he was and what he came from. She liked his status and that, maybe, I wouldn't repeat the same mistakes she had. She'd wanted me to make my marriage last. Not let the guy throw me away and basically outcast us from many sides of our family. We'd basically been shunned after the divorce, our dirty laundry out there. A scandal.

"Would have been a smart match," she'd said one day over her margarita. Once again, day drinking while she made me pancakes. She'd sighed. *"There's nothing you can do about it, darling? He's such a fine boy."*

Honestly, the whole conversation had made me sick. Sick that was all she thought I needed for myself to succeed, a man to carry me through life when clearly that hadn't worked out for her. I only kept my opinions to myself during our visits because I loved her and I knew, despite what she allowed me to believe with her active social lifestyle, that she was hurting. I called so I knew at least she'd been going to her therapy visits, and after that night she'd had to come get my butt at the club, she hadn't brought up my drunk escapade anymore. That'd be the last one as far as I was concerned, no time for it. I put my head where it needed to be.

Right back in the books.

After bringing my mom some groceries one day, I took the rest back home. I tended to shop for her too when I thought about it, getting her something better than booze and grapefruit. I tried to stuff her cabinets with essential food groups, and even though she gave me hell about it since she had "a girl" to do that, she took the food because she got to visit with me too. My mom held a strong upper lip after her divorce with Daddy, but she needed me. We needed each other. We always had the other, and that wouldn't change just because I was in school. She was the reason I'd moved home in the first place after all. I'd had a full ride to my alma mater on the coast, but I'd wanted to be home, be close to her. It was the only way I'd know she was okay, and knowing that kept me okay too.

I juggled the rest of my groceries with my key, closing the door of my Land Rover with my hip. It was gratefully not raining today since we were well into spring, and I was happy to see such sun shining days after such a cold and slushy winter. Another good thing about going to school on the coast was I didn't have to deal with the Midwest's sometimes temperamental weather. One day, it could be blistering hot, the next, snow, and that was all in the same season. Today, we'd gratefully had sun as it set, and I prepared for a long night of studying and *I Love Lucy* episodes.

Oddly enough, the classic playing in the background helped me focus, and I planned on making a homemade meal of fettuccine Alfredo to go with it. Sorting through my keys, I found the right one around my groceries, jumping as I approached the front door and noticed a man sitting on my stoop. He had his head down, playing with his fingers, but as soon as he heard me approach, he stopped.

I froze at the sight of my ex, still in his business suit from the day. Standing, he tugged at his suit, and despite wearing it and looking professional, he appeared too worse for wear. For starters, he had bags under his eyes, his cheeks hallow and his hair messy like he hadn't been sleeping or eating well. He approached, lifting a hand. "Hey, Bill."

Hey… Bill? I'd neither seen nor heard from the guy since he'd broken up with me toward the middle of the semester and he was here now?

Curious, I stayed put, and he noticed. He stopped right there in the middle of the walk, waiting for me. I hugged my grocery sacks. "Hi."

"Hey," he repeated, dragging seemingly restless fingers through his hair. He put a hand out. "Eh, uh. Let me help you with those—"

"Oh. You don't have to." To make the point, I waltzed right passed him, a visible drop to his shoulders. Finding all this fucking weird, I scaled the steps, and while I wrestled with my keys, a soft heat lingered behind me. He hovered close, and I shut my eyes. "What are you doing?"

Almost instantly, he backed off, and though he started to reach for my groceries again, he stopped. "Can I just help you with your stuff? I want to talk… please?"

"You want to talk?" I shifted around, completely forgetting about my keys and the door. "You want to talk now? What could you possibly have to say to me? I think you let me know exactly what your thoughts were when you tossed me on my ass."

Which still hadn't made sense to me. I literally played that conversation over and over again in my head, and I *definitely* should have been the one upset. For so many reasons.

He visibly tensed. "I know, and I know I don't deserve your attention, but I am asking for it. Two seconds. Won't take me long."

He was still terribly handsome despite how God awfully worn-out he looked, and I hated I still had a soft spot for him. We had a history, one where I did think that one day we may be end game. That all had come crashing down when he'd broken up with me out of nowhere, but nodding, I did let him help me by taking the groceries.

I was completely frazzled as I let him into my home, a place literally no one else had been inside but me the passing months. I had friends here, but they were all involved with other things, their own lives.

With Sinclair handling the groceries, I took off my jacket at the door. He knew right were to go, of course, heading in the direction of the kitchen, and sighing, I followed him after hooking my coat. I found him putting everything away in its proper places. Everything but the bread, and I stopped him. "I keep that in the fridge now."

It kept it fresher longer, at least that had been my logic. That's how we kept it at my parents' house growing up, but Sinclair had always left it out so I'd adjusted.

Nodding, he didn't protest before putting it inside the chrome refrigerator. After, he slid his hands in his pockets, and I invited him to come sit at my dining room table.

He gazed around before sitting himself in the oak chair. "Looks like you changed things a little."

I'd basically been living out of boxes before,

having just moved in, so I guess I had. Even still, I didn't want to talk about the state of my rental. I hugged my arms. "What's this about? Why are you here?"

The restless way he tugged and pulled at his dark hair told me he definitely had something on his mind. A heavy something. He laced his fingers together. "I think I made a mistake, Bill. A mistake about us?" He shook his head. "We never should have broken up."

Shocked, but honest to God I couldn't keep my laughter in. I sat back. "Well, that's nice. How many vaginas did you have to fall into in order to figure that out?"

His cringe was evident, and hearing that, I swore he actually looked sick to his stomach. He shook his head. "Don't say that. It wasn't about sex."

"Obviously, since we barely had any." I mean, I pretty much had to beg him to touch me, always an excuse about being busy or tired. "So you've figured out we're supposed to be together?"

"Yeah, I have, and I just want you to hear me out. I was confused."

"Confused about what?"

"I don't know. Us?" He waved a hand back and forth. "I mean, we got together, and it was like 'Hear Comes the Bride' was playing on loop after our first date. *Especially* from my parents."

"I never pressured you to get married."

"I know, but maybe you should have." Suddenly, his hands found mine, and for whatever reason, I didn't pull away. "Maybe you should have made me man up."

"That's not my responsibility, Sinclair."

"I know, and I also know now that the possibility of you and me being final scared me, but it doesn't now. You know my brother got engaged? Jack?"

I may have heard about it like *three times* from Mom. She kept up with all that stuff, stuff in our circles when I couldn't have cared less. I shrugged. "So?"

"Well, he's so happy, Billie," he stated, smoothing his hands over mine, and I *hated* that it felt good. I loathed that if felt familiar, and I latched onto it like treasure. I'd been so lonely lately, the only fire I'd had…

I forced stupid thoughts away, staring at my ex now. "He was happy. So what?"

"So I realized how stupid I was to let you go. *Us* go?" His hands tightened around mine. "I thought I was confused about some things, but I know we're right. We're perfect for each other, Billie. Your family likes me, and mine loves you."

That's what I'd thought too, which had been why *I* was so confused when he'd thrown us so casually away. I'd felt so bitter after, vulnerable, and I'd done stupid things.

I thought about LJ's hands on me, that fire burning and a moment that never should have happened. It should have always been Sinclair and me.

I guessed I'd been confused too.

"I just want a chance," he said, swallowing hard. "We can start fresh. Start from scratch."

I pulled my hands away, sliding back to me. "You hurt me. It hurt *a lot*, and I don't think I can just…"

"So how about we just hang out then?" He laced his fingers with mine, and this time, I didn't let go. He smiled a little. "We can come back to each other. Slow. Just hang out. Friends at first."

Gazing up, I wanted nothing more than that. I wanted it because it was easy and he was right, we were perfect for each other. We were a delightful little equation of pristine numbers and exquisite figures that ultimately added up to the perfect arrangement. Perfect was easy.

Perfect wouldn't get me in trouble.

Chapter Twelve

LJ

I spied them from my seat on the couch, Niko beside me and a girl under my arm while I drew off a beer. It took me a second to realize exactly what I was seeing, Billie and that asswipe ex-boyfriend of hers. Oh, I knew all about them, how he'd broken up with her after I'd basically busted out his ass right in front of her. He'd come to one of my parties all right, had a good time, and I'd made sure she knew about it. I'd heard he'd broken up with her shortly after that, though...

The breakup seemed to be long in the past as he got a hold of the back of her dress, sheer and as blood red as her hair. The silk barely covered her ass, her black stockings the only thing keeping her "boyfriend" from exposing her goods to me and just about every other guy in this room. The party was hopping, but a peek at the most delightful peach I'd ever seen would definitely get a few looks.

I growled, this dude basically flaunting her. Hand on that peach now, he hugged her up to him while they chatted with friends when he'd looked like nothing but a scared-ass Boy Scout the last time he'd been in front of me. And that had been at *both* parties, a timid little prick that didn't go around working up flames.

Those flames worked up tonight, my hand curling around my beer bottle, but my observance distracted when Niko nudged my arm. He noticed the pair too, smirking in that direction.

"Looks like she took him back," he said, his

smile coy before he took a drag off his beer. He swallowed it down. "Silly little Queen B."

Silly was right considering what her boy over there got up to that night at my party. At least, that's what I had heard. He'd made quite an impression that night, a *real* party virgin as he not only hadn't been able to hold his liquor, he'd completely let go of his inhibitions. I mean, he had a girlfriend, but she didn't seem to be in his sights at all that night.

At least, from what I'd heard.

My smile wide, I touched a hand to Niko's shoulder. "You know who he was hanging with that night? At our party, I mean?"

We'd been invited to this one, hence running into the beauty queen and her boy toy tonight. We obviously had some of the same friends and had I known she'd be here I would have stayed far the fuck away anyway. I'd been trying to avoid her since that incident in the classroom. I'd gotten what I wanted, her sweet little pussy, and I didn't need anything else.

My mouth dry, I gazed at my friend, the guy clearly scanning his brain like a super computer. My buddy cataloged people and good pussy away like a filing cabinet, but considering all the people he knew, he might have to dust off some of those files.

"Taylor, I think?" he said, then twitched a smile my way. "Why?"

Shrugging casually, I let go of the girl who'd found me on this couch. She'd been hinting at something promising so I let her stay, but at the present, I found something a little more tempting to bide my time with. Something a little more fun, and if I got to fuck with Billie's douche of a boyfriend in the process, so much the better.

116

I wet my lips. "You got digits?"

"Of course."

I shrugged again. "Shoot a text over," I said. "Maybe Taylor should know Mr. Huntington is here."

I got the look from my buddy I often got when I was up to no good, but also a fist tap when he went to work. He pulled that phone right out, shooting that text, and after kissing the cheek of the sweet thing who'd found me on the couch—Bette, I think her name was—I bid my leave, then got to my feet. Niko had finished his text at this point, joining and hugging me over by the arm.

"Taken care of," he passed off before taking another sip of his beer. We clanked them together, and with a look, I led. We stalked right up to the beauty queen and her dick of a boyfriend, the pair in heavy conversation. Perhaps that was what gave me the confidence to come over. Not able to see those bright, emerald green eyes of hers or get a whiff of that sweet floral skin.

Because the moment I had...

Jarring, point blank when she stared at me and even worse since it wasn't across a wide auditorium. Fuck me, if I wasn't completely and irrevocably *aware* whenever this girl was in the same room with me and had been ever since that day I'd fingered her into ecstasy. It'd been a game I'd been playing, one I'd told my boys all about that day at the gym. But I also told them I had control. *I controlled* her and not the other way around. I'd gotten what I wanted that day, yes.

But it hadn't been without collateral damage.

I was feeling that damage now, standing in front of her, and even though she was with another guy, all I could see was her. All I could do was *stare* at her, those sparkling greens wide and those pouty lips parted. She hadn't been expecting me obviously, but that was the only surprise she'd allowed herself to show.

"LJ. Niko." Too stubborn when she jerked that chin high and tried to physically grow herself in front of me and my boy. Those black stilettos *maybe* gave her an inch and a half, but nowhere near my nearing six-foot-seven. She waved a hand to Mr. Huntington. "You know Sinclair."

The guy puffed up too, an obvious attempt at intimidation, and I nearly laughed. He put out a palm. "Lance."

"Sinclair." I shook, as did Niko when he eased over. I pointed back to him. "You know my buddy."

"Right," Sinclair said, letting go of Niko's hand, then right back to his prize. Right back to *Billie.* He held on to her like a life force, and the whole thing was motherfrickin' hilarious. He stood in front of me now like he hadn't completely let loose in a house full of people mere months ago.

I wonder if he even told her.

Refusing to care, I passed a glance over the two. "Surprised to see you guys," I said, casual about it. "*Together.* We must know the same friends."

Emphasis on the *together* part, but neither Billie nor her boy toy gave me an in. Mr. Huntington merely smiled at what I said. He tipped his chin. "We must. And how have you been, LJ? Taking care of yourself?"

Better than he was of his girl, and fuck did I know that. How easy it'd be for me to blow his shit out of the water right now. *Especially* if he hadn't said anything to her. Lucky for him, that wasn't my way of doing things. I did things… differently, and I watched all that come to fruition right in front of me. All too suddenly, Mr. Huntington got a text, one I might have not put much stake in.

Had it not been for the look he gave it.

He bunched his hair right after, his teeth biting down hard, and I gave him the benefit of the doubt in that moment. He had a choice to make here if what he was looking at was all me, all my and Niko's doing. I had my boy set up a little something, but Mr. Huntington definitely could let it go. *Be a decent* human being.

"I got to take a work call real quick," he said, so obviously choosing not to, and I had to hand it to him.

He gave the consideration all of half a second.

This guy was an uber douche, and unsuspecting Billie let him be one. She frowned. "Now? We just got here."

"I'll make it quick, love," he said, kissing her cheek. "I'll come find you? Promise it will be quick."

As quick as he could get his rocks off, but I said nothing, smiling at him when he looked at me. I lifted a hand. "Later, bro."

Hell, if I got that salutation back the way he looked at me, and after he left, I tugged at Niko. I wanted him to make sure Mr. Huntington got to where he needed him to be. I jerked a subtle look to follow, and grinning, Niko backed up a little.

He lifted his beer. "Better go mingle," he said, casual about it. He winked at Billie. "Catch you later, Queen B."

She rolled her eyes at him, and when *she*

started to leave, I should have let her go. I should leave her life alone. It had nothing to do with me and maybe could even screw me, which had been why I'd kept my distance in the first place. My buddies had been right at the gym. Being seen or even spoken about in the same sentence with the kid of one of my business partner's enemies was a bad idea.

So why the fuck did I intercept her?

I cut right in front, shielding her from anything but me. "So you and the pretty boy," I stated, directing my beer bottle in that direction. "You back together then?"

No idea why I asked her that. No idea why I even let it be known I knew anything about her beyond the need to know. And clearly the information shocked her.

Her eyes twitched wide as she shifted on her heels. "How do you know we broke up?"

Casual about it even when the knowledge was far from, I shrugged. "Got my sources."

"Let me guess. You know a guy?"

Surprised by that, I looked at her.

Her eyes lifted. "Davey and Griff said you're called the Kingpin around here." Putting that out there, she eyed me down, and if that heated gaze didn't shoot activity straight into my dick. She hugged her perky breasts. "They say you run all and know all. That true?"

I'd been called a few things, Kingpin one of them, and I smiled before wetting my lips. I took a long drink, one she noticed as she watched the beer travel down my throat. Her gaze settled somewhere across my chest, and if she didn't hug those beautiful tits of hers more. I could basically see them above

120

that red dress painted on her body, a perfect valley I wanted to shove my face or dick between.

"Depends on who you ask," I said, only too wild. She wet her lips, and the activity in my jeans jumped from slightly uncomfortable to getting this girl into the nearest closet and shoving that skirt up above her sweet little peach of a bottom *now*. My fingers inside her hadn't been enough that day, and I closed space.

She immediately noticed, of course, removing it. Her arms covering her body like a lifeline, she backed against a wall. "Well, my sources say you're nothing but a bully, a brute who throws his weight around and apparently has Professor Douglas by the balls. So you're a drug dealer too?"

"I *deal* with dealers. So if that makes me one..." I shrugged, and she scoffed. "So you seeing the pretty boy now. Or what?"

"What's it to you?"

"It's not. Just didn't think you were that stupid."

"Excuse me?"

"You heard me." I put my drink down on a table, pressing a hand to the wall and looking down at her. "He threw you away, and you come right back."

"He didn't throw me away." She pushed off me, shoved me away, but I grabbed her wrist.

I jerked her to me. "He did, and any guy who does that isn't worth your time."

"And what? You are?"

She started to walk away, but I pulled her back, my hands full of her hips. I pressed her to the wall again, her throat jumping.

"I value what's mine," I said, too close. I

knew because I could taste her again, that floral scent deep in my chest and warming my blood. "And I may be a brute. I may be a bully, but when I have something good, I don't throw it away."

Red lashes flicked wildly over her eyes, her body shivering. Especially when I pushed off of her.

I grabbed my beer. "Don't be stupid, beauty queen. You're better than that."

Billie

All too quickly, he walked away, leaving me in his wake, and I dizzied yet again.

But he'd thrown me away too.

I hated that my thoughts even went there, and they confused me so much I did text Sinclair. I needed to get out of here. I needed to go home. This was our first public appearance since kind of talking to each other again. LJ was wrong. We weren't together, but we were talking.

Why did he even care?

Why did he know, and so confused, I shook my head. I asked Sinclair where he was via text, but when he didn't respond, I immediately sought out a bathroom. I needed to throw some water on my face. I needed a reality check.

"Bathroom?" I asked someone in the house. I didn't know this house. I didn't know these people. Sinclair had said he had some friends throwing a party, so we came out, the pair of us trying to do something different and me trying to be more adventurous. I'd basically cut myself off from the world after he'd broken up with me, become a hermit besides my visits with Mom, so I was trying to be better. Better only got me under the arm of Lance Johnson again.

"When I have something good, I don't throw it away..."

Needing to get him out of my head, I followed the directions to the bathroom and threw it open. I hadn't knocked first. For some reason hadn't bothered.

I should have bothered.

The space was preoccupied, two guys in there. One was balls deep behind the other, grunting wildly over the guy below, but the moment I came in, they both stopped.

"I'm sorry," I gasped out, backing away, but not before seeing the other guy's face, the one bent over the sink with his pants down to his ankles. Catching my eyes, the guy's widened, completely horrified.

That's because he knew me.

"Billie," Sinclair gasped, pushing the guy behind off him. Sinclair immediately righted himself, getting his pants back up. "It's not what it looks like."

It wasn't what it looked like? The fact that that was all he could come up with floored me, and I raised my hands.

"Don't fucking talk to me," I growled, shaking as I backed out of the bathroom. My eyes brimming with tears, I ran, looking for my coat, and the moment I found it, I shoved my arms inside. I hadn't driven, but I had one of Sinclair's car keys on my chain. He'd given it back to me once we started talking.

Such a huge mistake.

I was basically in tears as I ran through the

house, and by the time I made it outside and into Sinclair's car, my cheating ex had gotten his shit together enough to chase me.

He pressed his hands to the glass of the window of his own car, but I locked the door, keeping him out. He tugged at the door. "Billie, open this door and talk to me!"

So much made sense now. He'd said he'd been confused...

Shaking, I turned on his car, ignoring his roars on the other side as I pressed my foot to the gas and peeled away. I tried not to think about LJ's words about being stupid during the drive.

Because if I did, I wouldn't be able to stop crying.

Chapter Thirteen

Billie

A knock slammed against my door some days later, and though I thought I had a good handle on my curling iron, it slipped and burned the shit out of my finger.

I cursed, dropping the damn thing, and all the while, someone pounded at my door like the police. I managed to get my curling iron up, and after running my finger under some cold water for like a second, I rushed to the door. At this point, the person was ringing the doorbell like crazy, and I screamed I was coming.

"What do you want—" My voice screeched to an abrupt cut-off.

I thought the abs had something to do with it.

Glistening and sweaty, Lance Johnson stood at my door in a pair of gray running shorts hung so low I could have easily seen dick cleavage if he stood at the right angle. He was also shirtless, his shining pecs heaving with breath while he gripped my door frame in a pair of red running shoes. He looked around me. "Shit. You okay?"

Completely distracted by the glistening male in front of me, it took me a second to realize he'd shouted and was *still* shouting at me. I shook my head at the frenzy, and with wide eyes, he had hands on my shoulders and was then pushing me out of his way. I backed up. "What the hell?"

He darted inside my house like he had the right, like he had the gall to even do anything after the last time I'd seen him. That party still burned in my mind, for many reasons, and his part hadn't helped. He'd just been the dagger in an evening of stupid, an evening he'd called me out on and I still felt the burn.

Even still, I followed LJ, screaming myself at the jump of muscles that roved and shifted as he raced through my house like he was on fire. I turned a corner, and he was at my bedroom door. I just about grabbed him until I saw it.

Smoke curled from beneath my door in a thick cloud, and screaming for a different reason now, I launched myself at it. I went for the knob, but LJ jerked me back.

"Wait," he called, clearly the more well-reasoned between the two of us when he placed the back of his hand against the door. Clear, he went for the doorknob, and when he shot my bedroom door open, smoke billowed into the hall so quick I thought half the house was burning down.

I coughed, sputtering as I pushed my way inside. The room was so cloudy I couldn't see much, but the fact my iron blazed in a fiery glory on my ironing board let me know pretty quick it was the source. I immediately went for it, but I was jerked again, *LJ again* when he tugged me back and was once more the rational one between the two of us.

Out of nowhere, he had a fire extinguisher, one he worked like an actual firefighter when he fought the flames on my ironing board. He snuffed the flames out with like two, maybe three short puffs, not even wasting it, and coughing, I made my way over to my bedroom window to open it.

"What the fuck, beauty queen?" LJ growled behind me, and apparently, I was either too panicked or not strong enough to open my window. It didn't

126

budge, and LJ pushed me aside again, a sweaty arm into my side when he tucked the extinguisher under his arm, then forced the window open the rest of the way. I'd had it open a little. Though not much. He wafted the smoke out, and I took a towel beside him, doing the same.

Together, we got the smoke out to the point I could see my bedroom again, and once cleared, LJ was even more sweaty than when he'd started. He ran an arm across his glistening brow, frowning at me. "You trying to kill yourself or something? Good thing I was running outside."

Yeah, good thing, the charred remains of my ironing board beneath a smoking iron. I huffed. "I was trying to iron a dress."

"By setting it on fire? Jesus, beauty queen." He lowered the extinguisher. "I don't know how you iron, but when I do it, it usually consists of a few less flames."

I so didn't need this from him now, his attitude. Lifting my eyes, I propped my hands on my hips. "Where'd you even get that thing?"

He'd raced into the room so quickly with that fire extinguisher it'd been like he'd conjured it, and after a couple more puffs on the iron, I assumed for good measure, he stood back.

"All these rentals have them," he said, eyes narrowing at the smoke. "Mine was in the laundry room. Figured yours was too."

I guessed he'd figured right, and good thing. We might have been having a different conversation had he not happened to be running past. I wouldn't have gone for the extinguisher since I clearly didn't know about it. I grumbled. "I guess you saved my life or something."

"You guess?" He grinned a little, that smug grin that only Lance Johnson could manage to achieve and didn't fail to pulse activity into my nether regions.

The bastard.

I still hadn't forgiven him for basically calling me stupid that night at the party. I had been, but I didn't want him calling me that.

He wiped his brow again, his pecs jumping. He was a gorgeous male specimen, and worst of all, he knew it. His grin widened. "I guess I'll take that. You all right now, or do I have to worry about you burning the rest of your house down?"

Eyes widening, I ran out the room and into the bathroom. I'd, ironically enough, left my curling iron on, and once I got inside, I gave a breath of relief. Nothing was on fire there, a good thing, and I started to shut it off until a deep chuckle came from behind me. Lance Johnson was in my bathroom, that grin only too wide.

"Maybe I should stick around."

"Maybe you shouldn't," I stated, watching as he cut around me.

He picked up the curling iron. "Your presence around electrical appliances begs to differ." He shoved a thumb back. "I just unplugged your iron by the way. *The same* iron that just almost set your house on fire."

Fuck.

"What's your deal?" He lounged back in my space like a god on his throne, his biceps pulsing up and everything. "I've never seen you this scatterbrained. You usually have your shit together.

There wouldn't be trouble in paradise would there? With Mr. Huntington?"

I was sure he was well aware of what had happened at the party *he'd attended*. And I was sure he was even more aware Sinclair and I weren't together anymore. After all, he was the Kingpin, wasn't he?

"We're not together anymore," I said, putting things lightly. The moment I had gotten back to my house, I'd thrown Sinclair's keys outside of it. He'd pounded on my door for what felt like a lifetime before he'd given up, and that's when his calls and texts had started. I didn't answer anymore at the first. I told him I was done, *we were done*, and that was it.

I wet my lips. "But something tells me you already know that."

"I may have heard something," he said, scratching his neck before putting the curling iron down. He lounged back. "And if it means anything, I didn't want to be right about him."

He didn't? I found that hard to believe. Reaching over, LJ angled his long body over the box on the toilet, and before I could stop him, he was opening it up.

"Hey—"

The long dress fell out of it in shimmering waves, a sapphire blue silk. It came with a note, and when LJ picked it up, he frowned at me. "This is from your dad?"

"Yes, and it's none of your business," I said, ripping away both the dress and the card. I threw them both in the box. "And why are you still here?"

"Because I saved you and deserve a consolation prize."

"Which would be?"

His eyes twinkled before he jerked his chin in the direction of the dress. "An explanation for that?" He leaned forward. "And why you almost set your house on fire *twice*?"

Groaning, I nearly screamed at him before wrestling in my hair. Something told me he wouldn't leave either way. I huffed. "If you must know, the dress is a bribe."

"A bribe?"

I nodded. "My dad wants me to go to his wedding and thinks giving me things will convince me to go."

His other tactics hadn't worked, text, phone calls, and ultimately, the wedding invitation itself. I hadn't responded to any of it, my dad now desperate, but I didn't care. I didn't want to go to his stupid wedding.

LJ propped his sneaker against my wall. "So what's the issue then? You just mad because he's getting remarried?"

Because I'd be that sophomoric, that trivial, and the fact I was talking about this to *this* guy now floored me. "You know what? Thanks so much for saving me, but you can get out of my house now."

Instantly, he pushed off the wall, hands on my shoulders when he said, "Hold up," and hands coming *down* my shoulders, he made me stay. He looked right at me, his thumbs burning into my flesh.

It didn't help I was wearing a tank top.

Despite my dad sending me this gift I didn't want, I was going to try it on, taking the time to do my hair before modeling it. The decision had proved to be a huge mistake since I'd almost burned my house down with the iron.

LJ eyed me. "Did I say something to offend?" he asked, then noticed my hair. I'd started to curl it, nearly finished it. Currently, it sat in dead red curls on my shoulders. He twisted one. "Were you going somewhere?"

I groaned. "Since the dress came, I was going to model it. Naturally, I had to do my hair."

"Naturally."

I started to push him away, his body way too hard under my hands. His hands returned to my shoulders again and guiding me to the toilet, he moved the box and sat me down. "What are you doing?"

He worked quick, getting a bunch of products together from my basket above and even a few styling utensils. He grinned again. "I'm obviously going to help you with your hair to model the dress you don't want to wear for the wedding you don't want to go to." He winked, tapping my shoulder with a comb. "Just give me a sec. It's been a bit since I did this."

He'd done this before? My eyes widened. "When have you done this before?"

A wickedness in his eyes when he got behind me, lacing his fingers and cracking them before taking one of my dead curls. Getting it out to full length, electricity surged to my scalp when he touched it, and I attempted to ignore the fact he had his hands in my hair. He got behind me in the mirror. "Wouldn't you like to know?"

I actually would, amazed when he clipped my hair back and immediately went in to use the styling product. My hair never curled without it, and he somehow knew that.

"So you wanna tell me about this thing with your dad?" he asked, talking to me like a real stylist. The fact that this moment was truly happening right now blew my mind. He went for the curling iron and I froze up. He eyed me. "Seriously, beauty queen. I got you. I've probably done this more than you."

"How so?"

"Try three sisters and a mom who worked four jobs." Getting the iron on the curl, he held it, the thing steaming and perfect when he let go. The curl fell down on my shoulder in a way I hadn't even been able to do.

My lips parted. "Shit."

"Told you." Another wink before he got one more curl. This one came right out the same way, just as flawless. "Didn't know my curl game was so strong?"

He was easily over two hundred pounds of muscled male behind me and was doing my hair. So fuck no, I didn't know his curl game was strong.

"I guess I need to hire you," I observed, his eyes teasing through the mirror and his hands heaven.

Especially when he massaged my scalp.

He did it to get the product in, his long digits wrapping in my hair, and I looked away from his eyes in the mirror.

"So your dad's a dick or…"

"No." And I didn't want to talk about this. Not with him. I huffed. "He just did a dick thing."

I considered it that when you married a girl more than half your age. Also, marrying said girl who was half your age that you cheated on your wife and family with.

LJ's lip pulled into his mouth as he did my

hair, a slight frown to his lips. "Still bummed about the divorce then?"

I turned looking at him.

He shrugged. "I may have looked into you."

"Did you now?"

His look could have been guilty if he did such a thing. But Lance was nothing if not self assured. His shoulder lifted. "I was curious about you."

"Curious?"

A gravelly chuckle. "You handled me that first night at my house so I looked into you."

"And what did you find out?"

"I found out your dad seriously screwed you and your mom over," he said, going behind me when he grabbed my hair again. "And that said screwing over kind of made your mom and you the black sheep in your family."

He was right about that. My own grandma had the nerve to be mad at my mom for letting her marriage fall apart. That was just how it was in my world, people kept their dirty laundry to themselves. They didn't put it all out there for others to see.

I had no idea how I felt about LJ knowing so much about my family. About knowing so much about me.

"And your dad's the district attorney," he said, his expression a bit harsh when he said it. "Funny, he's out there fighting crime and he can't even take care of his own."

"And what would you know about that?"

"More than you think." His eyes narrowed. "There's a reason my mom had to work four jobs, and I was right there working my own beside her. I know a little something about self-serving fathers."

Silence behind me, steam rolling off his naked body. I hugged my arms as he continued to style my hair. I huffed. "What happened to yours?"

"Walked out on us." No emotion there. The comb back in my hair. "Never needed him anyway and still don't. I'm all my mom and my sisters ever needed."

Clearly, he had a bone to pick with his own dad, but he sounded more over the fact than anything else. His hurt didn't sound as fresh as mine felt.

But that didn't make his any less severe.

I obviously didn't know his story, nor did he have a right to know mine. But when I looked at him doing my hair, I couldn't helping wanting to share more with him.

"My dad's a good guy," I said, because he was. LJ was right. He fought to rid the streets of crime every day, worked his whole life when he could be making much more money in the private sector as an attorney. Truth be told, my dad's income mostly came from our family's businesses. Not his job as district attorney. The job was something he chose to do, wanted to do, and I'd always seen him as such a superhero because of it. I dampened my lips. "He fell in love with someone at the office."

"Fell in love?"

"Yeah, broke my family apart." That was one way of putting the colossal damage that had ensued.

"So he's not a dick because…"

"It was the last thing he wanted." The words chilled me to say, that last conversation I'd overhead him and my mom having. He hadn't wanted to leave her, the last thing he wanted.

"We don't love each other, Gen. Never have,

and you know that," he'd said, holding her as she cried all over him. *"Aren't you tired of pretending? Don't you want a chance? A chance to be happy for you and not someone else?"*

I then got to hear how my parents' entire marriage was a sham, chess pieces in their world of affluence and money. I guessed they'd met through shared circles and their parents had pushed them into it. They hadn't even wanted to get married, but had to appease. Dad had been all in, but just couldn't do it anymore. Not after he found Clarise.

He'd fallen in love.

Swallowing hard, I fought tears now, LJ's image blurring. The last thing I was going to do was a cry in front of this guy. He might use it against me.

"So he didn't want to leave," he said, thank God not noticing my tears. "But he did, beauty queen. If that doesn't make a guy a dick..."

"It's not that simple."

"Then what is?"

"Things can be complicated. *Are* complicated, but that doesn't mean I have to watch him flaunt his new love around."

My voice quivered after that, and I hated it, even more when LJ dragged his fingers through my hair. His touch was absolute heaven, and I absorbed it in.

"I think you should go to the wedding."

"I should?"

His eyes met mine through the mirror, my hair in perfect waterfall curls across my shoulders. He made me look even better than I possibly could on my own, a miracle as the curls framed my face. He smiled a little. "Because it's complicated, and you obviously love your dad."

Words harsh, though they hadn't meant to be. Still, they jarred my reality. I did love my father.

I was just mad that any of us had to go through this.

It angered me my parents had put us in this position in the first place, and I resented my dad. Resented him for being strong enough to choose his own path. The way in which he did it only made it worse, deceitful and behind my mom's back. That, outside of everything else, made it even harder for me to ever forgive him. I wasn't sure I ever would.

"It's lovely," I said, giving LJ a compliment. "What you did is lovely. To my hair?"

"Props from the beauty queen herself," he said, unplugging the curling iron out of the wall. He smiled a little. "I'll catalog that."

I was sure he would, my hand looping around his bicep. The flesh hard, I didn't know what I'd do with him once I had him.

I'd just wanted to touch him.

His eyes smoldered like raging fire, his hand reaching and propping against the wall. He had this way of completely closing me in, clouding my brain. His thumb touched my chin. "Now what?"

I didn't know what. I didn't know *how* or even if I should. This guy was so dangerous and was obviously mixed up in a lot of shit I had no business getting mixed up with. I mean, I was pretty sure my dad put away people like him, dabbling in some of the things he dealt with. A million thoughts traveled behind my eyes, and though I think he had some too, he came up with his conclusions a lot quicker than me.

He let go, his expression hard. "Try not to burn anything else. I might not always be there to save you," he said and then was giving me his back. He always did that, walked away.

Which made what I was considering not two seconds ago even worse.

Chapter Fourteen

LJ

Alexi Marvelli sat atop his actual throne, topless women cascading from the ceiling around him like greenery. They spun on shimmering silks, a lavish display in Alexi's crystal palace. Niko and I were presented to him here tonight, the Crystal Palace the viewfinder to the rest of Alexi's gentlemen *and* women's club The Cherry Bomb. The Cherry Bomb held the traditional flair for a club like this, fire eaters, animal tamers, and tits…

Lots and lots of tits.

Niko and I got an eyeful of them upon entering Alexi's Crystal Palace, the man's arms wide when he saw Niko and me.

"My boys," he proclaimed, having gotten up from his throne encrusted in jewels and glistening diamonds. The whole display was a bit much, but who was I to judge a guy for what he was into? Alexi obviously enjoyed nice things, and since I appreciated that too, I merely smiled once I approached.

He gave both Niko and me large and inviting hugs, part of the family until one wasn't. This was very much known to both Niko and me. A guy didn't fuck with the Marvellis. Not unless he wanted to be killed. This was precisely why Alexi was getting a generous donation today on top of what we owed him for his product on campus. Today was the last business drop, a day I'd been very much looking forward too. With the semester of my junior year winding down, I'd finally gotten to a place where I felt my family and I would be all right. I had plenty of money tucked away, and if I wanted a little something, I'd just promote my parties again. It was quick and easy money and held less of the stress of being the "kingpin" on campus.

I still can't believe Beauty Queen called me that.

Obviously, that was what people called me but *her* calling me that felt weird. A kingpin was in charge of his surroundings, called the say of the who and the what. He was also ruthless and willing to do anything to get his. I may be a few or more of those things, but I wasn't sure I necessarily wanted her to see me that way. I was also unsure, like many things, why I actually cared about her opinion, but I guess seeing her almost burn her house down the other day with herself inside had some kind of affect on me.

There was also her hair, soft and fragrant and nothing like doing my sisters' hair. I'd had to rub one off that night *badly* after touching it, and getting my head out of the gutter now, I checked back in on my meeting with Alexi and his bodyguards. He had them strategically sprinkled around the room like houseplants, "just in case."

Dual kisses on either side of my face from Alexi and Niko got the same when he came over to my buddy. Seeing what we held today, Alexi guided one of his goons, er um, bodyguards, to take today's large and final payment from us.

A nod and I had Niko hand the lot over, our hands behind our backs after that. We didn't typically come over to Alexi's clubs to conduct business exchanges, an exception made for today. Today was the last one so we did, and when we did do exchanges, we never stayed long. This was just how the pair of us did things, well-known on Alexi's end, but that didn't stop the man from inviting us into his sanctum for a drink after he got his money.

"Just one, my brothers?" he asked us, guiding a girl with glittery skin and gorgeous tits to get it started. Alexi's smile widened. "After all, it is the last time. Please? You'd do me the honor. We've had such a great relationship."

We had, and we wanted to keep it that way. Since he was right, today's drop the last time, I supposed I could break my limited contact rule—just once, of course.

Niko gave me a look, and when I nodded, Alexi clasped his meaty hands together, a large motherfucker in a suit the color of blood red, full crimson with black silk shirt and necktie. Alexi gestured toward his viewfinder, his private booth with an overlook of the entire club. "Please. My space is yours."

We took him up on the seat, the circle booth like a VIP section at a normal titty bar.

His club was gorgeous, high stakes clientele, and nothing like the smaller, more modest venues he had closer to campus. Those were more moderately priced to attract college students and the less affluent in town, but Alexi had people to oversee those. He maybe dropped in on them once a month for a check-in, something I knew since before Niko and I had started doing business with him, we'd seen him there on occasion. Of course, once we'd started working with him, he had given us the ins and outs of his business. This was a sign of trust, and I did take notes. I was nothing if not an entrepreneur, and though the guy and his family may have their hands in stuff I'd never touch, it couldn't be denied the Marvellis ran a smart and successful business. Alexi himself was head of the family, younger, but I'd heard his father had died of heart disease or something back in the nineties. He'd had to step up to the throne pretty quick, something I related to as well since I also came from a household sans a father.

Niko and I both clinked glasses with Alexi, but I nursed my scotch while Niko played with his. Alexi kicked his back right away, of course, grinning like the mob boss he was when he stamped his glass down. He lounged his big body back in the booth. "So sad to see you both go, but this will be a happy day, yes? How are your families? Niko, your mother? She doing well?"

We really were like family, and Alexi did know a lot about our lives. I guessed he had to, more of that trust, and we did know a little bit about his too. As much as he'd give up, of course, over our quick drop visits and check-ins about how our own business was doing.

Niko nursed that glass again, his smile a slight one in his gray suit. I was well aware of his mom's condition. She could definitely be better, but she hadn't been as bad as she was in the past. Her most recent clinical trial had been doing well. Niko pulled his drink over. "She's responding to her most recent clinical trial. She does have a long road, though."

"I can imagine." This saddened Alexi and upon getting his glass topped off, he clinked it with Niko's. "Cheers to you, my brother. I also had a mother with breast cancer. It will turn out all right. My mom's did."

"I hope so." The gruffness in Niko's words

worked at my heart, this guy *my own* brother since coming to college. No one could ever replace my boys from my hometown, Maywood Heights, but that family definitely could grow. Niko had done that for me, the guy my real fucking brother, and I hurt for him. Especially when he was hurting.

Alexi displayed a soft smile. "Never worry, friend. Never worry. Fate is on you and your mother's side. I know it is." Placing his glass down, he slapped his hands together. "I'm sure she has lots of medical costs. Perhaps I can help. I have many jobs coming up. A perfect way to help? I'd love to relieve some of those burdens for you."

Alexi never failed to push, create ways to draw us more and more into the dark underworld in which he dealt. The answer had always been a resounding no, but he never ceased to ask.

This was the biggest reason Niko and I never stayed for drinks, interaction best to be limited. I wasn't the type of guy to be drawn in easy. But even I had been tempted to touch the forbidden fruit of Alexi's exceedingly lavish life when we first started dealing with him. The man lived large and could make both Niko and I like him, struggling trash from small towns transformed into gods like himself.

The temptation was definitely there, always, and after an exchange with Niko, his eyes cut right back to Alexi. My buddy kept his head shake firm but polite, his hand tight on his glass. He passed that off by putting his hand back on the table, but I did notice it, the denial obviously hard for him, and I couldn't blame him.

How easy Alexi could fix everything in our lives? It was just *how* he fixed things that was the problem, and Niko knew better than to get in any deeper than we already had in the past.

Though this denial saddened our friend and brother, Alexi so obviously understood. After all, this hadn't been the first time we'd told him no. And smiling, Alexi got another drink before tipping his glass at me. "And you, Jay? Things well? How are those sisters? You have one on the way to college, right?"

"Yeah, and hell raising," I said, chuckling and making the table laugh. Dasha definitely had an attitude on her, strong-willed like me. As she was getting older and stir crazy to be out from under my mom's roof, the two were basically driving each other up the wall. Like a pair of titans constantly clashing, and without me in the household to keep them away from each other, I'd been getting more than one call lately from mom about her daughter's "attitude." I grinned. "She's doing well. Top of her class."

Dasha had already gotten into Woodcreek and was getting a full ride scholarship like me. She didn't even need the savings I'd put aside for her four years, doing her part just like I had to take the burden off our hardworking mother and, technically, me. My family was never a burden, though. I'd do anything for them.

My current dealings with the mob proved this, Alexi's smile strong on me.

"Of course she is. Gifted like her brother." He tapped the side of my neck before resting his arm behind the booth. "Well, if she or any of your family needs anything at all, let me know. We don't have to be done here today."

"Yeah, but I think it's time," I said,

exchanging a glance with my boy. When Niko smiled in agreement, I did too. I waved a hand. "It's time to be getting out on our own, Alexi. But of course, we appreciate all you've done for us. You know that."

"I do, but you both still have a full year left of school, Jay." He eyed me. "You have to account for other things that might come up. Some spending money perhaps?"

He nudged me with his elbow, and I chuckled again. I shook my head. "Got plenty of nuts stored up for the winter. Should be good."

And it was all locked down in more than one bank. There'd be enough for me to definitely start a good life post-graduation and plenty there for my other two sisters to get full rides to their own colleges. Mom also would be good and would never have to work herself to the bone again. This was basically guaranteed once I got hired on after school. I was studying to be an architect, something I didn't even realize I had a knack for until I went to school. I already had companies all over the country buzzing for me, ties I'd made *on my own* just by being good at what I did and having awesome relationships with my professors. They spoke around about me, something I'd earned with trust and had nothing to do with money or influence. Money couldn't buy everything in the end. Sometimes it took character, *heart* and something I always had a lot of.

I started to get into that with Alexi when a silver top caught my eye from the Crystal Palace. Normally, I wouldn't notice such a thing, but the girl's top was literally shimmering off the walls of this place. She paired it with a matching skirt way too short, that fiery red hair she had bathing her naked arms like The Little Mermaid. The only issue was this wasn't the sea but a din of danger and bullshit she had no business being a part of.

Especially considering who her father was.

Rage hit me as I realized The Little Mermaid down there was Billie, Billie at a fucking titty bar when she should be back in her cute little cottage with those breasts behind her sweater sets. I faced Alexi, and while he ordered another round for our table, I got Niko's attention.

Instantly, his gaze jerked toward the floor, and that let me know Billie was like a fucking beacon in this place. His eyes caught her right away, widening before facing me.

He mouthed, "What the fuck?" and I had the same thought. I didn't know if Billie was damn daft or just plain stupid to walk into a place where her DA dad had put away half this man's family. I looked her dad up after what my buddy Knight had told me about him, and the Marvellis had more than one family member behind bars because of that guy.

I casually excused myself.

"Hurry back, brother." Alexi waved after I did, grinning and already half drunk. Shit, he might be well on his way to shit-faced since I didn't know what he'd had before Niko and I arrived, and I only thanked the gods for their gift of alcohol and buffoonery in that department tonight.

In my own dark suit, I nodded at Alexi's henchman Darrell before walking past, the guy the size of a gorilla. I took the elevator to the floor, and needless to say, it didn't take me long to find the beauty queen.

Billie stood out like a fucking woodland fairy

in this place with her shimmering outfit, and it didn't help that she captured the eyes of pretty much every guy in the room. She had a flock of dudes around her, the girl all wide-eyed and innocent-like. She was innocent and didn't belong here.

Currently, Billie and her harem of suitors watched a fire eater, the dudes around her basically shoving drinks at her.

That was until they saw me.

A mere look and I parted the sea, and it took a second for Billie to observe the reason why.

Her gaze grappled on me like a kid with his favorite chocolate bar, the look and this place enough to make me recall why I'd stepped away the other day. The way she looked at me once I'd saved her from her iron and did her hair told me I could have gotten anything I wanted from this girl.

I'd just chosen not to.

It would have been so easy, so damn simple, and I considered it a victory until I saw all that damn debate behind her eyes. She had *to think* about me, and she probably should. I was the guy I was sure her daddy wouldn't want her having anything to do with.

Like she'd realized she was staring, she stepped back in her stiletto heels, and like the innocent little thing she was, she caught herself on them.

My hands launched out instantly, grabbing her and pulling her over to me, and I couldn't be more enraged. I was angry that she was here, yes.

But even more so at the feel of her in my hands.

I *hated* that I wanted to bathe in all that beautiful red hair of hers, that I wanted to kiss and suck on every lickable surface of her. No matter how dirty. Visions of her made my mouth water and my cock fucking steel inside my pants.

"LJ," she gasped, panting. She was actually *panting*. So goddamn needy. "What are you doing here?"

"What am *I* doing here?" I actually laughed, the sound literally booming my chest to the point I probably sounded crazed. Jerking her up to me, I growled. "What the fuck are you doing in a titty bar?"

Like a switch went off, she blanched, and though I thought she'd actually slap me, she settled for ripping her arm away. I found myself relieved by this. She shouldn't want me, and I definitely shouldn't be wanting her. Dangerous on both our parts. Especially with her being here. Her eyes blazed. "That's freaking rich. Last I checked, you're in this same titty bar, and I go wherever the hell I want. I came with *friends* if you must know, and you're not my keeper, *Lance*."

The hell I wasn't. In fact, when she decided to do her little dance of voyeurism in this outfit, she basically gave me permission. My jaw worked. "You look like you belong on the street."

"And you look like an asshole." She shoved me off of her.

At least, tried.

She was easily only a fraction of my size and basically couldn't move me at all. She crossed her arms. "You know, I don't get you. One moment, you're rushing into my house, saving me from my iron and doing my hair, and the next, you're manhandling me and pretty much calling me a whore. So which is it, LJ? Am I the damsel or something you're trying to break?"

She was right, of course, the lines blurring all the time and to the point where I constantly confused myself. I didn't know what she was, my curse or my salvation, but every day I felt this intense need to claim her, keep her and make her see that she was mine, and that remained current no matter what the day.

Most especially now.

"Is there a problem, Mr. Johnson?" One of Alexi's bouncers saddled up to my side, one I was actually very familiar with. I'd even been over to the guy's house for dinner once, eating with his family.

Billie chased his huge chest up to his eyes, looking a bit relieved by the guy's presence, but she shouldn't. He wasn't here to bat for her, only me.

The look of relief instantly wiped from her face when I grabbed her, doing so with more force than I meant to. I had to prove a point, though. She didn't belong here, not in this place. *Never* in this place. I basically threw her at Alexi's bouncer, and in her heels, she stumbled into him.

"Take care of this one," I grunted. "She's causing a disturbance."

I put my back to her after that, hearing her call me all kinds of things while she was dragged away. I was an asshole, a dick, and I could be anything she wanted as long as she was out of here. She needed to be safe, and here? She was anything but.

Chapter Fifteen

Billie

I was on fire by the time I got myself together enough to text my friends. LJ was so out of line it wasn't even funny, throwing his weight around at, of all places, a strip club. I'd been reluctant even to come out tonight, but after the whole thing with Sinclair, then LJ appearing and reappearing in my life, I'd just wanted to let off some damn stress. I had a few friends in some of my graduate film classes that were always talking about going out, so tonight I decided to take them up on the offer.

A lot of good it did me.

That bouncer had basically thrown me out on my ass, the place not my scene anyway. LJ was right. This really wasn't my scene. I'd just wanted to have a good time.

I shot what was going on with me in a group text to my grad friends, hoping they might like to go somewhere else tonight since I'd basically been thrown out. I waited for a response for a while, but when I heard nothing, decided to catch a ride-share. None of us had driven anyway since we didn't know who'd be drinking.

I used the app to call for a ride, then waited a few minutes before sitting down on the curb. My skirt was so short it rode up my ass, and I chastised myself for being able to be talked into wearing it by my graduate friends. They'd met me up at my house and told me to turn right back around and change, apparently the navy blue dress I'd been wearing not appropriate for where we were going tonight. It was only later after we pulled up to the club I realized we were going to a strip club. A nice strip club but a strip club nonetheless. Honestly, I guessed LJ had been doing me a favor in the end.

But never would he know that.

I growled, literally snarling over my phone app. I'd been assigned a ride, but for whatever reason it wasn't here yet, and I was getting more and more pissed off as I watched their little icon wander about town like it had no destination. I nearly canceled it for another when I caught the eye of a dude coming out the club. He fist pounded a bouncer, basically looking like one himself with his height and overall stature, and glancing at me, he grinned so wide I thought the club lights might reflect off his teeth.

Christ.

I groaned as *LJ's friend* Niko lifted a hand at me, then proceeded to saunter his way over to my corner of the street. He'd been wearing similar clothing to LJ, a suit that smoothed perfectly across his broad chest and big shoulders. Niko was basically big everywhere, looking pretty much like a football player at a draft party. He had his dark hair slicked back out of his eyes, his hand cutting into his suit coat to hold his tie. He was a debonair man of the world, and my mouth dried recalling how LJ looked in a similar suit. His had been a smooth navy, crisp and buttery in tone. Oddly enough, we would have matched tonight had I chosen to wear a similar color, drawing him to me even more, I supposed.

Stepping up to me, Niko bent his massively large frame, trying to find my eyes when he dashed a grin.

"Queen B, that is you," he said, then gazed

about the street. "Mind letting me in on what you're doing?"

"Ask your friend." I kicked my feet out onto the pavement. Where was that damn ride-share? "He's the one who kicked me out of your club."

"Our club?" Niko bumped a laugh like I'd said anything funny. He removed his hand from inside his jacket. "Hardly. But Jay actually tossed you out?"

The look I cut him let him know, and when he placed out his hand to help me up, I actually took it. I probably shouldn't be sitting on the street anyway, my goods hanging out. People might get the wrong idea.

"You look like you belong on the street."

LJ's words in my head sour, I hugged myself, warming my arms and seeing that, Niko took off his jacket. He started to give it to me, but I waved him off. "I'm fine. Just waiting for a ride-share."

"How long?" he asked, folding the jacket over his arm. All that remained over his burly arms was a black dress shirt and matching tie. He tossed a thumb back. "I'm leaving now and can take you home if you'd like. We *are* neighbors."

He leaned in when he said that, and I really didn't want anything from him. Before I could answer, though, he was handing a ticket over to the valet, and with only a few words into the valet's headset, a fire engine red sports car was literally pulling up in front of us. It also had spoilers glistening harder than my outfit.

Hopping out, the valet left the door open for Niko, and when he came around, he pressed a big hand on the top. He waggled his dark eyebrows playfully. "Coming or going, Queenie? I ain't got all day, you know."

I checked my phone app again, but since the driver was still wandering around the world, I canceled the thing and got inside. This received a chuckle from Niko, and after tossing the valet a wad of cash, he got in with me.

"Buckle up, Your Majesty," Niko teased, flashing a set of deep dimples at me. He worked the car into gear. "I drive fast and don't slow down for royalty."

Rolling my eyes, I did what he said, then shot back into the seat the moment he pressed his boot to the metal. I literally had to hang on to the car and might have shot through the window at every stop if not for the dashboard.

I slammed my hands on it every time, getting nothing but another chuckle from Niko. He rolled to a stop at most streetlights and ignored stop signs entirely, not giving a fuck. The time or two I thought he might were when we got closer to campus. The campus police were always out, but even then, he didn't care. He cruised right through, and the cops we saw didn't do anything about it when he zoomed past them.

Some even waved at him.

These guys even own the campus police.

Their pull seemed to never end.

All too quickly, we came up on our street, and the moment Niko started to slow in front of my house, I sat up. I started to gather my things but stopped at the sight of someone sitting on my porch.

What the fuck?

I left the porch lights on so I could easily see

the head of someone sitting there, a tall someone working his hands, and as we got closer, the fact my ex-boyfriend was sitting on my stoop couldn't be denied.

He had his hands cuffing his arms, facing the night and clearly waiting for me. Ducking immediately, I edged a look over at Niko. "Keep driving."

"What?"

"Keep driving!" I pressed Niko's foot to the gas, and he zoomed past the house, basically barking obscenities at me. I only lifted my head once we cleared the block, and growling, Niko put the car in park down the street.

"What the hell, Billie?"

"That was my ex."

"Your ex? Ex what?" Then his eyes flashed. "The one with that dude the other night?"

Framing my face, I nodded. "Yes. He's sitting on my porch, and I can't go back there. Not just yet."

As far as I was concerned, we could sit here down the street until he left. I had nothing for him, maybe not ever. He hadn't been shy about trying to talk to me via texts and calls, but I definitely wasn't talking to him. All that crap that happened, way too soon.

Hugging my chest, I hunkered down but shot up the moment Niko put the car back into gear and made a U-turn. My eyes twitched wide. "What are you doing?"

"We're going to have a little chat with that fucker," he said, almost gleeful about it, but then frowned seeing me. "What?"

"Um, *no*. I don't want to see him again. Keep

driving. No way."

"Billie, seriously. I'll make quick work of that shit. Anyway, Jay would kick my ass if I just let you go back to that house and didn't do anything."

He would? Yeah right, and I almost laughed but was too panicked by the fact that we were quickly rolling up to my house. I flagged down Niko, hunkering down again. "Would you please just *drive* or even better take me to your place?"

"My place?"

"Yes, I can squat there until he leaves. I'm sure he won't wait long." The fact that Sinclair was putting out this much effort to even talk to me blew my mind. He honestly never put much effort into our relationship when it'd been good, so yes, this now was surprising.

I guess when you lose something...

Chewing my lip, I felt Niko slow the car, and I thought he might ignore my request. But suddenly, his hand was on my head, cradling and pushing me further to lean down. He came to a stop, and when he rolled the window down, I thought I might vomit.

I saw him grin above.

"What's up, bro?" he asked, placing on that Niko charm. He dropped an arm on the wheel. "You looking for Billie?"

"Yeah. Have you seen her?" Sinclair's voice sounded way too close, my heart about to explode through my chest.

Covering my arms, I didn't mean to shake, but seriously, this guy definitely wasn't who I'd thought he was. It was one thing to call someone after a breakup, but to keep showing up out of the blue like he had the first time? It all honestly freaked me out and was warranted.

I hugged my body tight, shaking, and Niko immediately noticed.

Suddenly, his hand on my head went to my back. He tapped just lightly, as if to calm me, and definitely wasn't smiling anymore. He lifted his chin. "I haven't. But I'll let her know you were here. That you were looking for her?"

A clear warning was in Niko's voice, one I didn't understand, and being under his hand now felt way safer than going out there and speaking to my ex.

"Okay," Sinclair said, his voice sounding farther away. "I think I'll wait for her. I'm sure she'll be back soon."

I internally groaned, closing my eyes, and I noticed Niko's hand grip the wheel a little.

A quick nod, and he was rolling up his windows and before I knew it, he zoomed forward. The trip was quick, and when he pressed a button on the sun visor, I heard the garage door open up.

Niko slowed to a stop inside, and I let out a breath when he turned off the car, then closed the garage door.

I sat up. "Thank you."

"No problem," he said his smile returning as he unstrapped himself.

He came around the car, letting me out, and together, we went back inside the house that had left me mortified the last time I'd been there. He had entry through the garage, thank God, and I tried to erase my earlier visions of the place as I stepped inside.

The last time I'd been here, I'd been covered in beer and had to fight with people to make my way through. Now, the place glistened with the most beautiful sounds of quiet, the house truly lovely from both its modern decor to the masculine furnishings. The boys' rental had a lair-like quality to it but only in the most handsome way, dark undertones with umber sconces and crystal chandeliers all throughout. Whatever these guys had their hands dipped in financially was obviously doing well for them, the place almost lavish to the extreme. I didn't know about Niko's year in school, but LJ was only a junior. Not many undergrads could even afford to live in such luxury.

I took a seat on the boys' black leather couch, playing with my phone. Once Niko deposited his keys, he asked if I wanted a drink, and when I told him water, he came back with a bottle and had changed. He was out of his suit now and into a pair of sweatpants that hugged his muscular thighs and cuffed at his ankles, his feet bare and a tank stretching across his gargantuan chest. He really looked like LJ's bodyguard, a demigod incarnate, and not only did he have the bottle for me, but some bedding he handed out underneath it. Taken aback, I lifted my hands. "I'm not staying."

"The hell you aren't. Not with stalker douche across the street."

"He's not stalking me. He's just…" Seriously overstepping his boundaries and was now blowing up my phone. I had several texts asking where I was and when I was coming back and after silencing the thread, Niko smirked at me.

He ran his fingers through his ultra dark hair. "You're staying. At least for the night. You're not going back over there with that guy there. Jay would literally crucify my ass."

"Right. Because he cares so much about me." He'd said something similar before, and I lifted my eyes now like I had then.

Niko smirked. "Right. Anyway, you need anything else?"

Since I didn't, I said no, but imagine my surprise when Niko plopped his gargantuan ass on the couch beside me. Getting the remote, he tossed an arm back behind the couch, hugging up on me real good when he turned on the TV. I frowned. "What are you doing?"

"Watching TV."

"I see that, but why are you doing so down here?" They probably had like five TVs and I recalled one being in his room that night we walked in on the orgy.

"It's my house, isn't it?" he stated, dancing his eyebrows at me. After settling for reruns of *Ninja Warrior*, he relaxed back, cozying up to me like we were besties at a pajama party. "After all, I gotta make sure you don't go crawling back to that house and the douche canoe."

"Douche canoe? Really?"

"Really." He eyed me like this conversation was *very* serious. "He cheated on you, didn't he? Very openly, I might add. The whole party heard about that shit. The guy is a douche canoe. Look it up in the dictionary, and you'll see his mug."

I mean, he wasn't wrong, and I had assumed people heard about what happened. I'd basically been screaming at him that night as he chased after me.

He lowered the remote. "Where I'm from that's what that guy is. Sorry, but real talk."

I didn't know where he was from, but since that logic was the same from where I was from too, I sat back. Niko smelled nice so that made it easy. He'd also saved me tonight, and I guessed I could be around worse company.

And less attractive.

Jesus, he was gorgeous, almost as good-looking as LJ with his chiseled jaw and grin for days. Niko had eyes as dark and fine as a buck's fur and noticing me staring, he danced his eyebrows again. "Stare any longer, Queenie, and I'll be charging for the peepshow."

Rolling my eyes, I snatched the remote from him, changing the channel to a movie on Showtime. It was one of those rom-coms, but Niko didn't complain. I settled into the couch. "Where are you from anyway?"

"Chicago. South Side," he said, then smiled. "Very different from here."

"In what ways?"

"Well, for starters, it's not as easy to come up as it is here." He lifted his hand to the digs, letting me know he obviously didn't always have such luxury around him.

I couldn't assume anything, but rumors said drugs were involved and LJ basically confirmed that at the party.

Niko frowned. "But honestly, outside of that, I would have liked to have stuck around. Been closer to my mom." He snagged a pillow, strong-arming it between his thick arms. "She's sick. Breast cancer."

"Oh, I'm so sorry." I didn't know what else to say really, probably the wrong thing.

Niko lifted a hand. "She's doing okay with her

treatments. Doesn't want me to worry much, but I do wish I was closer. I plan on coming right back home after I finish school, and I send everything I can her and my sister's way. The least I could do."

Enjoying what I'd learned about him, I brought my legs up on the couch. "And here I thought you were just some meathead with a loaded wallet."

"Oh, my wallet is very much loaded." His arm dropped around me, those dark eyebrows waggling. "And though I'm not as smart as Jay, I'm far from a meathead. Grades back home got me a partial scholarship, but Jay..." He whistled. "Full ride. Guy's a fucking tank. I call him a genius, but he said it's just hard work."

Seeing his most recent efforts in school, I saw a glimmer of that genius. As far as hard work or lack thereof, I'd seen that too. "Well, he could stand to try a little in my class."

"Yeah?" He lounged back, hands tucked behind his head. "I guess I'm not surprised. You drive him crazy, Queenie. Frankly, I'm blown away he has any type of average at all with you around."

"Well, he drives me crazy." Taking the pillow, I tossed it at him. He fought me a bit with it before a barked throat clear made us both shift on the couch.

LJ, his tie loosened, had his jacket over his arm. He'd looked fucking sexy before, but now, his dark shirt labored at the seams, his shoulders thick and his golden chest exposed. He had the top button of his dress shirt popped open and basically smoldered before me.

I wet my lips despite myself and pretty much eased off Niko's lap since we'd been wrestling.

At least, I tried to.

Niko pulled me right back, dropping an arm around me when he grinned up at his friend. "Sup, bro?"

LJ twitched like Niko flashed him, his eyes cold. Tossing his jacket on the couch, he moved fingers through his perfect hair. "What the fuck is this? A hot tub party? You said you were just taking her home."

I angled a look over at Niko. He shrugged. "I texted him while I was upstairs changing. That I was getting you home—"

"And nowhere in that text did you include her ass basically all over you." Jaw clenched, LJ crossed the distance, and Niko lifted a hand.

"Give me a break, Jay. Her boyfriend's over at her house being a stalker—"

"*Ex*-boyfriend," I raised a finger, but even still, LJ's eyes flashed wildly for some reason. Before I knew it, he was striding in the opposite direction.

"Where the fuck is the fucker?" he charged, exiting the room completely. "I'm going to fry his ass."

I pushed Niko. "Shouldn't we go stop him?"

LJ looked *pissed*, and he might just kill Sinclair. Though I had no idea why. I started to get up, but Niko tugged me back.

"Like to see you try," he stated, chuckling. "Anyway, wait it out. I checked earlier and your guy is gone."

"So why am I still here—" Again, I moved to get up, but again, I was pulled back down. I pouted.

"Because he might come back?" he stated the fact like it was obvious, and I jumped at a door slam. LJ had obviously left, and at this point, Niko

162

chuckled, then pointed a finger at me. "Now, how about a real drink? Might be a long night with Jay all up in his feelings. Goes better with alcohol."

He started to get up, and palming my face, I nodded. "You got wine?"

"Sure thing."

A quick exit, and he eventually came back, a glass of dark wine in his hand. His arrival also happened to coincide with LJ, who entered the room with his shirt basically open, the guy amped the hell up like fucking Hulk. LJ's shoulders laboring with breath, Niko cut in front of him.

He handed him off a beer.

"No luck?" he asked, grinning at him before returning to the couch.

LJ frowned. "How did you know?"

"Just quick is all." Niko clearly tried to sound casual about it, but so obviously knew something when he plopped down beside me. He popped a cap off his own beer, being super flirty when he threw his arm around me again.

This didn't seem to particularly help the situation with LJ, but he did allow it before taking my other side. He didn't sit completely on top of me, but as big as he was, there was no way our thighs weren't rubbing the other. His extended limbs stamped out, my bare thigh touching his pant leg since I was still wearing a skirt.

He noticed, his gaze chasing up my legs before opening his beer and taking a long swallow. He forced it down hard. "Douche canoe's gone. Hopefully, with some protection because if he comes back here I'll shoot his dick off and feed it to him."

Niko eyed me before clinking my glass.

"What did I say? Douche canoe."

He'd said a lot of things, a few about his friend, but LJ was so hot and cold I had no idea what to make of him. Instead, I took the remote back, changing the channel again. The guys groaned when I found *Titanic*, but they were going to deal. It was my favorite movie.

And I needed a fucking break tonight.

LJ

The girl was hugged all up on Niko like he was her favorite toy, a drink in her hand while the two of them went on and on about some bullshit show for teens. *Riverdale*, I think she'd called it? Anyway, whatever it was had Niko all up in his feelings, hugging his beer bottle *and* Billie while he looked confused as fuck about whatever was going on in the show. All this followed the *Titanic*-fest since I guessed we only caught the tail end of it. Billie quickly acquired the remote again and now, was making us suffer through whatever this crap was on my flat screen.

Niko threw a hand out. "You've got to be kidding me. Why would the show's creators even pen this Betty and Veronica back and forth bullshit?" He lounged back, settling a hand on Billie's hip. "I mean, no contest here. Betty doesn't stand a chance, and if she thinks she does with my boy Archie, she's lost her damn mind. Veronica clearly reigns supreme here."

"I mean, I don't know." Billie rocked her little shoulders, still in that silvery little outfit that hugged her body right. In fact, every time she leaned against Niko's chest, I got a flash of her ass cheeks, the only reason I was entertaining him holding her at all, I think. She shrugged. "I'd do her."

I had to have gotten damn whiplash with as quick as I jutted my neck in her direction, and Niko, goddamn Niko, actually choked on his beer. Billie, on the other hand, gave her innocent little chuckle, smiling before taking a sip of her wine. Clearly, the Merlot had made her more cavalier than her usual perfectly put-together self.

She slid her basically empty wine glass on my coffee table, my eyes gifted with another flash of ass. I needed to get myself in check when it came to this girl. But I said nothing when she came back to Niko's chest.

He cradled her way too tight, my own hand about to crush glass at the situation presented. I wanted to whip her off him, take her to my room, and show her what the fuck was up. I wanted to do what I really wanted at the club tonight instead of forcing her away. But as the evening went on and the banter continued, I was well aware of my rights. I had no claim on this girl.

No logical claim anyway.

Instead, I chose to shake my head, wetting the top of my bottle before taking a drink. It went down in a tasteless lump, and I sniffed, passing off what Billie just said. "Sure, beauty queen."

"Sure?" She looked at me like I had nothing but audacity for what I'd said, her hands on her hips. "You don't think I'd do Betty?"

"Oh, I think you'd do her," I said, listening to myself. My dick suddenly awake, I lounged back in my seat, passing my discomfort off with a smirk. "But don't lie. Veronica does it for you too."

Both chicks were fucking hot, and I wouldn't lie, Betty did it more for me too. There was just something about a blonde as I smirked again, and Niko, well, Niko chuckled.

Putting down his beer, he threw his hands behind his head. He flicked his eyebrows at Billie. "Yeah, you'd do her. But come on, Queen B. You know brunettes do it for you. Take your stalker-ass boyfriend outside."

The very mention of the prick clearly with his own sexual frustration ran my vision hot, the same with Billie judging by the way her expression cut at Niko. Before I knew it, she was doing the craziest thing. She grabbed my buddy Niko's shirt...

Then kissed him right on the lips.

It was a forced kissed and surprised the ever-loving fuck out of Niko, his eyes wide and stiff in her hands. The whole thing happened so fast I was stuck in place, wondering what the hell was her deal, and by the time, I even got my head right to do anything about it, the whole thing was over. Billie had her mouth off my friend and Niko had his eyes closed, stunned the fuck in his seat.

Billie touched her mouth. "I think I need a comparison. Blond versus brunette?" she said, and then I found her sight on me. She stared directly into my eyes, so much intent, and I dared her. I fucking *dared* her to come to me.

On her knees, she did, her hands smoothing up my chest, and I passed the whole thing off as I looked at her. I wouldn't let her see the desire, the flames coursing through me like fucking lava. I wouldn't let her see how much I wanted to grab her too, toss her on her back and make a home between her legs. I did all that, it was over. I did all that…

Her arms settled around my neck, wanting me to come the rest of the way. Even still, I was stubborn. I wouldn't let her win, and she knew that.

"You want something from me, beauty queen?" I asked her, my voice heated and fucking aroused. I didn't want to be, couldn't help it. My throat moved. "Want me to do something for you?"

The rise of her supple chest told me what she wanted, that heat creeping up the side of her neck and flushing across the tops of her breasts. She wanted a kiss, maybe even more than me, but that taste might be the death of us. It'd take everything off the table, precisely why I held back now.

I honest to God thought she'd take her hands off me in the end, take that challenge back but with little effort she was closing the distance. And me?

I fucking gave in when she was only two-thirds of the way there.

I brought up that other third, groaning as I sealed our lips, and gripped into that sequence. Pulling Billie onto my lap, I tasted her tongue and went in for more before she could pull back. My lips fucking burned, tongue surging with the taste of Merlot and beauty queen.

Our lips parted before I was ready, all her and definitely not me. Looking dizzied, Billie touched her mouth like she'd done after she kissed Niko. And the girl basically looked drunk after maybe only having a glass and a half of wine.

She huffed. "Maybe I need another kiss," she said, looking at Niko who had a fucking grin on his face. He'd watched the whole thing, the fucker smiling only too wide. She smiled back. "I think I might need to compare."

She acted like she wanted to reach for him then...

And fuck that.

My hand at the back of her neck, I forced her to me, claiming her mouth and squeezing her shoulders. She moaned beneath me, settling on my lap and rubbing that hot pussy up against me.

The burn surged directly into my cock, the fucker steel against my fly. I ground into her through her panties, and the couch shifted to my left.

"Night, kids," Niko said, the couch rising. His deep chuckles sounded as he walked himself somewhere in the house, and I'd do something about that had I not had my hands full of Billie. He'd known exactly what he was doing tonight. Fuck, he'd known taking her back here in the first place would test me.

Fucking asshole.

Unconcerned with him at the moment, I kissed harder, shifting Billie and her supple curves on her back. I pushed that flimsy bit of top off her chest, the girl fucking bra-less, and her pink nipples arched right for my mouth.

I flicked one with my tongue, needing a taste, and Billie wriggled so hard beneath my mouth I thought my dick would snap my fly at the seam.

I drew her whole nipple in, laving on her flushed tits as I shifted my attention from one to the other. She tried to unbutton my shirt but I forced her hands over her head, her body arched and perfect and half naked on my black leather couch.

A sea of that Little Mermaid hair around her, she looked like a damn siren, and the last place I wanted to claim her was on this couch that'd seen more action than my bedroom. I didn't take many girls up here, a quick fuck downstairs usually enough.

This wasn't going to be a quick fuck.

I got off her, tugging her with me, and she stumbled in her heels.

"Where are we going?" she asked me, tits bouncing. We'd left that scrap of top she'd worn on the couch, nothing but her silver skirt hugging her ass and I groaned, picking her up by it. I kissed her on our way up to my bedroom, my mouth unable to leave hers.

"I'm fucking you in my bed," I said once we got there. I put her down, then kicked the door closed, turning her around.

I pressed her up against the door, my dick grinding against her ass as I forced that silver skirt up and over it. A perfect peach under my hands, I slapped the side of her ass, making it instantly as red as her hair.

"LJ," she gasped, my hand coming down over that cheek again. Unable to help it, I tugged her panties aside and bit, that sweet flesh in my mouth. She shuddered and I felt it through my whole goddamn body.

My tongue flicked against sandy freckles, drawing her in my mouth again and she moaned, quivering against the door.

"Take your panties off," I told her, rising, and she wiggled them down over her heels. I got rid of those too, the whole thing easy. Next thing I knew, I clasped a hand around her throat, rubbing against her bare bottom.

Her pulse point jumped beneath my reach,

something akin to desire in her eyes when she gazed back as well as a fair bit of fear. She should be scared of me.

I was fucking scared of her.

I was scared of what she could do to me, how she could sway my focus and make me see nothing but her. I couldn't do that when I had my own goals, a family to take care of back home. I couldn't get distracted.

I curved a finger along her throat.

"You're bad for me, beauty queen," I told her honestly. "I do stupid things when it comes to you."

Like now, needing to be buried in her so badly I could easily shoot my load off just at the taste of her. It was that serious, that dangerous for me.

Her mouth quivered, her swallow moving thickly against my hand. "I do too, Mr. Johnson."

I burned, so hot for who was basically my teacher.

Tugging her around, I covered her mouth, devouring her, claiming her to the point where she was basically a puddle in my hands.

Billie arched, shuddering against me when I jerked down her skirt, getting her completely naked. I unbuttoned and pulled off my shirt, then I was chest bare against her, feeling her softness and how she moved along every hard edge of me. I didn't move easily. But my body with hers did impossible things.

I took her on my king bed by the hips, her gaze raking down my body as I lay her back. They stopped where abs met my belt buckle, completely greedy, and I chuckled, pressing my body up against her.

"I dare you, beauty queen," I said, moving her

hand to my cock. I worked myself against her. "My queen."

I had no idea where that came from, again she made me do stupid things. Like close my eyes while she worked me sinfully in her little hand, my dick surging and fucking her palm. Her other hand gripped my bicep, making me growl at the scratch marks she pulled down my flesh. I forced her hands away, then spread her wide. Traveling between her legs, I believed I could die right there.

Especially at the first taste.

It made us both moan, Billie losing her fucking shit when she tugged my hair.

"Oh, fuck. LJ. Fuck!" Her thighs locked my head between them, and I got aggressive, my tongue flicking wildly between her folds. Her heat so sweet, I took both her legs and tugged them over my shoulders, my mouth sucking her lower lips right into my mouth. She called out, her fingers gripping my scalp, and that's when I added digits, one, then two.

I arched deep, tasting sweet juices with every come hither movement of my fingers. My strokes maddened her, the woman wild in my sheets. She bucked, and I thought she'd come right there in my mouth. The only thing keeping me from taking her over the edge was that I wanted to do the pleasure, *take her pleasure* and make it mine.

I got up before I could finish the job, leaving her hanging, and she panted in frustration.

At least, until she saw my cock.

I unzipped, my hand filled when I pulled my boxers down. So greedy, Billie rose up on her elbows but I forced her back.

"*I* take *you*," I promised, working myself but

fuck if I needed any help. The hard steel pulsed at the tip, my thumb rubbing precum all over the mushroom head. Leaning forward, I pulled the crown along her slit, Billie's eyes rolling back in her head.

"Don't play with me, LJ. Jesus."

So, *so* greedy. I chuckled again, reaching into my bedside table. I didn't want to talk about who was clean or not at this point. I just wanted to claim her, but next time we did this… fuck, if I'd have anything between us.

For now, I did the responsible thing and actually groaned at only the thought of being inside her. To her surprise, and I think a little of mine, I fell to my back, pulling her on top of me. I wanted her up there, riding me while I watched her tits slap up and down against her chest.

I got a handful of one while I guided myself inside her, my eyes rolling back, and I nearly came like a teen at nothing but a feel. This wouldn't last long, that I knew, and I got to work, arching my hips while Billie moved hers.

She grated her nails down my chest, and I growled, the girl looking like some kind of mythical goddess on top of me.

Hair a fire red, it swept across her flushed skin, those perfect tits bouncing like something out of my most erotic visions. When she'd been in this very room before, reeking of beer with her tits springing out, I really had thought she'd been a stripper. But fuck, if I didn't want her to be a little something more. I never paid for sex. Never had to, but if this girl would have let me that night she could have charged whatever she wanted. That's exactly why I'd kissed her in the first place. I'd just needed a taste, and that kiss had proved to do nothing but help me meet my maker, what we were doing now completely inevitable.

I rolled my hips as Billie dropped her back and cried out. She felt on her breasts, and I roared, holding her up and fucking her from below. She was a sea of legit emotion while she rode me, and I knew I was tying her to me with every thrust.

We were doing something dangerous here, tying ourselves to each other. Quite frankly, I didn't think either of us could stand the other, and I think a little alcohol may have lowered inhibitions—on both our parts. We were both sober enough to make the decision, though. And I think that was the scariest part about all of this. We chose this for ourselves.

No matter what tomorrow would bring.

Billie came first, gripping her hair and calling my name. Rolling her hips, she milked me for all I had, and I did the same beneath her, my balls tightening as I flooded the condom between us.

I groaned, actually biting my arm when I came down from the high. This left me with nothing but an exhausted and sexier-than-fuck redhead on top of me, a redhead I should have left the moment we'd gotten done screwing. After all, I'd had my taste.

Instead, I reached over, pulling her with me under the sheets. She wasn't fucking leaving me, not tonight, and the way her arms curled around my body beneath my biceps, I knew she wasn't trying to leave either. I think that was the only way I got to sleep in the end.

Fuck what tomorrow would hold.

Chapter Sixteen

Billie

What the hell had I been thinking last night was my actual first thought when I woke up the next morning. Hip to surging hip, I had my leg curled around LJ's firm ass and could only slightly blame screwing his brains out last night on the booze.

I hadn't been that drunk.

I hadn't been drunk at all. I knew drunk, and last night wasn't that. I thought to move away. Escape while I could since he was still sleeping, but then, LJ's large hands settled tight against my bottom.

He hugged me right up on him, hot against his hard chest, and fuck me, if I couldn't resist burrowing myself in the man's scorching heat. He smelled like sex, all sin and heat, and I actually sighed, drinking him in.

He was a wash of male perfection, all hard angles and chiseled features below a mess of tousled blond locks. His lips parting, he yawned but didn't wake up, letting me go a little to lie on his back. One of those gladiator thighs fell out of his bed, the sheets sliding down and revealing a cock sent by the very gods, who had no doubt chiseled out each and every one of his hard formations. That steel rod glistened at the tip, his hand scrubbing his face as I so innocently stared.

God, he's hung like an animal.

My second thought, since last night had been a mess of crazy decisions and sexual tension. I could gripe all I wanted that I was inebriated, that he'd taken advantage of me, but at the end of the day, I hadn't been drunk and was completely aware of what I both did and didn't do last night. *I* came on to LJ. *I* kissed him, and we fucked because that was what I wanted to happen. I gave in to him, completely sound of mind.

Just like I was now.

A smirk and a chuckle as LJ's eyes flickered open, a fan of blond lashes blinking over clear aqua colored eyes as he woke up. Settling back, he draped a muscled bicep above his head, eyeing me with that challenge in his eyes he liked to do. He grinned. "Don't stare at it unless you're going to do something about it, beauty queen."

For emphasis, he pulled the sheet completely away from his thighs, presenting his dick to me like the most coveted prize. With his long digits, he fisted it, working it hard beneath his palm, and my mouth watered as he let go and played with his balls.

I had the sudden desire to suck them into my mouth, my pussy lips tingling at the mere thought. He let go, tucking both arms behind his head, and without much thought, I took him into my mouth.

"Fucking shit," he grunted, clearly not expecting it as I sucked him deep. He groaned. "What the fuck, Billie? Shit."

Funny enough, it was the first time I think in a long time where there'd been no teasing between us. I wasn't the "beauty queen," and he wasn't trying to get one over on me. That was when I realized *I* had the control, and hovering over him, I took him as deep back into my throat as I could.

Forcing back a growl, LJ lifted his knees and trapped me between them. He got a fist full of my hair at the root, guiding me up and down over his mass, and when I peeked up through my lashes, he had his eyes closed. Garbled phrases of curses and my name flew from his lips, especially when I popped his dick out of my mouth and sucked his balls.

He tugged harsh at my scalp. "That's it. Fucking fuck."

Working me over his cock, he bit his lower lip, sighing before angling me back over his velvety flesh. I let him guide me how he needed and took great pleasure being the reason he fell apart, the reason he let go of himself a little. His hips raising, he slammed himself into my throat, and I gagged over the sheer length of him. I really couldn't get him all the way in, but I'd done my best.

"Open your throat," he guided, going much harder as I did. Eventually, I did get him all in, and he groaned. "That's it. Fucking take me."

I played with myself between my legs, about to come too, which was wild to me. I never got off giving a blow job, but this was turning me on clearly as much as it was him. My finger rigorous against my clit, LJ shot his eyes open, grunting as he looked down.

"Hell, are you touching yourself?" he asked, and when I moaned, giving him my answer he literally shattered apart.

His hips stiffened, literally on the balls of his feet as he exploded his seed down my throat. He hadn't lasted long at all, not like last night, and funny enough, I got great pleasure in that.

Drumming my sex, I attempted to take myself to the edge, drinking him down and swallowing every bit of his salty flavor. I was just getting myself there when he pulled me off his satisfied cock.

"Up here," he said, kissing me and so obviously tasting himself on my tongue. For some reason, he didn't care, guiding me to sit across his waist. He worked my hips in a way that nearly made me come right there, but stopped, suddenly biting my lips. "Shower with me? I'll take care of you in there."

It'd been the way he said it to make me shudder, like he actually cared and was completely serious about it.

Without much acknowledgment from me, he picked me up in his arms, damsel style. We were both completely naked, but he rushed across the hall and immediately into the shower. He had like five shower heads in there, all with various pressures, and after getting the heat on us both, he was on his knees and between my legs.

Tongue flicking wildly and mouth sucking, he made me come with his mouth, the orgasm ripping its way through me. My hands pressed hard to the glass walls, he made good on his promise to take care of me.

And he did so on his knees before me.

Later that morning, or maybe even afternoon since I'd lost track of time, LJ made his way with me downstairs. There was clanking in the kitchen when we came down, and it must have still been morning because Niko was frying eggs over the skillet. Shirtless, he had his actual shirt over his shoulder, his body glistening with sweat while he wore nothing but a pair of basketball shorts. He looked like he'd just gotten done working out, and since there was a basketball on the kitchen island, I assumed he'd just finished shooting a few hoops. The pair did have a small court in the back that could be seen from the street.

Upon seeing LJ and me over his shoulder, Niko chuckled, I was sure a sight to be had in front of him. Not only did I wear one of LJ's shirts that basically came down to my knees, I'd worn a pair of his boxers too, but it wasn't like I had a choice. I'd attempted to put at least my skirt on from last night with my top being somewhere downstairs, but LJ basically growled at me.

Before I knew it, he was tossing me his own clothes. As I did, he jerked on a pair of sweats, along with a cross chain for his version of a full outfit. He made sure to put that weird-looking gorilla ring he always wore over his finger too, then the next thing I knew, he was grabbing his phone, and we were headed downstairs.

Niko smirked. "Good morning, kids," he said, flipping the egg in the skillet. Placing the skillet down, he picked his cellphone off the counter. "Or I guess I should say good afternoon?"

Shit, *had* we been in his room all freaking day? Well, the shower and his room. After he got me off in there, we ended up in his sheets again, just a couple of times before he growled and said he was hungry. I hadn't fought him because I was hungry too. He made me crazy, and I couldn't seem to get enough.

Sliding his phone across the counter, LJ flipped his friend off, eliciting another chuckle from him. *This* got Niko a hit in the head before LJ shifted around and placed his hands on the counter, crowding in on me. "Want me to have Niko make you an egg? Or I can make you something else, whatever you want."

The proposal had Niko gazing over his shoulder, smiling away. How I managed to keep my own in I didn't know, but I had. I ended up telling LJ toast was fine, and he smiled at me before joining Niko by the skillet. The toaster was nearby.

While he got started on that, I checked my phone, getting all the social media out of my system before setting it next to his. I watched a titan and his dutiful demigod make food after that, all roving back muscles and sex on legs the pair of them. I bet some girls would pay good money to watch the kingpin himself making brunch for a girl, for me, but then I got annoyed. Thinking about other girls seeing him that way bothered me, I guessed.

Whoa, where had that come from?

Getting territorial when it came to this guy was dangerous, something I definitely knew when suddenly LJ's phone started blowing up next to mine. He continued to cook with Niko, the two of them distracted with some kind of debate whether fried eggs or scrambled were better. All the while, texts kept coming in on LJ's phone, and since they were, I couldn't help sliding my gaze over.

Dasha: Hey? What are you doing right now? I need you. Can you come get me?

Another buzz.

Dasha: Seriously, where have you been at all morning? I need you...

And then another, more of the same before the next.

Dasha: LJ? What's going on? This isn't like you.

"Something important for you on *my phone*, beauty queen?"

A frown below narrowed blue eyes, LJ pulled his phone out of my sight and away from me. All humor from his earlier debate with Niko was gone now, his expression harsh and cold as he stared at me.

I lifted my hands. "No. I was just…"

"Yeah," he said, then studied his phone. Seeing who it was, he appeared to not give much emotion toward the person, but then, he was putting a hand on Niko. "Eh, I gotta go take care of something. Make sure she gets home?"

She as in *me*, the girl he just got done fucking for the better part of several hours. The girl he was now ditching because another girl was blowing up his phone and saying she needed him.

Niko frowned, gaze flicking over my way before looking at his friend. "Now, bro? I mean, we're about to eat."

This didn't seem to concern LJ. Not one bit before he finally faced me. He popped a chin in my direction. "You all good? We good?"

Are we… good, and just like that, he let me know where we stood.

And how incredibly stupid I really was.

I got it wrong twice. Two different guys and two different scenarios, but wrong nonetheless.

I nearly laughed as I passed my shrug off, and without much thought, LJ escaped from the kitchen. A door slammed shut not long later, probably only the time it took him to put a shirt and shoes on. Soon after that, a car started outside somewhere, and sighing, Niko scrubbed his hand through his hair.

He platted my toast himself, and after getting the jam out, he put it all in front of me. His smile was small. "Coffee with your toast?"

Chapter Seventeen

Billie

The only difference between my relationship with LJ before we had sex versus after was he'd actually started showing up to classes again. Though, this change in effort may have had more to do with the fact that the semester was winding down and he wanted to pass than it did with seeing me. He'd said very few words to me since we hooked up and he caught me looking at his phone, and though he did participate in recitation, he did only the bare minimum. He spoke up when required, then sat back on his phone the rest of the time, like he was biding his time and really didn't want anything to do with me. He'd literally fucked and dashed, no doubt his MO, but what frustrated me the most was that I'd fallen for it. I may have come on to him, yes, but I didn't deserve to be treated in such a way.

Even if I had peeked at his phone.

He'd gotten so frustrated, and I thought, maybe, illogically. Of course, I didn't know his reasons, not my business, but if he was going to another girl only moments after heating up the sheets with me, he was nothing but a goddamn player and someone, you'd think, I would have known better to stay away from. I wasn't a college freshman anymore and long past the naïveté of an undergrad.

At least, I believed I was.

As we headed into those final weeks of classes and I started to really get focused on my own studies, I was happy to soon be rid of my TA experience with Professor Douglas. The man did nothing but load on the work and had frequent check-ins with me about his students. This started right after the incident in question with LJ, of course, but I'd been happy to assure him LJ had been honestly doing well. LJ did his due diligence in class, and as I handed out final term papers back for the students to use to prepare for their final exams, I stopped him at the back of the room. He had his earbuds in, barely paying attention as per usual, but at least his grades fared well.

Light toned eyes drifted from his paper in my hands up to mine. He'd not only passed his final essay with flying colors, but he'd aced it.

I let it fall to his desk.

"Crazy what you can do when you actually attend class," I said, all I could really give him.

Picking up his paper, he studied it, but I didn't stick around long enough to see his response. I continued on, passing out the rest of the term papers, and once I cleared my stack, I returned to the front and gathered my things. It took me a second to realize I was being watched, but once I had, that heat blazed.

I found those blue eyes again as I stared ahead, LJ the last person in the room besides me.

He stood at the door, hands on his shoulder bag. I thought he may come forward, but as quick as he stared, he was even quicker leaving. The door slammed shut behind him, and I passed whatever his deal was off.

I had to.

Later that night, I loaded a grocery cart for one, my mom off at another party. She was proving to have a better social life than mine these days. Always out, and she was actually consistently going to therapy now. I came over to find the house clean most weekends and hadn't found her passed out on her couch in what seemed like months. She must have been feeling better.

I was the only fuck-up these days.

I hadn't been drinking, but I had been completely up in my feelings lately. I could blame many things, but at the end of the day, I had to take ownership of my own mess. I chose to get involved with D-bags.

My phone buzzed in my grocery cart.

Daddy: Hey, kid. How've you been?

The same since the last time I hadn't answered his texts.

Another buzz.

Daddy: I know you're not talking to me, but I really hope you liked the gift I sent over. You can do with it what you wish, of course, but I wanted you to have it.

I cringed.

Daddy: Anyway, I love you. And I really hope I do see you at the wedding this summer. Things didn't go the way I hoped with your mom. But I think things can be better the way they are now. I wasn't being fair to your mom, and I'm just so sorry I hurt you. Hurt both of you.

I was sorry too, sorry that they'd both gotten involved, and he'd wrecked our family with his decisions. I just couldn't easily forgive him. Even if my parents *hadn't* ever loved each other.

My stomach sour, it took me a second to realize someone was speaking to me. I followed my phone up to blue eyes and paused at seeing them, so familiar, but not the owner.

The young girl tapped her sneaker at me, like

maybe eighteen or so. Eyeing behind my cart, she studied the cookies I currently stood in front of, and stumbling, I backed up so she could get them.

"Thanks," she said, her earbuds in and a bomber jacket on. She looked ready to dance in a music video, barely passing me another glance before leaving.

I bit my lip behind her. "Sorry about that."

But her music must have been too loud. Cookies in hand, she walked away without another glance, and I was embarrassed having just been caught standing there in the middle of the aisle. I hated when people did that to me, and pushing on, I refused to let my dad be a hindrance in my life anymore. I continued to grocery shop, making it to the produce and getting my items there quickly. The last thing I needed was some apples, and as I reached for them, I bumped a hand.

"Sorry—" Once again, I hit those same ocean-clear eyes, the young girl. I had no idea if I just kept hitting her because I wasn't paying attention or because she had music in her ears. Either way, she appeared *annoyed* at *me*.

She took an earbud out. "You go ahead."

"No, you're fine."

She took me up on the offer, grabbing a couple that totally weren't ripe, and since I didn't want to overstep, I let her. I did, on the other hand, come ready with a bag to help her, though. She hadn't grabbed one.

"Might make it easier?" I asked, and this surprised her, eyes blinking.

"Thanks." So obviously curious about the gesture, she eyed me. She shrugged. "And sorry about

186

the bumps before. I wasn't paying attention."

"No, I wasn't." I held up my phone for emphasis. "These things are like crack."

A snort, a light and bubbly snort when she'd been a little cold before. Well, my joke made her laugh now, I guess, and nodding, she agreed.

"For sure," she said, and when I grabbed some apples, she noticed mine. "Those look better than mine."

"Well, the trick is the color. And the feel too. See." I pressed down, then let her. "I think the ones you have just aren't quite ripe. Let me help you."

"Yeah?" She appeared shocked, and I grinned.

"Yeah, no problem."

Between the pair of us, we got a real good set together and got her bag so full she'd be eating apples for days. I had no idea where her parents were or if she was shopping herself, but she appeared to be alone.

"Don't tell me you're actually getting something healthy, Dasha—"

At least, I believed she was alone, alone until another set of bright blue eyes and a cool grin came my way. It faded instantly upon seeing me, LJ with a cart in his hands and looking all domestic.

And how good he looked, leather jacket on and pushed up his mighty arms. He accompanied the ensemble with a set of well-worn jeans that sagged low at his hips and crisp white sneakers that matched his T-shirt. His hair was also a darkened blond, wet like he either put product in it or was just out the shower.

He swallowed upon seeing me, and this girl, Dasha, rolled her eyes at him.

"Don't be an asshole," she stated, making *me* blanch. No one talked to this guy like that. I was sure not even the police. Cradling the bag of apples, she propped a fist on her hip. "I was just trying to help you out since you eat well, Jesus."

Judging by the contents of his cart, he didn't, the thing filled to the brim with pizza bagels and cereal. I tried not to look at it, my attention mostly on him, and wetting my lips, I severed the attention back to the girl. She deposited the apples into the cart, then smiled at me.

"Thanks for your help before," she said, truly shocking the fuck out of LJ, whose head snapped back. She directed a thumb at him. "This one's no fucking help at all."

"Watch it, attitude. Or you'll be walking your ass back to the house."

The girl merely jutted her shoulders at the LJ I'd come to know and love, and I had to give it to this girl. She had real moxie.

Giving him a little wink, Dasha waltzed right past LJ, moving onto some grapes and I considered the name as I looked at her.

Dasha...

That'd been the girl blowing up LJ's phone, this girl.

Like LJ realized my thought process too, he studied me but made no comment. He nodded at my cart. "Doing a little grocery shopping?"

"Trying," I said, all this so very awkward. I literally hadn't talked to this guy outside of class, and the last time I had, we'd been screwing each other. I pulled down my hair, letting the red fall in thick tumbles, and LJ noticed.

His pupils dilated just a bit, his hands gripping his cart. Seemingly bothered, he glanced around, and *I* attempted to keep my heart in check. This guy screwed with my insides something awful, always did. He wet his lips. "You helped my sister?"

Confirmed, that she was indeed a relative, *a sister*, I felt really silly for how things did go down. I'd been wildly jealous, but then again, he hadn't acted right either. My jaw moved. "Yeah. She didn't know what she was doing. Picking apples?" But then I eased a look into his cart, smiling a little. "Seems someone hasn't taught her much about produce."

Eyes cut back, possibly a retort on his lips, but then that wicked grin that teased my heart. He rubbed his neck. "That obvious? I'm trying here but find myself giving her what she wants instead of what she actually needs. It's always been that way. With all my sisters."

A pushover, this guy?

As if he knew my thoughts again, his cheeks colored. Lance Johnson... *flushing*. Someone had to be playing a trick on me. He grinned. "I admit I could do better. Dasha's staying with me for a little while. Albeit, *temporarily*."

A middle finger lifted from the grapes area, Dasha when she flipped her brother off, and I had to bite back my smile.

"And as you can see, she has a hell of an attitude," he grunted, then sighed. "She and my mom have been bumping heads lately so..."

She was staying with him.

"I need you. Can you come get me?"

And hence the text messages. Feeling even more stupid, I covered my arms, but I noticed LJ glance away as well. I may have jumped to conclusions, yes, but I wasn't the only party involved that day at his house.

He let me go to that place after all.

"Anyway, I better get back."

"Of course," I said, starting to let him walk away, but then something had me intercepting him.

His eyes followed me over to a quick dinner kit, one the store put together with veggies as a feature. I held it up. "Maybe better than pizza rolls?"

Chapter Eighteen

LJ

Billie was good with my sister, which said something considering what a sarcastic little shit my sister could be. I loved Dasha, I did, but I equally wanted to strangle her most days. Especially since she constantly gave lip to Mom. The two fought like cats and dogs, and since I wasn't there now to play referee, they'd been getting into it more than usual. Dash only had to get to the end of the school year.

But she couldn't even manage to do that.

I watched her with Billie now, the beauty queen teaching my sister how to make gravy. As far as my sister was concerned, Billie was just a friend, and that friend managed to get all kinds of messy cooking with my sister. The pair played with shit like cornstarch, getting it all over each other since it was messy. Billie literally had some on her nose and Dasha on her cheeks, smiling at Billie in ways she didn't often. All my sisters had their issues, just like me, but I think it'd been Dash to take Dad's leaving the hardest back then. She remembered him just like I had, and even though she tried pretty good in school, she had a fair amount of bullies and a temper that could match mine most days. She didn't make things easy for Mom, but for whatever reason, Dash was able to put that shit away now and cook with Billie. Her first rounds of gravy had been truly awful-looking, lumpy and shit, and just when I thought she'd go into a Dasha meltdown, Billie was able to talk her off the ledge. Billie was patient with her, truly listened to her, and I could tell that meant so much to my sister. She put that attitude right away and cooked beside Billie, listening to everything she said.

I didn't know how I felt about that, watching them from the kitchen island while I tried to do some homework. Honest to God, I thought Billie and I were over, my fascination with her done when I'd deliberately put space between us. Things were getting too heavy for me, and my sister needing me had been a good excuse to cut things off. I hadn't planned to step back that day, and really, I'd been completely obsessed with the beauty queen at that point it wasn't even funny. I couldn't see where she ended and I began, and it took my sister's text, family needing me, to show me my priorities. Billie was still linked to her dad, and though I wasn't tied to the Marvellis anymore, that fact still remained. I wasn't trying to work up any shit with the Marvelli family for getting involved with enemy ties. I literally couldn't for the sake of my family, which meant Billie Coventry was trouble.

But fuck me, if I didn't want to take a walk on the wild side.

Currently, Billie wiggled her little bottom behind my laptop. Mashing up potatoes from that veggie kit she'd bought, she pretended real damn good she wasn't aware of me staring at her. She laughed with my sister, teasing her on occasion, but every so often, I did get a glance over her shoulder in my direction. She was well aware of me, just as I was of her.

Why can't I get this girl out of my head?

A spoon in her hand, Billie sprinted on over to me in her black leggings and sweater that hung off her freckled shoulder like the ultimate tease. I wanted to drag my tongue across every freckle, flick and sample that sweet skin. I wanted to make her quiver and sweat just like I had that day in my bed, but I pretended not to notice her coming over.

She pushed the spoon in front of me, something orange on the top.

"What's this?"

She nudged it with a grin. "Just try it."

As aloof as my ass pretended to be, I didn't need to be told twice. I took that spoon right into my mouth. Pure heaven, I actually groaned, and Billie giggled, shooting heat action straight into my pants. The fucker couldn't seem to keep his mind on anything serious, cramming for exams apparently not as big of a deal as Billie's ass wiggling in skintight leggings.

"It's orange marmalade for the biscuits."

So much pride flashed across her glittering eyes. In fact, so drawn our gazes clashed, *hard.*

A lip chew and Billie passed her attention back over to my sister, who looked pretty fucking hilarious in an apron and oven mitt. One would have thought she was Suzy Homemaker outside of that expensive ass jacket she wore and designer kicks, all gifts from me. What could I say? I loved treating my siblings. Currently, sis pulled some biscuits out the oven, and Billie grinned at her. "Dasha made the marmalade. The biscuits too."

Shocked to hell, my brow jumped, and Dasha happened to catch that after depositing the biscuits on the counter. She shot her middle finger up at me. "Don't look so surprised."

I raised my hands in defense. "Didn't say a

word."

"You didn't have to." An eye roll before she smiled at Billie. "Can we make dessert now?"

A little Gordon Ramsey when she'd never made anything she couldn't defrost or nuke in her entire life. At least, as far as I knew.

Duty calling, Billie got right to work at the request. The pair pulled out a cookbook I didn't even know I had, and I was so busy watching them I nearly missed my buddy Niko. He came sliding on into the kitchen, his jacket on and a set of keys in hand. He appeared to be going when I didn't even remember hearing him come in.

"Something smells damn good." Fucker dipped his pinkie in the mashed potatoes, sampling with a pop in his mouth.

Billie growled at him. "Seriously?"

"Seriously, what?" He winked at her before tipping his chin at Dasha. "Sup, little Jay?"

His nickname for her and never ceased to shoot my sister's cheeks up like ten degrees in color.

Forgetting about dessert and the cookbook completely, Dasha leaned over the counter at him. "Hey? You eating with us tonight?"

"Nah, I can't." Bouncing around, the asshole literally tasted everything in the room. As he reached an actual hand for the potatoes, Billie hit him with an oven mitt and that seemed to keep the garbage disposal at bay. He chuckled. "Got some business to take care of. Otherwise, I would."

"Business?" Curious, my eyes flashed up from my computer screen. "What kind of business?"

I felt like I hadn't seen him in forever, which kind of meant something considering finals were around the corner. The only place he should be was either here or at the library.

He definitely wasn't going there in a nice jacket and a pair of his best Jordans.

Catching me looking, Niko waved a hand. "Nothing much. Just meeting some friends."

Friends must have been real important. Again, we were coming up toward the end of school, and that'd always been priority. It was the most important—for both of us. Family didn't get fed off partying, but jobs after school with degrees did. As far as Niko, the stakes were even higher, his mom being sick and all that.

Like I hadn't said anything at all, Niko fisted a biscuit before pointing at Dasha. "Save me some leftovers, little Jay?"

"Of course." My sister actually sighed, all doe-eyed and dreamy in her gaze, and my fucker best friend winked at her. I told him about entertaining her fascination with him. She clearly had a crush, and he shouldn't be giving in to it.

Ultimately, I let him off the hook since he was headed out, but I would have to bring up how I hadn't seen him around lately. I mean, neither of us were homebodies or anything but when it came to finals and shit, we didn't play around.

With him gone, the girls ended up making berry cobbler for dessert, and after we ate, I did them both a favor and washed the dishes. This was something they should definitely document considering I didn't even do my own fucking dishes. I had someone come a couple times a week to do it, a cleaning service.

While I did that, Billie helped Dasha with her

homework. I called the school back home about her fleeing town, and they agreed to let her do e-learning until she got back. Since it was her senior year, she hadn't had much to do anyway, and my sister rocked in school like I did. I was just finishing up the dishes and going back to my own assignments when Billie returned to the kitchen.

She had her arms stretched above her head, her little navel exposed with her stretch, and I couldn't fight a smile in her direction.

"My sister tire you out?" I asked, passive about it.

Her shoulder lifted as she took a barstool. "Nah, I can handle her. She's a good kid."

"When she wants to be."

"I can hear you, asshole!" came Dasha's voice from the living room. "Like literally, I'm in the next room here."

"Yeah," I tossed. "And you should be doing your homework."

"Basically done!"

"Well, get it *all* done."

A groan and Billie's chuckle beside me. The laughter made her face red, a huge flush all over her cheeks, and I hated I wanted to kiss it. That I wanted to *kiss her*. We really shouldn't be doing this.

And yet here we were.

"You don't have to stick around, you know?" I stated, my last ditch effort here. Weak, I even heard that in my voice. I wanted her to stay, as long as she liked.

Her lips parted as she wet them, another shrug and that bare shoulder. Christ, if I didn't want to push that sweater up, make her warm. She looked at me. "I know and before, I didn't mind helping. You needed the help."

"I can handle my sister."

"I didn't say with her."

We collided again, our gazes. Hugging her arms, she leaned over the bar. "Why didn't you just tell me that was your sister that day? On your phone?"

My gaze passed over to my computer. "Didn't seem relevant."

"Didn't it?"

Not at the time, and it'd been a very good reason to cut all ties. It'd been my reality check for dipping into shit I had no business tasting. Billie Coventry was forbidden fruit for me. "Look, I appreciate you helping—"

"Don't do that."

I looked her, all joy gone from this girl's face.

She reached for me, but when she hesitated, I let her pull back. Her barstool scooted out, and I got to watch her walk away from me.

She tugged her sweater back up over her shoulder. "I'm just going to go say goodbye. To Dasha?" She stepped back. "Then I'll be out of your hair."

My eyes closed as I was left by myself in the kitchen, my thoughts completely plagued. I wanted nothing more than to go after her, tell her things were complicated with me. Nothing could come between my family and me. They were the most important thing, always, and if I thought for a minute any involvement with someone else could complicate that, there'd be no contest. My family and my priorities would win every time.

"LJ?"

But still, I came when she called me to the living room, ran right to her like a fucking weak-ass little shit. Billie stood in front of the couch, and I had no idea why until I arrived.

Billie stared at my sister, *my sister sleeping on the couch*. Dasha managed to actually look innocent, her textbook across her chest. Billie grinned. "I was going to wake her up and say goodbye, but…"

She looked sweet, goddamn her. I scrubbed into my hair. "I get it. She actually manages to look innocent."

"She does."

"But she can't sleep on the couch." I had my sister set up in one of the guest rooms upstairs. I started to go for her books, but Billie grabbed them first.

"I'll help," she said, doing that for some reason. I'd given her not one, but she was there right with me. She got Dasha's books while I picked my sister up in my arms, carrying her upstairs and to the guest room. The place was a mess with her living in there, but I managed to get around all her things.

Billie pulled down the bedding, and I tucked her inside.

"'Night, ingrate," I whispered, kissing her brow, and in her sleeping daze, my sister gave me her middle finger again. She immediately curled on her side, and I chuckled, letting her have that one. I drew the bedding over her, and when I got up, I noticed Billie at the desk in the room.

"You did these?" she asked, showing me my own sketches. I had them papered all over the desk since I usually worked in here. This was normally a guest room so no one came in here.

"Uh, yeah," I passed off, some of my older designs in here. Simple stuff for commercial buildings and some modern family homes. That's why this rental actually appealed to me. Reminded me of my own stuff. "That's what I'm going to school for. Architecture."

"Really?"

I grinned. "Yeah, didn't know I was really good at it until, well, I came here."

I honestly hadn't known what I wanted to do when I first came to Woodcreek. I just knew I wanted my degree, needed to do something profitable for my family. Architecture and design work just came easy for me.

Billie picked up one of my notebooks beside the loose designs. Opening it up, she thumbed the pages, a small smile on her face. Her hand stopped on another family home I designed, many elements of chrome and granite in the design. "These are really good, LJ."

"Thanks," I said. "I tend to sketch in here since this is usually a guest room."

"Well, now I see why you don't like film," she stated, laughing a little. "Clearly, it's not your thing."

"What gave it away?"

Her laughter faded as I reached around her, turning to some of my best work. Her soft smell consumed me, and my fingers danced from the pages to her fingers.

They looped around them, her digits so small compared to mine.

I angled a look at her. "I have more back in

my room if you want to see them."

I had no idea what I was doing, inviting her to my room and deeper into my life, but once my lips got going, I couldn't seem to stop them.

Billie

Flipping through LJ's design portfolio, it was hard not to notice him hovering over me.

I mean, we were in his room now.

We'd managed to keep our hands off each other, but we were and I truly had to be an idiot. I'd put myself in this position far too many times before. The most recent, only seconds ago in the guest room down the hall.

My gaze drifted to a set of baby blues staring at me, LJ's big body crammed into the window seat with me. I hadn't gone anywhere near his bed. This was safer, and as it happened to be near the bookshelf where he got his design book, I'd been okay with this.

I turned another page. "You really are good."

Had I been in the market, I might have hired him myself, his smile coy beside me. He studied his work over my shoulder, but I felt like he was more so studying me. He *watched me* study his work, fingers to his lips. "And here you just thought I was a lazy shit."

"Oh, you're definitely a lazy shit."

A deep chuckle, his chest rumbling against my back. *That* was how close he was, smelling like aftershave and the ocean. He grinned. "I try when I feel like it. I'm pretty much set up after school. I've made some contacts and my professors have put in good words for me."

I closed the book. "Well, I'm glad you have your thing. I wanna teach, so yeah, that's where I'm at."

"You'd be good at it." He raised a foot to the window seat. "Nothing but a hard ass."

"As long as none of my students are as arrogant as you, I think I'll be good." I shoved him, and he took my hand, a way too dangerous action. "LJ?"

A warning in my voice, but more for myself. I was warning myself I needed to stay away from this guy. I was warning myself he hurt me before and was probably about to again as soon as he could.

Even still, he didn't let go, playing with my fingers. "You fuck with my head, you know," he stated, looking up at me. "You're not good for me."

"And you're good for me?" I started to pull my hand away, but he kept me. He wouldn't throw me away.

"...when I have something good, I don't throw it away."

"I'm the worst for you," he admitted, his words cold. "Probably even worse than the other way around. Surely, your daddy warned you about people like me. Thugs? Kingpins…"

He hadn't, but he would. He would if I let him.

I wasn't currently on speaking terms with my dad, but LJ was right. He would *not* want me to be with someone like him. Besides the fact that he was completely self-involved and *arrogant*, he was also dangerous. No, my daddy wouldn't like this.

My hand flatted on LJ's heart with a press, his racing muscle beneath my hand. I frowned. "Why am

I bad for you?"

He looked up, and so much flashed across his eyes, so many words, but all of them unsaid. He wet his lips. "Because when it comes to my life, I have one priority. *Family* and that'll never change."

But what did that have to do with me? I didn't understand.

He let go, but I grabbed his shirt, a warning in his eyes now. "Beauty queen..."

"It's Billie," I said, getting on my knees. I shouldn't cross this line, and he obviously had his own reasons for not wanting to do the same.

He grabbed my hands. "Billie then," he said, his thumbs touching my chin. "I'm really not good for you."

"Then try to be." Completely blinded, I took his mouth, wishing, *praying* he could be that very thing. That he'd choose to be so...

That this was worth it.

What we felt, at least on my end, always felt right. I couldn't stand it, but that didn't mean I could deny the feeling. This guy and I were literally liquid heat, physically unable to flow in a different way.

Believe me, I'd tried.

LJ's lips hesitated against mine, slow, but sighing, his hand covered the whole back of my head.

"I want to be," he said, kissing me harder and pulling me onto his lap. "Fuck, do I want that. Crave it."

Then why couldn't he? Absolutely none of this made sense. Hell, *we* didn't make sense, but always, there was that heat. There was *this*, his hands on me, and there was no stopping it once it happened. I'd die first.

Guiding my mouth open, I ground my hips against him, and not only did he hold them firm, he shifted me on my back.

Angling over me, he delved his tongue into my mouth, pinning me between his arms. I moaned, and he absorbed the sound above me, reaching back and gripping his shirt.

He jerked it free and his hair was a mess of blond, the length flopping over his eyes. He was so goddamn sexy I couldn't even stand it, my fingers digging into each hard crease of his firm muscles.

LJ growled as he picked me up and took me to his bed, and crowding over me, he appeared like the Greek god he was.

His abs tightened and strained beneath his tanned skin, his cock thick and probing his sweats. He'd changed into them when he'd gotten home, working himself through the material before tugging me beneath him.

He placed nearly his full body weight on me, lacing our fingers together and pressing them into the sheets. My thigh hugging his hip, I rubbed up against him, and he groaned.

"This won't last long if you do that, beauty queen," he teased, his tongue flicking mine. He hugged me close after that, just holding me as he kissed me, and I sighed at how slow and wonderful each stroke was. This wasn't like the first time we were together, like he wanted to claim or even break me. This time, it was like he wanted to keep me.

And damn if I didn't want to keep him.

These thoughts were foolish, of course. There was something he was obviously keeping locked up, something about his family, and whatever that was, he'd strategically placed a fair amount of distance between us. He wanted this, maybe even needed it, but maybe that wouldn't be enough.

I didn't know what plagued him, but at the moment, I didn't care. I needed my own release in a way. I had my own bullshit I was dealing with, issues with family and all that crap with Sinclair. I just wanted to feel something, and this passion with LJ was truly the only consistent thing in my life. My body's need for him, I recognized.

It was so familiar it scared me.

I drew in a breath as he bit down on my neck, reaching to shove his hand beneath my sweater. He palmed my breast, the flesh tight beneath his working hand. Dipping his head, he eased my nipple out of my bra, suckling, and I gripped his back. "LJ…"

"Beauty queen," he hummed, moving to the other breast when he eased it out. He teased that one too with gentle flicks, his eyes closing. "Billie…"

I burned, wriggling in his sheets, and he tugged my sweater completely over my head. Tossing it, he wrapped my hair around his fist, tugging while he sucked me.

I bucked against him, my back bowing off the bed, and he unstrapped my bra. He threw it somewhere, then he was picking up my legs, jerking my leggings and panties off. He would have gotten my shoes too, but I left them at the door when we'd come in.

A mighty growl, and he dove between my legs, kissing my sex before sucking. He pulled my pussy lips right into his mouth, drinking in my taste and I spread my legs.

"Oh my God." I clinched the bedding beneath

my fingers, sighing when I rubbed my head back into his pillows. They smelled delightfully of him, all male and whatever sea breeze scent he used in the shower. Gripping my thighs, he drew me up, tongue diving inside my heat. His tongue spun around inside me, a come hither motion before he sucked, and I called out. "LJ, stop. I'm going to come."

He didn't stop quickly, his body basically shaking at retreat before working his sweats down his thighs. His cock sprung free and when he kicked the sweats off, he sat back on his powerful thighs. He got a firm hand on his length, working his balls. "Can I come inside you? I'm clean."

If he was asking me if I was on birth control, I was. I nodded. "We're good. I'm on birth control."

Exactly what he needed, he kissed me with what could only be defined as animalistic vigor, moaning deeply into my mouth. Gripping my hips, he turned me on my tummy and I was ass up when he hovered over me.

He caged me, guiding himself inside. A hard slap and his powerful thighs hit the back of mine.

I groaned as he thrust his hips and gathering both of my arms, he fucked me wildly.

"Yes," I sighed. "Yes…"

His wingspan came around me as I sighed him on. His embrace tightened, and he really was hugging me, holding on to me as if almost for dear life.

I hugged him right back, my face buried into his pillows to contain my scream. His sister was maybe two rooms away, and biting the material, I gave readily into the release.

I crashed with stars behind my eyes, LJ's hand around my throat as he too submitted to the fiery flames.

His body quivered and shook as his cum filled me. He milked me hard, riding out his high until he collapsed nearly on top of me. The only thing keeping him from falling was the fact he pulled me flush up against him. He found a home for me within his arms, and I stayed there.

I closed my eyes to the sound of our breaths, LJ's lips tugging mine apart with soft but intentional kisses. I honestly didn't remember when I fell asleep.

I just remembered kissing him even in my dreams.

Chapter Nineteen

LJ

My sister bitched really fucking good on the drive back home to Maywood Heights, our small town. She couldn't stay with me forever, and if she actually wanted to graduate and go to college next year, she needed to go home. This was something she knew but wasn't necessarily happy about. She literally pouted in the back seat of my Beamer and would have sat up front had Billie not been insistent on coming along. I told her it was a long drive. Like five fucking hours, but for whatever reason, she said she was cool about it.

I watched her from time to time sitting next to me, the hours she spent in my car gauged between messing with the radio dials (which drove me fucking crazy) or chatting it out with Dasha. She was keeping my sister very cool. I knew because the bitching about coming home and seeing Mom had stopped around the three-hour mark. Turned out Billie Coventry was really good with my family, at least my sister.

And I didn't know how I felt about that.

We had the physical thing down. I wanted her like I needed my next breath, but emotionally... that shit was hard. I couldn't deny having anything to do with her at all was dangerous, but still, I kept dosing myself in kerosene and walking right into the flames with her. Eventually, she fell asleep, and when she nodded off in my direction, her hand easing over my bicep resting on the console, I didn't pull away from her. If anything, I tangled our arms a bit more, drawing in her sweet heat.

Fuck, I was screwing myself.

An innocent drive home was all this was, and hot fucking sex last night was all it could be.

At least, that was what I kept telling myself.

I tapped my Court ring against the steering wheel of my car, both girls asleep as I passed the welcome sign into my hometown.

In actuality, I visited Maywood Heights more than I liked. I did so for my family, because my mom and sisters were all still here and I knew, in the end, this was where I'd be too. My family was the most important thing to me, and I hadn't been lying when I told Billie that. I wouldn't deliberately do something stupid that could compromise them or their well-being. That made this thing with Billie all the more complicated. Billie's family was the enemy to people I'd done business with, and hanging out with her in any capacity was walking on thin fucking ice. Regardless of whether said business had concluded.

I didn't know how I was going to handle that, or really do anything about it at all. The easiest thing was to turn Billie loose and not take the chance of pissing off a previous business tie, but that was obviously very complicated. Things always were with her. This wasn't about breaking her anymore.

It was about how she was breaking me.

Billie woke up as I parked in front of a mid-Modern-style home, the house sandwiched between two more in the nice cul de sac. Mom didn't live in the fanciest neighborhood, but it was nice, *safe*, which was most important to me. With as much money as I was sending home, she could afford more but refused to upgrade the house I'd lived in as a boy.

My mom *believed* I just had a really good internship while I was in school. All she could know. I wouldn't tell her anything she didn't need to know or could compromise her. I wasn't always dealing with people who were completely on the up and up, so it was just best for all if I was the only one in the trenches. I'd take any burden I had to in order to take care of her and my sisters.

Dasha opened her eyes too once we'd arrived, and though she unstrapped, she didn't do anything. She just sat there, staring at the house, and turning, I put my arm over the seat.

"So what's it going to be?" I asked her, talking with her briefly before this. My sister was obviously going through some growing pains, some crazy shit that started happening when she reached around sixteen that I personally hadn't had to deal with. It was something about moms and daughters when the kid reached a certain age. I thought they'd rip each other's hair out when I'd lived there.

She frowned. "You don't know how she is. She's so hard on me."

That's because Mom loved her, fiercely and was afraid. She was afraid of losing her, all her babies going off to school. It'd been different with me being the first. She had three others back at home, but now with Dasha about to leave, Gwen and Lia right around the corner…

I started to go into that when Billie turned around. She had her cute little leggings and sweater on, that shoulder bare, and it heated my blood so bad I thought I'd tackle her. She smiled toward the back seat. "You know that's normal, right?" she stated, shrugging. "You and your mom have, what? A few months before you go off to school?"

Sitting up, Dasha nodded. "Yeah, and it's gotten worse. She's just so grating and hovers."

"My mom and I went through the same thing," she admitted, then hugged the seat. "I literally thought we were going to kill each other before I went to college."

"Seriously?"

"Yes, and we were so close before. Still are." She grinned. "It totally gets better after you go away. I think you guys need that space, you know? To breathe? She's probably just holding on so tight because she knows you're going to leave. That's how it was with mine anyway."

The words pulled directly from my lips, from her, this girl.

I sat back, awed when my sister actually reached forward and gave Billie a hug.

"Thanks, Billie," she said, actual laughter in her voice.

"No problem. It'll be better. I swear. Just give it time."

Billie

Hoping the advice helped, I sat back and truly forgot in all this time LJ had been there. He'd been idle, sitting quiet, and when I pulled back from his sister I realized why.

He'd been staring at me, and something about his observant gaze made me shy for some reason. Chewing my lip, we severed eye contact, and before I knew it, he was getting out of his seat.

"I'll be right back," he said. "Just going to

help her in."

I nodded, this not my family, and it might be a little awkward following him anyway. I mean, I didn't know what this was or if there was anything at all between us.

Still, I turned toward the window, watching him help Dasha gather her things. She only had a small bag and LJ got it, helping her to the house. She stopped just a moment to wave back at me, and leaning toward the window, I did the same.

"Good luck," I mouthed, receiving her grin. This got a glance from LJ, a quick one before he put his hand on his sister's back. It was so weird seeing him this way. He truly was nurturing.

I guessed I found his kryptonite.

This was confirmed when his mom appeared, the woman opening the door before the pair got there. He got an arm around his mom, a larger woman, and though I sat back, a more than kind face shown above his shoulder. She was tall, just like him, and when she pulled Dasha in without hesitation, something told me I'd been right about my earlier theory. There was obviously a lot of love between these people, family.

"...when it comes to my life, I have one priority. Family, and that'll never change."

So obvious as he literally held mom and daughter together, the glue between them both. Dasha needed space, and he came to her rescue but was also the one to do the reuniting in the end. His commitment to family was obviously very important to him.

Still, I had no idea what that had to do with me.

Something about this side of his life made him

wary when it came to me. It was a wariness I didn't understand, and sitting back, I watched as LJ's mom cradled Dasha inside. She literally wouldn't let go of her. Reaching for a hand, she grabbed LJ too, but when he held back, she let go. Some words exchanged between the two of them, then suddenly, she was gazing over at me.

Pinned to my seat at this point, the woman with the kind face looking at me. A broad and clear smile stretched across her face, her hand instantly waving in my direction.

I waved back, albeit shyly, and beside her, Dasha did the same. The pair both started to wave me in, but LJ raised his hands.

More words I couldn't hear, but every second passed squeezed my stomach. LJ had his arms braced, his head shaking and incessant about it. He obviously was saying no, *no*, I wasn't coming in.

No, I wasn't going to be a part of his life.

"I have one priority. Family, and that'll never change."

I sat quiet as he got back inside, and strapping in, he started the car. A wave over the wheel and he gestured goodbye to his family, wide smiles on both Dasha's and his mom's faces. Soon, the pair were joined by two others, strawberry blondes just a little shorter than the others. They spoke to LJ's mom and Dasha, then they waved too, just as stylish as Dasha in glittery bomber jackets and nice tennis shoes.

"Fuck, if they wouldn't let me leave, let *you* leave," LJ said, sometime later. We were on the road now, heading back to Indiana. His family lived in Illinois, and it'd been basically a five-hour drive to get to their town. I'd wanted to go, though. Say goodbye to Dasha. LJ smirked over the wheel. "Mom wanted you to stay for dinner. But I told her the drive, you know?"

So he *hadn't* minded if I stayed?

Chewing my lip, I found his eyes, but just as quick, LJ had flitted them back to the road. He went on to say that the other two girls I'd seen were his younger sisters Gwen and Lia. They were in middle school, and once he got going, he couldn't stop talking. I got to hear about how they were doing in school, all the activities they were getting into, and then, he was showing me pictures.

"You must be really proud," I said, grinning as I swiped his phone. He'd actually given it to me, trusted me with it to look through.

A shoulder lift. "I'm glad they're not delinquents, will make something of themselves. Shit's not easy in that town, not for the poor anyway."

His hand rubbed across the wheel, that chrome ring on his finger. It had that scary-looking animal on the front and was something he always wore.

I wondered about it, also what he said. He wasn't poor clearly, and his family wasn't either. I could probably pay a bill off the value of Dasha's shoes alone, the same with what I'd seen his younger sisters wearing. I came from opulence, my mom a prime example. I grew up in a world around people who had an affinity for nice things, myself included.

That'd just been my world.

With the way LJ talked, I felt maybe that might not be his, and I wondered if his story was similar to Niko's. He'd said he grew up pretty rough, obviously not the case now since he'd come into some wealth. He and LJ lived pretty large.

I handed his phone back. "Does that ring mean anything? You always wear it."

I had been wondering about it, and smirking, LJ gripped it.

"Just means home," he said, his eyes kind on me. He had those same eyes I'd just seen on his mom.

I guessed I knew now where he got them from.

*

On the road, we stopped for dinner, and when we finally did get back to town in front of my house, I assumed LJ would peel away. The magic was gone, and we were back to reality. We were back to the real world, but not only had LJ turned off his car, he rounded it, coming over to me. He tugged open the door, and when I gave him a look, his shoulders dropped.

"You gotta be fucking kidding if you think I'm letting you go back inside that house alone," he stated, eyes serious. "You got a fucking stalker, and I need to take a look around first."

I rolled my eyes, but did get out of the car. I huffed. "He's laid off. I haven't seen him since that night I stayed over."

Hadn't talked to him either. Though, that may have been more to do with the fact I silenced his texts. I just wasn't ready, told him that, and eventually, he had stopped trying to call me. I think things just ended really badly. We *both needed* time, and Sinclair wasn't unreasonable. He stopped, and hopefully, when I was ready, we could talk again.

LJ peered down at me. "Right. Well, I'm still coming in. A quick look around. I'll leave after that."

I had too much pride to say I didn't want him to—leave, that was. Eventually, I knew he would and whatever this side of him was would be over. His family appeared to bring out the best in him, a strong unity of people around in his life. I supposed that was something I'd come to miss with my own family drama. I still saw my mom, but if I was being honest, I really missed my dad. I missed what we had. We'd been close.

Coming inside, I allowed LJ to do his sweep. He got right to it, easing his long frame through the house, and while he did, I deposited my purse and keys. He wouldn't find anything, my ex not that crazy, but LJ obviously needed peace of mind. He returned to the living room as I'd been lighting candles.

"All clear?" I smirked, but he frowned. His denim jacket caused him to appear way too heavenly for my eyes, snug on his thick shoulders and formed perfectly to his hard frame. He rocked a pair of black jeans to go with it, and they grappled his muscular thighs like life support.

He grunted. "All clear, but you text me if you see anything suspicious. I'm not joking, beauty queen."

I knew he wasn't, and where I'd normally say something smart, I found I couldn't.

His hand reached out, taking full ownership of my shoulder. Grappling the other, he gripped me tight to him, but I flattened my hands on his chest.

"Don't do it," I said, his shirt twisting under my fingers. "Not unless you plan on staying."

I meant this in more than one way, my heart so fragile with this guy. Last night had happened, yes. But I couldn't do any more of this back and forth.

I just wasn't strong enough.

Before, my pride might not have allowed me to admit that, but here, in his arms, I had to let him know. It all just hurt too much any other way.

"Billie…" Rough fingers smooth down my chin, a clear debate in LJ's eyes. I didn't know exactly what it was, but when he cradled my face, for a second, I thought he may tell me what I needed to hear. He'd tell me what was on both his mind and heart. *He'd open up* and give himself to me.

But then we weren't alone.

"What the hell is this?"

A presence pulled us apart, my ex-boyfriend at the door. Sinclair had a box under his arm, a key in his hand, and I thought I just might lose my shit. I'd *taken* his key, and with a growl, LJ tucked me behind him.

"What the fuck are you doing in her house, man?" LJ literally had grown two sizes, seething, but before he could do anything, I tugged him back.

"What the fuck am I—" Sinclair's eyes twitched wide, just as wild as LJ's, but he wasn't nearly as put together. He had bags under his eyes, had lost weight again, and his clothes didn't even fit him. They hung off his big body like rags, and I couldn't even recognize this guy before me. His eyes blazed in my direction. "Billie, what is this guy doing here?"

"Why are you here?" And because I could fight my own battles, I pushed my way between the two men. Within reach of that key in Sinclair's hands,

I snatched it. "Is this a key to my house? How do you have this?"

"Under the mailbox," he growled and wasn't even looking at me. He stared way up at LJ who had at least a head of height on him. His expression darkened. "The one you keep for emergencies? I came to bring over some of your stuff since you clearly won't speak to me."

"Well, can you blame me?" I cut, equal parts annoyed and tense. I'd been lax about the whole stalker thing, but this was a new level. Him taking my spare key to get inside my house? My nostrils flared. "You had no right."

"You need to leave." Pushing in front of me again, LJ went chest to chest with Sinclair. His expression chilled. "I won't tell you again, man."

"Really, Billie. This guy?" Sinclair grunted. "I fucking knew it. *Knew it.* You act all perfect. *Get on me*, but this whole time you've been fucking this guy—"

"Who I fuck is *my* business, and I had a right to be mad! I never cheated on you."

"No, only kissed this son of a bitch while I was a floor away from you. And then, there's that shit I walked in on in your office." His chuckle was dry. "You're just as bad as me."

"Okay, you need to go." I shoved at him, but despite looking completely a shell of who he was, I couldn't budge him. He was too big, but LJ behind me got him moving toward the door.

Sinclair lifted a hand. "All right," he said, placing the box of stuff he had at the door. "I'll go, but not until you know what kind of a piece of shit you're dealing with."

"What are you talking about—"

"Go, man." LJ shot a finger toward the door. "Before I *make* you go, and believe me, you don't want that."

"Oh no. We wouldn't want that." Sinclair rose palms in a mocking fashion. This set LJ's eyes a blaze, but since I was still between the guys, he wasn't getting any traction. Sinclair chuckled. "What? She doesn't know your dark secrets? How you set that shit up the other night?"

"Back the fuck off," LJ barked, but Sinclair merely tossed his head back.

He placed a hand on his chest. "Of course, she doesn't know, and I had no reason to tell her because I never thought she'd ever have anything to do with your criminal ass—"

"Sinclair. LJ. Stop!" I had my hands full of LJ at this point, pushing him off and away from Sinclair.

Sinclair pushed against my back. "Your boy told all, bro. He *confessed* after she walked in on us."

I shook my head. "*What* are you talking about?"

"He set it up, Billie." Sinclair raised a hand. "Everything from getting me to go to that initial party of his in the first place, and later, getting that guy to find me for a second hook-up."

"A second hook-up?"

Sinclair sighed. "Yes, and I'm aware that's on me. That's where I met that guy you found me with. Met him *at his* party. We hooked up, but I wouldn't even have gone to the party in the first place had your *new boyfriend* not coerced me to go."

"How did he coerce you?"

"He sent word to my office." He wrestled with

his hair. "Said he wanted to make up for the noise and being a bother that other night. One of my clients happened to be there when I got the invite and wanted to go. LJ's parties are one of the hot things to do, I guess."

LJ smirked. "Thanks, bro."

"That wasn't a fucking compliment!" He raised his hands. "You got me to go to that party, then pushed so much pussy and drugs in front of my face it wasn't even funny. I was completely wasted when I hooked up with that guy the first time."

"So what was your excuse the second time?" This guy was a goddamn liar. I shook my head. "And how is LJ asking you to come to a party, then *you* hooking up with some random dude his fault? Either time?"

"Because he knew what would happen." He shook his head at LJ. "Like I said, he coerced me, and the kicker was when you and I did get back together. He found that same guy I hooked up with at his party and called him to come hook up with me again! Had Niko do it. The guy admitted the whole damn thing after we were caught."

I froze, chilled to the bone, and Sinclair took that in, approached.

He jerked a chin in LJ's direction. "This was all a game to you, right? A sick game?"

LJ said nothing.

Sinclair wet his lips. "All just to get into *my girl's* pants—"

LJ's fist came out of nowhere, a swing and collide. He clocked Sinclair so hard his eyes crossed, and launching for him, Sinclair took his own swing.

A miss, one LJ dodged easily, and when he

reared back again, I knew he'd take Sinclair's lights out. I screamed, and LJ hesitated just long enough for me to get his hands.

"This asshole fucks around on you and starts throwing shit at me?" Eyes an electric blue, LJ struck the air with his hand. "Real classy, bro. Real fucking classy."

"Better than you, and you'll never be enough for her. *Ever.* You criminal piece of—"

"Would you both stop!" Hands in the air to both of them. I faced Sinclair. "You had no right."

"Billie—"

"And you." My hair flipped in LJ's direction. "Is what he's saying true? Did you get that guy to come on to him?"

Because I didn't believe it. LJ was capable of a lot of things, but that…

That?

He said nothing at first, scrubbing into his hair, and I thought I might be sick. Especially when he found my eyes.

His expression sobered.

"What do you want me to say?" he asked, actually asked me that. He lifted his hands. "This guy fucked around on you."

"But it sounds like *you* did it first." I recalled that night in vivid detail, his words about me being stupid. He obviously knew Sinclair had cheated on me. I shook my head. "Did you invite him to that first party on purpose? To hurt me?"

He sighed. "I invited him."

"Invited him *knowing* you were going to 'throw pussy' in his face?" Sinclair obviously ended up with a guy that night, but LJ created the scene. *He* started this.

LJ's lips moved. "I feel like it doesn't matter what I say."

But it did, it really did…

And somehow he'd said enough.

More laughter behind me, Sinclair when he barked it out.

"I told you, Billie," he said, coming forward. "This guy's nothing but—"

"Get the fuck out of my house." I shot around, his eyes twitching wide. I shoved him. "I said get out of my house. And you." I paused, looking at LJ. I pointed toward the door. "You follow him."

I was completely serious, completely done *with both* of them, and though LJ didn't move, Sinclair did.

"Let me know when you finally want to talk," he said, leaving out the open door, and LJ may have stayed, but I wouldn't let him.

I pushed him too, his stumble back obviously one of surprise. He lifted his hands. "Beauty queen…"

"Don't you fucking *dare*. Get out." I shoved him again. "Now, and take your win with you."

"My win?"

I swallowed. "Yeah. I guess this is congratulations. You got to both break *and* fuck the beauty queen."

He blanched, like he'd been the one just punched across the jaw. I might have had he not finally left, cutting around me.

He stopped at the door, and when I thought he'd say something, he merely shook his head.

The door closed behind him with a soft click,

and I threw my shoe at the wood. After, I hit the door so hard I felt the ricochet through my entire body. What sucked the most was I knew this was how it was going to go down from the jump. I mean, he'd told me himself.

He was bad for me.

Chapter Twenty

LJ

The colors of Woodcreek's campus shifted once term
ended, flowers springing up, and that hard heat of
May sliding in. I'd crushed the semester, like always,
and came away not just with passing marks to signify
the end of my junior year, but aces across the board.
I'd even managed to pull an A minus in my film
class, putting in the work on my final exam. Billie
had given me an A in the end, a victory and a perfect
way to end the term. I thought I'd see her more those
final days of classes, but she'd been mysteriously
absent outside of recitation. She hadn't even shown
up at our final exam in lecture.

With not much to say to her anyway, I hadn't
put much thought into not seeing her. And I assumed,
eventually, she'd get over what happened with her
boy enough to talk to me. We were neighbors after
all, and I figured we'd cross paths. We ended up
doing so a couple weeks after the term ended.

I basically almost ran into her.

She had a box in her hands, her vision
completely obstructed, which was why she almost ran
into me. *I* nearly collided with *her* because, despite
being distracted by the music pumping from my
earbuds and my morning run, she still entranced me.

She was wearing these wedge heel things,
stamping the earth with her shapely legs. They eased
smoothly beneath her floral skirt with her strides, a
summer top on that showed her bare midriff. It was
hot as hell today, and she was showing off her tight,
little tummy. Her red hair was also sticking to her

neck with sweat, and I thought about how she used to sweat beneath me. I'd made her shiver into a quivering mess when I fucked her, the pair of us like animals that last time.

My stomach tightened, thinking about that last moment more than I liked and how it'd all fallen apart in the end. It'd fallen apart because of me and a fair bit of pride. Truth be told, Sinclair had done me a favor, the asshole. I should have cut all ties with Billie long before that moment due to the Marvelli thing but hadn't been able to. I'd gotten wrapped up in her, and though things had started one way with us, they'd obviously shifted. She wasn't my game anymore, nor simply my obsession to break. She'd become my beauty queen.

And I'd screwed her over.

She granted me with more of her attention than I deserved, her gaze dragging over my abs before finding my eyes. I always jogged without a shirt on. Most especially these days since it was so damn hot. Her chin lifted above her box. "LJ."

The words "beauty queen" started to leave my lips, but I held back. I wet my mouth. "Hey. You need help with that?"

"No, I'm—"

I got it for her anyway, taking it. With a sigh, Billie directed me to her car, and she had all the doors open, several boxes inside. They all had words written on them too, things like *bathroom* and *bedroom*. I got the box in, then draped an arm over the top of her car. "You going somewhere?"

"Moving actually." Literally no emotion on her end, let alone in her voice. Apparently, she reserved none for me. She covered her arms. "Moving to an apartment for next year. Broke my lease early."

So she wasn't even staying the summer, something I was doing. I planned to go back home here and there but, for the most part, was staying around here. I lifted a shoulder. "Isn't that a bit of a downgrade?" I angled a finger over to her house. "I mean, because you had a house before."

I literally sent this girl running for the hills, because I had my foot up my ass so far I couldn't even take ownership of what I'd done. I'd played with her. Played with her and her ex-boyfriend. I couldn't apologize for that douche canoe, though. Dude fucked around on her now, and I'd saved her from that shit later. What did bother me, though, was that I'd hurt her in the process.

Pride really was a son of a bitch.

Because with her standing here, for some reason, the words just wouldn't come. For *some reason,* I just couldn't say what needed to be said, that someway, somehow things had changed. I'd stopped trying to chase her down.

And just wanted to stay with her.

I didn't want to play the game anymore and ended up being one of the ones who got played. I'd played my damn self, my own fault.

"Depends on how you look at it," she stated, answering my previous question. She shrugged. "A change of scenery might be nice."

I supposed for both of us really, probably the best thing for her, putting a few miles between us. For a few reasons.

I closed the door for her, and casually she asked how my semester ended but was passive about it. I gripped my arms. "Did okay, I guess."

"Just okay?" Her eyes lifted, all the red breezing across the tops of her bare shoulders. "I'm sure you aced everything."

Because I had, I couldn't help my small smile. I scratched the side of my neck. "Yeah. You do okay?"

"Not all As, but good." She leaned back against the car, chewing her lip a little before looking at me. "Just one more year now. Same for you too, though, right?"

Yeah, which was crazy. About to begin my life, do the adult thing for once. I nodded. "Dasha's coming in as a freshman next year. She's been asking about you."

The fact that her whole demeanor changed at the mere mention of my sister caused my stomach to squeeze. Honestly, my sister had asked about her *a lot*. Wondered if, when she came down to visit over the summer, they could see each other. I hadn't had it in me to tell her the truth, that Billie wasn't around anymore. That she wasn't in my life. My sister had just believed Billie had been my friend, now we weren't even that.

Billie's smile was small. "I miss her. Give her my number if you haven't. I'd love to talk to her again."

My brow jumped up. She would? I nodded. "Sure. Yeah, sure. Of course."

"Cool."

I shouldn't be surprised she cared. She'd been so good with my sister. Hell, I bet she'd be good with my whole family.

Don't do that. Don't.

The time for all that had passed, and I'd made

sure of that. This girl wasn't just not in my life anymore. I'd completely kicked her out of it.

I guessed, in the end, that was what I'd wanted.

*

A beer in my hand later that night, I had every intention of getting drunk off my ass. Niko had ditched me tonight, something about being busy, so instead of wallowing by myself, I decided to blend in at one of Alexi Marvelli's strip clubs. I figured a lap dance or two might get me out of my head, make me not think so much about earlier events.

Immediately upon entering the joint, I was swarmed, tits and ass in my face right away. I spent a fair bit of money at these clubs when I went, so I wasn't surprised. I was tugged by a couple girls to take the show elsewhere, and though I'd intended on spending my money privately tonight, I ended up at the bar with the rest of the patrons.

I came to a less flashy club tonight, one where I could blend in closer to campus. My hand gripping my beer bottle, I lounged back and watched the show, trying to clear all the shit raging around in my head with perky tits and shaven pussy. When I felt compelled, I tucked a twenty between the breasts shoved into my face, mostly to get the girls to back off. I felt a vacancy behind my eyes as I watched them, unable to concentrate on anything else but Billie and the fact that she was moving. I hadn't said shit to her today when she told me.

I just let her walk away.

Fuck, I'd packed her car for her, never one to

give an inch. I couldn't get over my own self enough to apologize to her, easier than admitting the truth.

The truth being that she broke me in the end. Hell, she nuked her way through my entire life.

I pulled out my phone, that bored in the strip club. Apparently, I'd rather scroll social media than watch the girls on the bar.

I kept off Billie's feed entirely, not really wanting to know what she was doing to put more space between us. It was none of my business anyway, the beauty queen not my concern anymore.

Swallowing hard, I dashed a thumb across my phone and ended up with her name under my digit. I told myself I hovered over her name to copy her contact and send the information over to my sister. She had told me to give it to Dasha after all.

But then I pressed the call button, and I knew my reason for finding her contact had less to do with my sister and more with me. I'd wanted to talk to her, about what I didn't know.

I almost allowed the call to go through before another came in. I clicked over, ending that call when I saw it was Niko.

I frowned. "What the fuck you want?"

My "friend" had ditched me tonight, ditched me every goddamn night. I felt like I hadn't seen him in goddamn weeks. He was always out with an excuse, a party, social engagement, or whatever. And after finals week, I basically hadn't seen him at all.

Some panting hit the phone, and I narrowed my eyes. "Nik—"

"Jay?" He huffed, heavy breaths dragging into the line, and I rose up. Niko moaned. "Jay…"

"Niko?" He had my full attention now, not

228

sounding right at all. "What's going on?"

"I fucked up, Jay." His voice sounded so weak, strained. "I messed up, man. I need your help."

Warning bells shot off in my brain and so loud even the club music couldn't drown it out. I wet my lips. "Okay. What's going on? What do you need?"

"Can you come…" A harsh growl, then a groan. "Come to me? I need help, man. I've been shot."

Shot…

I was off my barstool, asking more questions with my valet ticket in my hand. Outside, I exchanged it for my car, my buddy telling me exactly where he was as I got behind the wheel.

I thanked fucking God I hadn't drank more, able to cut away from the club completely sober. I hit my foot to the metal with complete adrenaline turned on, Niko sounding so weak in my ear. I told him to stay with me, to not panic, but I couldn't in good faith tell him everything was going to be okay. I didn't know, hadn't seen him.

And he'd been shot.

He didn't tell me much, mostly because I told him to save his energy for when I got there. He instructed me to come to some motel, a sketchy-ass place on the other side of town. I must have gotten to the right place because when I rolled up, Niko's red Mazda was parked outside.

I passed the car and nearly cringed at the sight of blood on the door handle, fingerprints. The same was on the door knob of the room he'd told me to go to.

I twisted the knob, working the door open, and when I found my buddy, he was lying on one of the beds in there. He had a wad of bloody towels to his abdomen, stretched out with his phone pressed weakly to his ear. In actuality, the bed was more so keeping the phone to his ear, his bloodied fingers hanging off it limply.

My face had to have paled. "Niko…"

I rushed to his side, cringing as I tossed my keys on the bed and held the towels to the wound for him. "Bro, what the hell? Why aren't you at a goddamn hospital?"

I started to pull towels away, see the damage but the terry cloth was completely caked to the wound. How long had it been before he called me?

Niko roared, and I pressed the towels back. I reached for my phone to call goddamn 911, but he hit my hand away. He gripped my hand over the towels. "No hospitals. Can't. I'll get arrested."

Arrested? I shook my head. "The alternative is you might fucking die. What did you do?"

I tugged off my shirt, too much blood for the towels. Peeling some of them away, I replaced them with my shirt. At this rate my buddy might bleed out, and I reached for my phone again.

"No, Jay. No!" His arm hit wildly at mine. "I can't, man. It's the cops who did this. Shot me."

"What the *hell* happened?" We were both covered in blood at this point and so much fear ran rampant in my brain, I couldn't see straight. I had no idea why we were even talking and not in my car driving to the hospital.

"I messed up, bro," he said like he had on the phone. Cringing, his hand bunched over mine holding down pressure. "I took a job for Alexi. The police got in the way."

"A job?" Hot fire in my veins, my fear for him worse. "What kind of job? Why?"

"I had to, man." He bit down on his lip, pain retching across his entire face. He rubbed his head back. "Mom's medical bills have gotten insane. It got so bad I took out a loan from Alexi. I was working to pay the debt off."

I closed my eyes. "All right. Well, what went down tonight?"

"We were moving some cars for him. But usually the jobs aren't that big. It's usually smaller stuff, nothing flashy," he said, letting me know this clearly wasn't the first time he'd worked for Alexi. His chest heaved, heavy with breath. "This last one had to have been a set up. Alexi's guys and I barely got to the warehouse before the cops were shooting the place up." He sucked in a breath, gripping the wound harder. "I just barely got out."

"Niko, this isn't getting out. You've been shot, man."

"I know, but I can't go to the hospital, Jay. They'll arrest me, and I can't go away. My mom, my sister… I'm all they got. You know that. I can't go away. They'll have nothing. And with my mom being sick…"

"Maybe you can cut a deal with the cops?" I said, nodding. "You've obviously been working with Alexi. Give the police something on him. They'll work with you."

"Then Alexi will come for me." He groaned, his roar basically filling the room, and I got my phone again. His eyes flashed wild. "Jay—"

"I'm not calling 911," I urged, the phone ringing in my ear. "I have a buddy. His name is

Royal, and he knows people everywhere." A phone call, and my boy could get us a doctor here in minutes, lesser tasks easier for him. Royal had resources all over this country, always the one with the hook-up in our group. Even if Niko and I were across state lines. "He'll get you a doctor over here."

"Can you trust him?" he asked, panting heavily, and it wasn't about trust at this point. It was about fear and if my buddy *could* get someone here in time. I trusted Royal with my life so trust wasn't the problem. It was time, something I wasn't sure Niko had much of.

Especially when his eyes fell back in his head.

Chapter Twenty-One

Billie

My new lease didn't start until the first of the month, and I didn't know if I could wait that long. That run-in with LJ last week was just about my undoing, and I didn't know if I'd be able to handle bumping into him during another one of his shirtless runs. The guy still affected me despite myself.

I sighed, my lungs full of steam in the shower. My hands scrubbed lather across my stomach and lower, thoughts of LJ still sending a tingle between my legs. We were like oil and water, undying heat and harsh cold. Whatever those differences, we still burned. And as much as I tried to put him in the same asshole category as my ex, I found myself hard-pressed. LJ may have set up the chess pieces, but Sinclair had acted on his own. That in itself put Sinclair in a completely other asshole ballgame, and though it didn't let LJ off the hook for the role he'd played, I couldn't deny some of the moments we'd had together. Those raw moments of all-consuming and undying heat. That passion and attraction I knew had definitely been lacking when I'd been in a relationship with my ex-boyfriend. I'd loved Sinclair, really had, but there'd always been something missing between us. A part of it was obviously him and other details he had going on in his life, but there was also me. We never held the kind of fire I held with LJ the second he kissed me. A fire I felt from day one and every moment since. Being with LJ was an adventure. It was exciting, freeing and something akin to free falling.

Somewhere along the way, I guess I'd just forgotten to put my parachute on.

A noise crashed, and I jumped in the shower, immediately turning the water off. Ripping the curtain away, I forced my head out. "Hello?"

No one should be here but me. I was still in the old house until the first. I'd only stopped by my new apartment last week because my super allowed me to bring some stuff over to make the move easier prior to the first.

With caution, I put my toes out, well aware I was naked and had no weapons. Making do, I grabbed my loofah with the hard handle. It was the best I could do under the circumstances.

"Sinclair?" I called, hoping to God he wasn't trying to test me by breaking into my house again. I guessed he technically hadn't broken in the first time, but he had come in uninvited. I grabbed my towel, wrapping it around my body. Pushing open the bathroom door, I called again. "Sinclair, is that you?"

Still nothing, but *I knew* I'd heard something. I padded lightly, immediately heading toward the bedroom. I had my phone charging in there, but in my frantic escape across the hall, I clipped one of the moving boxes.

Pain shot though my toe almost instantly, and losing my footing, I tumbled toward the ground the same time a set of strong hands grabbed me.

Niko frowned above my head, *freaking Niko*, and after slapping my way out of his arms, he let go of me.

"What the *hell*, Niko?" I growled, hobbling on the floor. I stubbed my toe pretty damn good, the thing pulsing.

A wide chuckle and Niko shrugged an arm against one of my boxes. This hall was wide enough, but he was so big he filled nearly all of it. His eyebrows jumped. "Nice to see you, Your Majesty," he said, his gaze raking over my half-naked body. "Nice look. That just for me?"

Groaning, I threw my loofah at him, making him chuckle again. I stomped down the hallway and into my bedroom, getting on a shirt, sports bra, and a pair of bed shorts before returning to the living room. When I came in, Niko had made himself at home, now filling half my couch with his entire frame.

He frowned. "Why were you calling for that douche canoe before? He still bothering you?"

No, but he was. I hugged my arms. "Why are you here? How are you here? How'd you get in my—"

He held up a key, his dark eyebrows wiggling. "Jay said you had one under the mailbox. Though I did knock first. You didn't answer."

Yeah, totally needed to find a new place for that. Leaning forward, Niko placed that key on the table, but when he sat back, he grabbed his side. Discomfort etched deeply into his face when he leaned back, and I frowned. "What's your deal?"

"Eh, uh nothing," he said, but it didn't look like nothing. He even had to breathe out when he relaxed. "Just a little accident I had last week."

"What kind of accident?"

He passed it off with a grin. "Seriously, nothing. It only hurts when I breathe."

My eyes twitching wide, I started to prod again when his attention fell on some of my moving boxes. His smiled faded. "So you really are moving?"

Obviously, LJ had told him, and really, I hadn't seen either of them coming or going since that day I'd seen LJ. At least, for the last week anyway. Honestly, I'd been so relieved by the fact I hadn't thought much about it.

"What's going on? Why did you sneak into my house?"

He moved slowly to angle his body in my direction, and each shift flashed a clear sign of discomfort across his face. Again, he had to breathe just to *move*, and I eased in. "Niko… are you okay? Can I get you something—"

"No." His bite shot me back, and seeing that, he sighed. He lifted a hand. "I mean, I'm good. But yeah, I'm here for something. I need a favor."

"What kind?" I took up the seat beside him, being slow and more than careful. Obviously, he was in some kind of pain here, even if he didn't want to admit it.

Another sigh and he was moving that silky dark hair around. "It's for Jay," he stated, my breath instantly stalled in my throat. "He's about to walk into some trouble, trouble for me, and I need your help getting him out of it."

That breath didn't do anything to move, the lack thereof racing my heart. "Trouble?"

"Yeah, the major kind. The life-threatening kind, and it's all my fault."

"What do you mean? What—"

"He's going to a crime family called the Marvellis for me," he stated, making my brow jump high. He shook his head. "I owe these guys a lot of money, and Jay's going over there tonight to settle the debt. The thing is, they won't let him walk out of that

236

bitch. That's not how this works."

"Wait. Back up." I was still trying to get over the fact he was asking me for help about LJ. That we were even *talking* about LJ. And then this? "You're saying you owe these people money."

"Yes, a lot. I fucked up." He was breathing into his hands now, worry etched all over his face. "I took out a loan from the Marvellis. Remember how I told you my mom was sick?"

"Yeah, she has cancer."

"Well, I've never been good with money. Not like Jay. I didn't have all my ducks in a row, so when those bills starting getting bigger, I didn't have the cash. But my mom got so sick... she had to keep doing those clinical trials or she'd die, Billie."

"Okay, so you took out a loan."

"Uh-huh." A hard swallow, but when I offered him water, he waved a hand. "A big one, but I was working it off for them. Things were going fine, but then this job I took last week went sour. The police shot the whole place up."

He lifted his shirt then, revealing a large bandage across the side of his abdomen.

My mouth parted. "Are you saying they shot you?"

"Yeah, nearly clean through." He lowered his shirt. "Jay took care of me. Had his friend get me a doctor to fix me up so I didn't have to go to a hospital. I've been hiding out ever since."

"What the hell, Niko?"

"I know." A nod and his head sagged. "I didn't ask, but fucking Jay... He doesn't stop. He took care of me. He's *still* taking care of me. Even now."

"What do you mean, Niko?" I asked, and when he shook his head, I touched his arm. "You said he's going to settle your debt. You mean, he's paying them?"

"It ain't that simple, Billie." His words sobered me up, chilled me to the bone. He drew fingers down his mouth. "That debt was my responsibility. I have to work it off. They won't just let him go in there and walk."

"So why don't you take care of it?"

"Jay." He raised and dropped a hand. "The Marvellis called me while I was laid out about working another job, and he freaked. He urged me to go to the cops. Maybe work with them, you know, but I wouldn't budge. I have a family, a sick mom, and I can't risk going away. I mean, I'm their fucking livelihood. Anyway, we had a huge fight about it. He wasn't happy, but I thought that was the end of it."

"It wasn't?"

His head shook. "I woke up this morning, and he was gone, Billie. Picked up to take care of it himself. He left me nothing but a text message about what he was doing, but he can't. It's my debt, and I have to pay it. He said in his message everything would be fine, but I'm scared out of my fucking wits he's not going to come back."

"Well, what can we do? We can do something, right?" Panic shook my very limbs, my swallow hard. "Tell me we can do something. The cops?"

His hands gathered mine. "There is something you can do. That's why I'm here. I need your help."

"What? Anything."

A long breath. "I told you Jay wanted me to

238

cooperate with the police, and that's what I want to do, but I need you to reach out to your father. He's got a history with the Marvellis. Fuck, he's responsible for putting half the crime family behind bars. I could go to the police, but if I had him…"

My hands left his. "How do you know about my dad?"

"Jay," he said, like it was obvious. His throat worked. "I could talk until I'm blue in the face to the cops, but at the end of the day, I'm still some snot-nosed kid from the South Side of Chicago. A kid with a crime history. They won't listen to me, and by the time they did get their heads out their fucking asses enough to help Jay… Jay…"

His emotion came back, and mine did too, all over my body to the point where my vision clouded. He was most likely right. No one would listen to him, not like they'd listen to me.

Not like *my dad* would listen to me.

Niko touched my hands. "Your dad's the DA. He can just make a few calls, Billie. A few calls to the right people…"

"My dad and I don't talk, Niko." I raised my head, tears actually blinking down now. "We… We haven't physically spoken in forever."

"But you have to," he pleaded. "I honestly don't know how much time Jay has. He might already be there. He'd need to get the money together, but after, he'd go right to them."

Goosebumps covered my arms.

"Please, Billie," he said, urged. "I don't know what will happen if we don't do anything."

Chapter Twenty-Two

LJ

I dropped the black leather bag filled with cash on the table in the downtown warehouse, one of Alexi Marvelli's places. Guys in work coveralls pushed all kinds of the hard stuff around me, crack cocaine, crystal meth, and other shit Niko or I had never touched. We had to draw the line somewhere, and that was it; the stuff we did was enough for us. That'd always been okay for Alexi since every facet of his business had to be attended to. We stayed on our side of the yard, doing our thing, and as long as he got his cut, he was good.

A wave and Alexi himself had one of his suited gorillas check the bag. I didn't recognize this guy, tall and maybe even a new one. Then again, Alexi had all kinds of people around him all the time, and he had a lot of people here today. Where there weren't guys in coveralls, there were armed guards, dressed to the nines in the finest, but they didn't fool me. They were here for Alexi, *his* men, and I minded my *P*'s and *Q*'s. I was here for one purpose and one purpose only, to get one of my best friends off the hook, and then I planned on walking the fuck out of here. I hadn't even come armed, a sign of trust, and Alexi's guys had understood that when they'd checked me at the door.

After the new guy basically fondled my cash bag, he shoved it over to Alexi, his hand catching it. This deal today would cut a sizable chunk out of the savings I'd put aside for a rainy day, but if it got my buddy off the hook, then it was worth it. I figured money talked, and in this situation, I hoped I was right. Alexi smiled. "We have love, don't we, Jay? We're family?"

I nodded. "Of course, Alexi. I've always had a soft spot for you and your family."

"But do we have *love*?" A wave of the hand, and the new goon took the cash, standing at my side. The guy got hella close, basically shoulder to shoulder, but I stood my ground. I had to. Alexi frowned. "This bag is awfully light to settle your friend's debt."

I dampened my lips. "I'm in the process of moving some money around." Niko owed a lot, and I wasn't able to draw it all today. I lifted my chin. "You'll have the rest first thing tomorrow. I'm good for it, and you know that."

After all, he was the one who paid me. Of course, I took my own cut, but he knew what was coming and going from Niko and I. He provided the goods, always had.

Sitting down, Alexi pretended not to notice all the activity around him, guys on forklifts and rolling dollies filled with so much coke a crackhead would shoot his load off. This was just a day in the life for him, a complex and complicated life. How many times had he tried to rope my buddy and me in? Become a part of this life with the glitz and glam on the outside. He always said he could make us very rich men, and though I'd always been tempted, I kept my head in the books and thinking about the women in my life in Maywood Heights. They were where my loyalties lied, and as much as I considered Alexi family, at the end of the day, I only had one.

They were a pretty good one too.

"Yes, I know you're good for it." He set a hand on the table. "I just don't understand why we have no love. Where we lost it?"

The goon beside me, the new one, moved. He pressed up against me again, and my hands curled behind me.

Very slowly, Alexi got up from his chair, the frown hard on his face. He touched a hand to his chest. "You pain me, Jay. You really do. I thought we really did have love."

"We do." I angled a look, our small party of Alexi and this new guy suddenly growing by five or six. Each one was in a suit, each one with their hands posted behind their backs. I faced Alexi. "We never lost that."

"But didn't we?" He flicked the bag's leather strap. "You know, I suspected we may have lost love a little… but to do that to Niko. *Your friend*…" He tsked before looking at me. "There's no honor in that. There's no honor in betraying your friend or your family, *me*."

"Alexi, I don't understand."

But then a photo was slid in front of me by one of Alexi's goons. It was a picture of someone I knew, someone that made my fists squeeze behind my back even more, as I took in the photo of soft lips and vibrant red hair. He had a picture of Billie in front of me.

I just didn't understand why.

"You know, when I first heard whispers you were seen with Dean Coventry's kid, I figured maybe you just knew the girl. Especially since our business relationship ended on good terms. The girl was maybe an acquaintance to you. A quick fuck even—"

"Alexi—"

His hand lifted, and I stopped. His chin jerked up. "But then the raid. The cops knew exactly where I was conducting business that night with Niko. Why do you think that is, LJ?"

"I don't know, Alexi." My eyes fought a twitch when the goon beside me got even closer, his hand on my arm. I faced forward. "I don't know how the cops knew—"

"You're *fucking* the DA's daughter." His voice shook my insides, the sound ricocheting off the walls in my head. His hand touched the photo. "I know because we had you tailed. Your relationship with that little Coventry bitch has obviously jaded your judgment."

It took all I had not to reach across this table and clock this motherfucker straight. But I did that and it was over. I did that and *I* wouldn't be walking out of here, so instead, I ignored his goon's hand on me.

I stared right at Alexi. "I do have a relationship with her. But I assure you, it's nothing but pussy."

A dry chuckle called me on my bluff, Alexi's hand leaving the photo. "You take me for an idiot, Jay. A simple screw doesn't have you seeing this girl as much as you have. Remember, I had you tailed."

I shifted, but the hand on my arm squeezed, holding me back. I looked up at the guy, but he wasn't looking at me, only Alexi. I huffed. "She's nothing to me."

"Nothing, huh?"

A click, a silencer twisting onto a gun. The goon beside Alexi himself had done it. The guy on his left already had his together.

They both lifted in my direction.

Alexi grinned. "Here's to family."

"Police! We have you surrounded!"

People in coveralls pulled out guns, nearly all of them flashing badges around us. They honed in on us, honed in on *Alexi*, and there were just as many as the suits suddenly surrounding us. The suits were Alexi's guys, and in seconds, the silencers went in the direction of the guys with badges. Those first shots fired, and I jumped, suddenly jerked to the ground. I hit with a slam, gunshots ringing around me.

"Stay down, kid!" came from my side, the new goon in a suit who, just seconds ago, I'd thought had been Alexi's.

He covered my whole body, clearly not Alexi's. The guy had his hand on my head, his own gun out, but he wasn't able to use it. Those shots popped off like fire crackers above us, bags of crack exploding like fucking sugar.

I covered my own head, the pair of us just waiting this shit out while gun casings hit the floor around us. I closed my eyes, thinking about faces, and five hit my mind's eye like nothing else. They'd been my mom and sisters, of course, but there'd also been Billie.

Billie Coventry.

I prayed I'd get out of this. I prayed I'd get to see my family again. I'd done some stupid things, but this, by far, had been the worst. Eventually, those gunshots silenced around us. Eventually, I could lower my arms and lift my head. I did, and I found a set of eyes. Alexi Marvelli was on the floor too.

But he was pinned to the ground by a man in

coveralls.

One of the cops had gotten him down, and after he yelled, "He's down!" the man on top of me slid off. Before I knew it, he jerked me to my feet, rushing me away and out of the fray. Those gunshots started again, and I covered my head, obviously all this shit not over yet.

Outside, flashing lights took my vision, blinding me, and I was dragged through it all. I was rushed right past the cops holding like a million guns on the place and taken to a black sedan.

The guy with me opened the door for me, sliding me inside.

I noticed right away I wasn't cuffed.

This didn't seem to be a priority, a cop behind the wheel and some guy in a suit next to them. Since they faced forward, I couldn't see either of their faces.

"This is him," said the guy who put me in the car. He slammed the door shut, and before I knew it, he was running back inside the building with his gun drawn. I had no idea what the hell was going on, but suddenly, the officer behind the wheel was peeling out of the lot.

I belted in, bumping around and it took me a second to realize someone was yelling at me.

"You Lance Johnson?" The guy in the passenger seat yelled at me, the one in a suit. He had red hair and wild eyes. "Lance Johnson, yes or no—"

"Yes." I sat back, confused as fuck as the gunfire continued on behind us. It started to fade as we pulled away, but still, sounds of the shooting ran goddamn rampant in my scull.

"Just sit tight. We're headed to the precinct,"

the guy in the suit said, and though I did what I was told, I couldn't help the growing tension in my limbs. I heard my heart in my fucking head, and like Niko probably did that night he got shot, I considered the totality of what I may be about to lose. I wondered if I'd ever get to see my family again outside of steel bars.

I wondered if I lost my whole life as I knew it.

Chapter Twenty-Three

LJ

I studied the guy in a suit from the side-view mirror. He'd put on some dark sunglasses during our drive, completely obstructing his face despite the fact it was pitch black outside.

I sat back, my fingers laced when I dropped my hands between my legs. I felt like I was totally screwed here but didn't know for sure. After all, they hadn't cuffed me…

Panning to the dark streets, I thought about the events tonight and how they'd gone down. The guy who'd saved me tonight and kept me out of the crossfire of Alexi's guns clearly had been a cop. He'd not only saved me but seemed to know something about me too. That exchange he had with the cop in the driver's seat and that guy behind the shades was an obvious indicator. Shades definitely knew who I was, knew my name at least anyway. Since he was in a suit, he could be a detective or something, but I didn't know.

I glanced to the mirror, and Shades appeared to be looking in my direction. Though I couldn't gauge that by the sunglasses. Whatever the case, he and the cop driving us stayed silent, and the moment we pulled up to the downtown precinct, I took in a sharp breath. I figured a rough arrest was next for me as Shades got out. He stood idle while the cop in the uniform opened the door for me. Surprisingly, they both allowed me to get out on my own, and neither put their hands on me once I hit the pavement.

I looked around. "What's going on?"

Maybe a stupid question since these guys were cops, but whatever. I had rights and should know what was going on. The only response to my question was from Shades when he put a hand out. He guided me to walk ahead, and he and the cop flanked me. Cop got the door for both of us, and that felt... weird. I wasn't arguing since I still wasn't in cuffs and appeared to still have my freewill.

Once inside, I followed behind the guys. Again, weird. They put their backs to me and let me follow.

I did, staying close as I watched other guys and women being escorted very roughly through the place. After all, this was a police station. Still, I wasn't one of them. I stayed quiet the whole time, not trying to make waves. Eventually, the pair took me down a quiet hallway, and the regular cop stayed behind while Shades put a hand out.

"Right through there," he said, sliding off his glasses. Light-colored eyes bored down on me, narrowed distinctly in my direction. Inside now, this guy also had hair as bright as his necktie, a darkened red but bright nonetheless. His gaze settling hard, something about this guy struck me as familiar. I might have questioned it had I not turned the corner.

I saw similar eyes.

A darkness was underneath them, Billie chatting to Niko. The pair of them sat in some kind of interrogation room, but the moment they saw me, they launched out of their chairs.

And Billie launched right at me.

She came for me, no other thoughts given in a pair of little shorts and a tank like she'd just gotten out of bed. I had no idea what the fuck was going on, but the instant she hugged her tight little body against mine, I hugged her back. I *drank her in* and braced her so hard I thought my body would literally fuse into hers.

"Thank God, LJ. Just… Thank God."

She was happy to see me, forcing her fingers through my hair. Her racing heart beat wildly into my chest.

Mine matched.

"Beauty queen?" I questioned, awed that this girl was even standing in front of me, let alone in my arms. She peeled away quickly, and I noticed right away how goddamn beautiful she was. Not a stitch of makeup on freckled cheeks, lips red and flushed. I wanted to bruise the shit out of them, kiss her until I couldn't anymore. I reached to touch her, and she pulled away, eased away by Niko when he pulled me in.

"What the fuck, buddy? What the fuck?" Tackle-hugged by this guy and chuckling, I embraced him back. I think I got him a little too hard with his injury because he cringed a little.

"Sorry, bro."

"Hug me however hard you fucking want, dude. You're alive. Let me look at you." He did, holding me out, but the whole time I was staring over his shoulder. Billie lingered on but wasn't close enough. In fact, she was adding space.

She made her way to the door. "I'm just going to get some coffee."

And then she was leaving, cutting out of the room before another thought could be had. She passed Shades in the hallway on the way, her head down, and he almost went after her. He started to and everything, but in the end, put his hands in his pockets. A shake of the head, and he headed in the opposite direction down the hall. Meanwhile, Niko was handling me and looking at me like I was the missing link.

"God, bro. You're so fucking stupid. How could you go out there to the Marvellis? Fucking stupid."

It was, but not for the reasons he believed. He just hadn't wanted me to go because he didn't think they'd honor a financial exchange with me for a loan he'd taken out. The thing was, I had a very good relationship with Alexi. He would have forgiven Niko and let me pay, but that hadn't been what put me in the crossfire when it'd all been said and done. It'd been my link to Billie, my obsession with her and the whole reason I'd tried to keep my distance from her in the goddamn first place. I'd put her in danger. And honestly, the only good thing that had come out of tonight was that they'd gotten to me in the end instead of her. I'd never forgive myself if it'd been any other way.

I really had been stupid.

"What's going on?" I asked, wanting to go to her now just to make sure she was safe. My jaw moved. "How are you and Billie here?"

"How are we…" Niko started to chuckle. He put hands on my face. "You're only even here because of that girl."

"How?"

"Dude, you scared the fucking shit out of me when I woke up and saw you were gone. I didn't know what to do so I called her."

"Why?" I left him, going to the glass window.

Billie was out there, down the hall just a ways, but I could see her. She'd returned with that coffee, but wasn't drinking it.

Pacing, she chewed her little lip, waving her hands around and talking to herself. I couldn't hear her since the door was closed, but she looked frustrated as fuck. I didn't know if the frustration lay with herself, the situation, or what, but whatever she was doing, I smiled at her.

She looked cute as hell.

"She called her father, man. Called him for you."

I found my buddy's eyes. "What?"

Grinning, he folded his big arms. He too spied Billie through the glass, her drink up to her lips. "I wanted to go to the cops, but I didn't think they'd listen to me. I went to Billie instead, told her everything and she got her dad involved. The DA? Anyway, he made a few calls, and after he did, the police got a team together to go get you..."

"Does her dad have red hair? Wear aviator shades?"

He frowned. "Don't know. Haven't seen him."

I think I had, and I think he was here tonight, which meant *he'd* gone to get me when he definitely didn't have to. I mean, he wasn't a cop.

My mouth dried, staring at Billie again. She'd sat down now, staring at her lap. I swallowed. "She called her dad for me?"

"Yeah." Niko dropped an arm around my shoulders. "I don't know what would have happened if she didn't."

I did, in the middle of that goddamn shoot out.

She called him...

I stared at the beauty queen once again, and this time, she stared at me, her head up. Lifting her coffee, she waved her cup a little at me, and I raised a hand back. This girl saved my goddamn life tonight.

And she spoke to the father she hated to do it.

Chapter Twenty-Four

LJ

Niko drove Billie and I back since the police wouldn't let me get my car until morning. As a result of working with the police, Niko and I were both told we were able to go, but I had a feeling that may have had less to do with our cooperation and more to do with Billie and her dad. Of course, we weren't told this. We were just told we could go, and neither one of us argued. We were just happy to be out of that place and that Alexi was in custody. I was told I personally would be hearing from the police soon regarding him and his arrest. I was told not to worry. As long I was available, I wouldn't have any issues regarding the police, and I was just happy to be done with all this shit. I just wanted to finish school and forget about that part of my life.

Of course, I wouldn't have had the option at all if it hadn't been for Billie. She hadn't had to help me, but she did.

I just didn't know why.

I'd fucked up royally when it came to her, but still, she'd helped me. I wanted to talk to her, but with Niko around, I hadn't felt it appropriate. He was going to drop her off at her house, but since I had wanted to talk to her, I'd been able to convince her to come back to our place for dinner. It was the least I could do, but I also had an evening's worth of metaphorical crap on me I wanted to scrub off as soon as possible.

I left Billie downstairs with Niko to chew the fat and shit while I showered. He was supposed to call in takeout.

My hand on the shower wall, I let all the stress and shit fall, my hand somehow finding my cock when I thought about the redhead downstairs. I couldn't help but think about her and what she'd done for me. It'd been a brave thing she'd done tonight. From what I understood, she and her father had a history she wanted nothing to do with. This history sent her running, but she came right back to him. She did it for me.

Grunting, I almost got myself to that peak, but ended up stopping. Fuck, it'd be too easy but I didn't think I had the right. I didn't have the right, not with all the drama I'd made sure she'd gone through in the past. I'd hurt her, something I needed to own up to.

My own history plaguing me now, I let go of my dick, then turned the shower cold. This tamed the madness within, calming me down enough to ultimately finish my shower, then towel off. I had clothes waiting, sweats and a white tee. I shrugged the sweats on with no boxers, but held the t-shirt in my hands as I came downstairs. Billie was still where I'd left her at the kitchen island. But surprisingly, there was no Niko in sight.

"Where's Nik?" I asked, and her sight lifted from her device. She'd been playing with it when I came downstairs, but she wasn't now.

A heat touched her gaze that simmered all those rogue thoughts again, a flush crushing her cheeks. Her attention drifted down my damp chest and lower, stopping at the midpoint of my abs before finding my eyes. Red lashes blinked. "He went out to get the food."

All too quickly, she fluttered those lashes back

in the direction of her phone. Honest to God, I hadn't left my shirt off to tease her. Though, that'd been my nature in the past so she probably assumed.

Being real, I'd still been amped up from thoughts upstairs, *hot*, and the way she eye-fucked my chest just now didn't help.

I eliminated space between us, freckled thighs crossed atop my barstool. So supple-looking, I wanted to thrust myself between them, and her wearing her night shirt the way she currently was didn't help. She had it bunched at her midriff, her hair tie doing the holding. Set free, her red hair fell in thick waves across her shoulders, and I wanted to wrap them around my fist and crush my mouth against hers. I had all these words in my head, all these goddamn words I'd mulled over in the shower, and not one of them made it out of my mouth now. She made it hard, never easy with her.

Her eyes glanced up to me, literally not an ounce of space between us. Her chest heaving, she stared up to my eyes. "What are you doing, LJ?"

What *was* I doing? I had no fucking idea, sliding my shirt to the counter and looking at her. My mouth parted. "I just want to know why."

"Why?"

I nodded. "Why did you do what you did? Why did you call your dad?"

I just… needed to hear it, couldn't believe it. *Why are you doing this to yourself?*

I didn't deserve this girl, not in a million galaxies with all the shit I'd done to her. Even still, I was torturing myself. Still, I allowed myself for hope I most definitely didn't deserve.

But if she gave me an in…

The ball was completely in her court now, and I think she knew that, turning away from me.

I bought her back by the chin, my thumb sliding across her lip. "Why, beauty queen?"

"Why do you think?"

I shook my head. "*Why?* Tell me."

The ultimate question that somehow caused tears to form in her eyes. Her lip trembled, and when I tugged at it, she wet it.

"I was scared," she breathed, my heart punching the walls in my goddamn chest. "I was scared for you. Scared I'd never see you again."

The lump in my throat thick and hot, I choked it down, *made* myself look at her. Framing her face, I dragged her gaze up.

"LJ…"

"Want to know what scared me?" I asked her. "The last thoughts I had when Alexi Marvelli had me staring down the barrel of more than one gun."

She cringed, her hands coming to lock around my wrists. "What?"

"Well, it wasn't school," I said, waving the hair out of her face. "And it wasn't just my family. Though, I thought about them too."

I thought about so many things, and yes, my family but she'd been right there with them. It'd been her face I found there too in the night. She'd been right there with them, a heavy fear that I'd messed up and never got to see any of them again for decisions I made. My jaw moved. "You were there in my mind, Billie. *You.* I had thoughts of you as one of my last, and I hate myself for that. I hate what I did to you. I hate that I hurt you."

Tears finally fell as she trembled in my hands,

her eyes closing. "Then why did you? Why did you do those things?"

"Because in the fucked up spaces of my mind, I thought I was doing it for my family. I worked with Alexi Marvelli, had a good relationship with him. He was a business partner, and I couldn't have anything come between that. I'm all my family has, and the Marvellis and your dad are literally at war. Having anything to do with you would have been bad. Your dad's that family's enemy."

"But what does my dad's relationship with them have to do with me?"

"Because you're close to him, Billie." I dragged my thumbs across her cheeks. "You know, the Marvellis showed me your picture tonight? Alexi Marvelli had your goddamn picture in his fucking *hands*. He knew who your dad was, your ties to me. He knew I love…"

I stopped just short, unable to go there. Because once I said that, it was over. I was hers, but she could never be mine. Not after all the things I did.

I said the words anyway.

"He knew that I love you," I said and not past tense. I swallowed hard. "I love you, Billie."

She was trembling so hard at this point, quivering. It drove me so fucking mad my mouth fell down on hers, claiming it.

A gasp and she gripped my shoulders, basically fusing our mouths and bodies together.

"I love you," I breathed over her mouth, unable to hide it anymore. This girl had me undone to the point I thought I'd collapse beneath my own weight.

Her tears wet my cheeks during the kiss, that

same passion I felt coming right back to me. I had no idea when all this had changed, but it had. She'd claimed me.

And I marked her.

"I love you, LJ." Her hands seared over my body like hot wax, each touch the best fucking burn. She sighed when my tongue flicked out, tasting hers. A reach and I forced everything off the island, picking her up and setting her on it.

"I'm so sorry," I gritted, unable to get enough of her softness and taste. "I'm so fucking sorry for everything I did to you."

I couldn't be sorry enough, her body quaking in my hands. I tugged her shirt off and saw just a sports bar hugging her full tits. The thing gave her cleavage like a motherfucker, the swell of her breasts flushed and heated.

Growling, I dove between the pair, licking from one swell to the other. She gripped my hair as I worked the bra off, releasing her breasts. I drew a nipple instantly into my mouth, laving, and she dug her fingernails in my abs.

"Christ, beauty queen. Christ." I bit *hard*, and she cried out against my teeth, the sound literally reverberating through her entire chest. Yanking her shorts off, I realized she wore just as few undergarments as I did.

My groan hit the room at the smell of her sex, a glistening heat between her legs when I widened them. I dragged my hands down her legs. "I need a taste."

And I did, sucking her lower lips right into my mouth. So sweet, my tongue tunneled directly into her heat, drinking her in.

Her thighs squeaking across the island, she fucked my face, laying back while I worshiped her. Taking her thigh, I brought it over my shoulder and made a home between her legs, Billie calling out as I flicked her clit.

"I'm going to come."

"Fucking do it," I groaned, shoving my sweats down, and my cock sprang free. I fisted it. "I'm coming with you."

I didn't even wait before claiming her, guiding myself inside her. She'd told me she was on birth control before, and that's all I needed.

I physically shuddered inside her, and pulling her up, I thrust my hips, fucking her wildly across the counter.

Her lips parted, and I bit down on them, making her call out. She dragged her nails across my back, and I roared, working my hips so hard and fast I felt like I'd split her in two.

My mouth claimed hers as I picked her up. Kicking off my sweats, I walked with her into the living room, my dick still inside her. I had to walk slow but I wasn't leaving this pussy for a second.

I made it to the couch still inside her, pressing her down on her back. Her thighs hugged me, and I rocked my hips, her breasts bouncing as I slapped my body against hers.

"LJ…" Her eyes rolled back as her body arched, mine too upon reaching that high. I grunted, filling her completely with my seed and didn't stop until I emptied inside her.

Pulling out, I eased down from the high with Billie beneath me, kissing her sweetly into the couch. Before her, I didn't think I did sweet. I didn't have to, not before her.

I hadn't cared enough.

I loved her, drowning in her heat as I fastened her to me. I only let go of her a little when I picked her up to take her to my bedroom. She wasn't leaving tonight.

I wasn't letting her go again.

Chapter Twenty-Five

Billie

I was by myself in the morning, a place that might have worried me had last night not happened. LJ and I fucked two more times last night, then after, we made love. It was different. It felt so different, and by the end, he hadn't let me go until he literally got up this morning. He had a phone call, but I was so tired I'd turned over and went back to sleep. Achy, I still felt him inside me.

This was all different.

I didn't feel like we were in the same place we were before, and I think last night really just put things into perspective for the both of us. There were no more games. No more who was going to break who. There was just this and what we did last night.

That was what ended up allowing me to get up with confidence that morning. I had no clothes here, of course, mine sprinkled downstairs no doubt. I found some of LJ's, though, so after I got dressed in a band tee and a pair of boxers I found from his drawers, I came downstairs.

LJ sat at that same kitchen island he'd fucked me on, and the tingle instantly blazed between my legs. Shirtless, he had his back to me as he spoke to Niko, the demigod standing next to him. They both faced forward, talking to someone else but I couldn't see who that person was. I moved closer, and by the time I came completely in the kitchen, I had no time to turn back.

Some people have told me I looked like my father, and I used to like that before he'd left my mom. I used to relish in the fact I looked like him, feeling that connected us.

Now, our similarities just angered me, those same light eyes staring back at me. My hair was darker than his, both my grandparents redheads on his side.

Daddy saw me first, lounging back against LJ and Niko's range. He stood tall in my presence, his hands working. "Billie..."

His throat jumped following my name, and both Niko and LJ turned. Upon seeing me, LJ's hand came instantly out for mine, and had it not, I know I would have turned right around. I'd seen my dad last night, sure, but I sure as hell hadn't talked to him. I'd barely even spoken to him on the phone when I'd called him for help last night. I'd told him what I needed, and that was it. Call ended. He'd ended up doing the rest after I'd given him the location Niko believed LJ was located at.

"What's going on?" I asked, tugged by LJ. His presence only slightly distracted me from the existence of my father, then fully when a strong arm looped around my waist.

He popped a kiss on my brow, a trail of heat drifting directly from his lips. He was so very handsome, sexy from his broad shoulders to his bare feet. He'd only put a pair of sweatpants on when he'd come downstairs, his hair a mess of lazy blond. He cradled my hip. "Your dad came to talk. I guess the police have some concerns. Ones about the Marvellis?"

That crime family? I frowned. "Why? Didn't that guy get arrested? Alexi?"

At least, that was what the police told Niko

and me last night. During the bust, we got a call that they'd gotten LJ on time and were bringing him to the precinct. I'd been so relieved. I just wanted him to be safe ultimately, regardless of what happened between us before.

Us getting together after had just made everything that much better.

"Yes, sweetheart, but the threat doesn't stop just because he's off the streets." Daddy pushed his hands into his pockets, the frown hard on his face. He appeared completely at war with himself as he rocked back on his patented leather shoes. Like he wanted to come closer, but didn't want to jinx it.

Probably best.

Daddy's jaw moved. "The police believe he's more dangerous now than he was before."

"LJ?" I questioned. I wouldn't look at my father, let alone listen to him.

I think LJ understood that, his arms falling around my hips. His attention drifted to my dad. "Alexi Marvelli is very powerful. Your dad says the police feel there might be some danger there. That Alexi might try to retaliate for his arrest. He's head of the Marvelli family. Might cause some trouble."

My insides jolted. "Wait. Are you saying you're in danger? Could he hurt you—"

"No, baby. No," he said, my insides instantly calming but not because of his assurances. It was because of what he called me. What I'd somehow come to mean to him. This guy went from hating me to loving me, the same on my end as well. I didn't know I ever could, but I had somehow. His thumb dragged across my cheek. "The police have sent a detail for me. I'll be safe."

"So what is this then?" I asked to both LJ and Niko. Niko stood quietly, peering on during this whole thing. I jutted a chin at my dad. "Why is *he* here?"

"Sweetheart…" Daddy started to cross the room, but when I stiffened, he stayed in place. His hand lifted. "I'm here because I had some concerns for *your* well-being. Lance let the authorities know that you're on Alexi Marvelli's radar. They might try to go through you to get to him, and I can't have you in danger."

I frowned, looking at LJ, and he had so much war in his eyes it raced my heart. His throat constricted. "We need to put some space between us."

"What are you talking about?"

"It would just be temporary. Babe—" He grabbed my hands, holding them when I tried to pull away. "Billie, it wouldn't be for very long. It'd be short term, until things cool off around here for a little while, and I think it's best."

"Is that you talking or him?" I grunted, jerking my chin in Daddy's direction.

"It was your dad's idea, but I agree. You don't know these people like I do, Billie. The Marvellis aren't anyone to fuck with."

"He's right, Billie." Niko forced his hands into his pockets. "We gotta get you off the grid."

"You'd go to a safe house, honey." My dad now came in, his expression grave. "And you'd have complete monitoring. I've spoken with the police, and they're backing me up on this. You'll be completely safe."

"And Niko's even going with you," LJ chimed in with, his hand framing my face. "He'll watch over you."

"The least I can do, Queenie." Niko shrugged with a smile. "And hey, we'll have fun. Play board games and shit."

"But what about you?" I pressed my hands to LJ's chest. "Aren't you going with us?"

"I've agreed to work with the police." He gathered my hands. "I do that, and they give both me and Niko immunity for some of the other things we did. Our involvement with Alexi himself. I am going to meet you. Just not right away."

"When?"

"Billie, honey?" My dad redirected my attention to him, and though he spoke to me, he didn't move an inch in my direction. He didn't dare, a sigh falling from his lips. "Lance will be safe. I've spoken personally with the police commissioner. He's pulling out all the stops. Lance will be safe."

He had?

"I'll come right to you as soon as I help the police get what they need. I promise you, Billie." LJ brought his arms around me. "I just need you to go along with this plan of your dad's. I can't worry about you."

A plea deep in his eyes, and I knew that was the only reason I was agreeing to upend my entire life. It had nothing to do with my father.

I looked my dad. "I'm only do this for him. Not for you."

A blink before my dad nodded, but with that blink, so much relief hit his eyes. In fact, it was the happiest I'd seen him in a long time.

I didn't know how I felt about that, looking at him. I just knew if something happened to LJ in all this, I couldn't even think about what I'd do. I just knew my dad wouldn't just be able to bank on me not coming to his wedding in the summer.

He'd be lucky if he ever saw me again at all.

Chapter Twenty-Six

Billie

My dad arranged for Niko and me to be housed in Woodcreek University's Grey Woods, which were about twenty miles outside of campus. Since the term had ended, no one would really be around the area for hiking or anything. There were also many cabins for rent, a good place for Niko… or I guessed *for me* to lie low, but still, I believed this whole thing was ridiculous. I understood the threat, obviously. It was a real one but what I didn't understand was why the authorities were allowing my dad to put me away like the president's daughter. Meanwhile, LJ, the real person in danger, was out there on the streets. He was basically helping my dad's cases and being punished for it. His freedom was being used as a bargaining chip, and as far as I could see, my dad was only to gain from the scenario. Like I said, it helped his cases with LJ being out there and helping the police.

Things were obviously more complicated than I could see, but I couldn't help but make things personal. Especially since things were personal. There were a lot of lives just being tossed around, and from what I understood, LJ hadn't even been given access to his own family. He'd had to make up some excuse about staying on campus to take a summer class. Meanwhile, his family had no idea what was going on. They'd at least been given a police detail from what I understood. The detail was assigned to keep an eye on things, and Niko's family got one too. Thank goodness.

As for me, Mom believed I was taking a

summer class too and needed to focus. I couldn't tell her anything else for her own safety, and gratefully, she hadn't asked. She'd been doing really well lately, pretty much stopped her heavy drinking, and I didn't want to mess any of her progress up. She was finally healing, so with all this going on, I made sure to keep close to the cuff for her sake. Dad arranged to have someone go over there too for me, but the police didn't feel she was in any immediate danger. *I* was the main focus here, and my dad sure let me know it.

One really would have believed I was the president's daughter the way my dad had things set up. The police were on rotation in the woods, about four squad cars coming and going. Though suffocating, I dealt with it. I really wanted to cooperate for LJ's sake and his peace of mind. I got to talk to him during designated hours but not nearly enough for my liking.

A cool month passed by like this, time spent in the woods and with not many updates from LJ himself. He honestly couldn't tell me much, not allowed, but one thing I did know was he'd been supposed to meet me out there around this time. When that deadline obviously came and went, I thought I'd lose it the next time I spoke to him.

"Just a bit longer," he said today, his honeyed voice through the line while I sat by the window. I stared at the swaying trees, not much to see beyond that. Besides the cops, I had Niko, who, when he wasn't bugging me about playing board games, was playing video games on the cabin's flat screen. He was either doing that or upstairs in his room watching internet porn. I knew because I caught him a time or twelve.

The quarantine was obviously getting to him too.

Currently, the guy shot zombies in my ear, winking at me from the couch when I passed him a look. Despite being trapped together for over a month, we had bonded. I found out he made a mean grilled cheese sandwich.

Though smiling a little, I let out a sigh in the phone. "I'm not sure how much longer I can do this. I thought you'd be here days ago."

"I know, and I will soon." It was hard not to be wrapped up in that deep voice, a smile in it. "Actually, it should be sooner rather than later. The police have arranged a meeting with the Marvelli family. There's a new head with Alexi in prison, and the police are assuring me whoever it is seems agreeable."

"How agreeable?"

"I hope enough to not retaliate for their family member being thrown in prison."

"Which wasn't your fault."

"I know, beauty queen." Another smile in his voice that literally made me burn. I could just see it in front of me, touch it. "Billie?"

I leaned my head on the window sill. "Give me an exact date. You said you didn't want to worry about me, but that's all I do here."

It was all I could do, not really much else to do.

A sigh on his head.

"How about I ask around about that today? And as soon as I hear something, you'll be the first person I call."

"Promise?"

A light chuckle. "I promise. I love you."

Weeks of hearing him say that and the same smile still appeared on my face.

Tugging down my hair, I told him the same before hanging up, and Niko chose that moment to stretch out his wingspan.

He'd decided to wear less and less clothing during our time together, nothing but workout pants hanging low on his chiseled hips. But where most girls would probably swoon in this situation, this guy had become nothing but my younger brother. And since he watched porn in his free time instead of looking hotly at me like he used to, I could imagine the understanding was shared.

Grinning, he did a little gorilla thump when he tapped his balled fists against his chest. He really was a riot, and I shook my head at him. He pointed. "Time for lunch? I can make my famous grilled cheese."

It really was about the only thing he could make, and since it was tasty, I didn't complain.

Getting up, I stretched out myself. "I'm actually going to go for a jog I think. Stretch my legs."

Absolute delight took over his face. He backed toward the stairs, shooting a thumb back. "Let me just go get changed. We'll go together."

"Yeah, that wasn't an invitation," I said, watching all that elation fall. I'd spent every waking hour with this guy. Even during my runs and I needed a break. I put my hair up in a ponytail. "We got the armed warriors outside, remember?" I stated, referring to the squad cars on constant rotation. "They'll stalk me so you don't have to."

"Yeah, Jay totally would have my dick in a jar

if I let you go by yourself." He jogged backwards. "Just let me get my sneakers on. Two seconds."

"Niko, come on—"

And like every other guy in my life these days, he ignored what I wanted, sprinting up the stairs two by two.

Rolling my eyes, I popped on my own shoes at the door. I had a pair of shorts on as well as a sports bra and tank already, planning to go for a run after my call with LJ.

I headed outside, then stretched once more in the day. The fresh air was my fuel, and as I stretched, Niko came outside to join me.

"We'll stay on the trails," he said, dropping his foot after stretching his thick calf. He had shorts and a red tank on. "That way the cops won't lose track of us."

Nodding, I figured that'd be the case. It always was, and with that, we headed off the porch. He hit the trail right away, and after, I texted our police detail to let them know we were going out. They liked us to do that, so I did. After getting confirmation, Niko and I headed deep into the trail. We were only about five minutes into the jog before Niko cursed, though. He jiggled his pockets, and when he came up empty, he shoved back a thumb. "We gotta go back to the cabin. I left my cell phone."

"I have mine."

"I need to track my steps, Queenie. Two seconds."

Him and his two seconds. I started to follow him, but stopped.

He did too. "Aren't you coming?"

"I'll wait." And when I got his eye, I raised

and dropped my arms. "Dude, I will be fine. I'm not going anywhere."

He frowned. "Promise me?"

"I promise you. Now go. So we can go." The sooner he went, the faster he could come back.

A heavy sigh before he bunched his hair. "You better not go anywhere. I'll be right back."

I mean, where would I go? I nodded like that fact was obvious, and only after I did, did he sprint back. I lost his back through the trees, scrolling through apps on my phone. I had my own workout apps I liked to monitor and brought one of them up.

Leaning against the tree, I played around on the device, but the snap of a twig behind made me jump.

"Can you help me? I think I'm lost."

I turned around, feeling like I recognized the voice, and the moment I did, my eyes twitched wide.

A man, a disheveled man wearing a dirty T-shirt and sweatpants. About a month or two of coarse hair on his face, it took me a second to realize I knew the guy.

But by then, he'd grabbed me.

Sinclair covered my mouth, smelling like booze and smoke when he normally didn't do either. I screamed, but his hand muffled the sound, and before I knew it, he was dragging me across the woods. He had a car parked off the trail, way off and far away where the police normally did their rotation. It wasn't just a car, though. It was a *van*, a white one, and opening it up, he threw me inside it.

"Help—"

The door slammed in my face, cutting off my sound from the world. I scrambled on my front as a door opened and closed. Sinclair hopped in the front seat, and the next thing I knew, he was peeling away, my body sliding and slamming against the side of the van.

I groaned, hugging my impacted side. I tried to get up on my knees but didn't have the need when Sinclair reached back. Getting a hold of my arm, he dragged me up and between the seats.

"Get the fuck up here and sit down," he growled, dark circles under his eyes. I barely recognized him, his facial hair patchy and completely unkempt. He pointed toward the seat. "*Now.* That's not a request, and don't even think about going for the doors or windows. They don't open on your side."

Shivering, I stayed where I was, but then he went for the handgun shoved into the front of his sweats.

He pointed it at me. "Get in the fucking seat, Billie. I won't ask you again."

Chapter Twenty-Seven

LJ

"You're doing great, Lance. Just great. Remember to stay calm and don't obstruct the wire."

The detective working the Marvelli case coached in my ear while I strode down the street. I'd told Billie that the police planned to meet with the Marvellis.

I'd just left out the fact that person would be me.

The Marvelli family had asked to meet with me specifically, sending a representative on their behalf. I hadn't told Billie because I hadn't wanted to worry her, and the police assured me they had my back on this. They said they'd have me completely surrounded at any given time, and I think the only reason I trusted them was because of Billie's dad. He made sure I always had someone around me, security detail out the ass watching over me. He'd fought for me and my family, as well as Niko's. He made sure people were there keeping an eye on things, an eye on them, and as far as I was concerned, the man made good on his promise to his daughter.

Her dad did right by me, had me covered enough that I felt safe in this situation, a downtown cafe today's meeting spot. The Marvellis wanted neutral ground, and I did too, but I wouldn't go without the police in my ear. They had a wire on me, but I highly doubted this rep wouldn't know about it. In fact, they probably assumed, which was why they wanted to meet on neutral ground in the first place. Out in the open assured no trouble.

On both parts.

Letting out a breath, I headed down the street toward the cafe. The cops dropped me off about a block away, well within view of the cafe, and they had another car positioned on the opposite side of the street. Any trouble and they'd come in, but I didn't expect any trouble. These people weren't stupid, and the cops had already gotten Alexi, so I highly doubted they wanted to make waves. I came upon the street crossing before getting over to the cafe, but had to stop when the light changed, a cluster of people around me.

"Not long now, Lance," Detective Guthrie said in my ear. "We got your back. We're watching."

I looked out for them. Though I couldn't see the authorities, I supposed that was the point. Breathing hard, I waited for the light to change when suddenly a guy brushed my arm.

I glanced over at him, the man in shades talking on a cell phone. Shrugging the brush off as nerves, I stared ahead, waiting for the light change.

That was until he touched my arm.

"Pass the cafe," he said, letting go and sliding his hand into his pocket. He kept the phone to his ear, a young guy like myself in jeans and a graphic tee. He didn't look out of the ordinary, but maybe that was the point. He lifted his head. "Then keep walking and get into the first black sedan you see. It'll be waiting for you."

Frowning, I glanced up, and with no voices in my ear, I supposed the cops hadn't picked up on what this guy clearly said to me on a crowded street corner.

Tension brewed immediately in my veins, and bracing my arms, I shook my head at the guy. I knew the cops were in my ear and didn't want to incriminate myself with whoever this guy was.

The guy must have seen what I did because he nodded. After that, he shrugged a little. "Suit yourself. My employer would just like a solution that suits everyone's interests. Keeps *everyone* safe."

My heart jolted as the light changed, and before I knew it, this guy was on the move. I stood there, frozen and jaw slack. It took a moment for me to realize the detective was in my ear, asking what was wrong.

"Lance?"

"I'm good," I mumbled, sprinting across the street in my jacket. The cafe sign with a peach and fancy lettering came up pretty quick, but without a thought, I kept walking. The guy said something about *both* our interests, *safety*, and that sure as hell stuck with me. They knew about Billie obviously, and if whatever this was kept her okay, my family...

"Lance, where are you going? You've passed the cafe. Lance?"

"Just trust me, all right?" I whispered, though I hoped he could. I wasn't a betting guy, but at this point, I was all in here.

I found the black sedan easy, the thing was literally parked just beyond the cafe. Since it was out in the open, that made me feel only slightly better. The cops could see where I was going and follow if these people took me someplace.

Coming upon the ride, the front door clicked open. A man got out, a driver in a suit. He opened the back door, then put a hand out for me to go inside.

"Looks like he's getting into a black sedan! Lance?"

I lifted a hand, but only just, swallowing before getting inside. Right away, I heard the detective's voice again.

"He waved us off. Just… keep eyes on him for now," Detective Guthrie said. "The windows aren't tinted. Just one perp inside."

The detective was right, only one man inside, and with the windows not tinted, this whole meeting was terribly obvious. Whoever this guy was, clearly wasn't trying to hide.

Dressed sharp, the guy had dark hair, his look inquisitive. His legs crossed, he shifted a glance toward the window. Outside, a maroon-colored van took his attention, the words *Sullivan Bros. Electric Co.* marked on the side. He ticked a finger toward it. "I'm assuming your friends. Let them know you're fine. This won't take long. We aren't going anywhere. I assure you."

My mouth dry, I stared at the guy, clean-shaven and a cigar in his hands like he'd stepped straight out of *The Sopranos*. He had an air about him that screamed Alexi Marvelli and even looked like him, his face narrower and more physically fit in general. Alexi was a little on the hefty side, but this guy looked like some kind of politician. A slow breath eased from my lips. "I'm good, guys."

"You're good?" came into my ear.

"Yes, for now," I said, then returned my attention to the guy sitting across from me. He wasn't smiling, wasn't doing anything really. He just stared right back. We were the only ones in this car, not even a driver in the front seat. The guy who let me in stood outside, his back to the door.

The man crossed his legs. "Do you know who

I am, son?"

I didn't, but assumed he was from the Marvelli family. I shook my head, and he nodded.

"Leonardo Marvelli." He reached for my hand then, a hard shake I took before he sat back. He lifted his chin. "Though to the public, I go by Leo Pearson. My mother's maiden name."

Well, that name I definitely recognized. Leo Pearson was like a senator or some shit. I mean, he used to be. I'd heard his name a lot freshman year, since that was when the elections were and new people were taking office. My lips parted. "You were a senator."

"Yes, hence the name change." He chuckled, the sound light. "My family name hasn't always had the best associations with it. And I'm sorry for all the cloak and dagger." He lifted and dropped his hand. "I'm not in politics anymore, but people still know my face. I just wanted to meet somewhere I wouldn't be recognized, and definitely not at a police station. I've heard my name in the papers enough over the years and don't really want to add another byline to it. I figured here, the police could still see you while at the same time, give us a little privacy."

"Privacy for what?" I asked. The dude made me get in his car and that didn't sit well with me.

A smile touched his eyes now, an array of genuineness there this guy definitely hadn't earned from me. At least, not yet. Even still, he attempted to give it to me, his fingers lacing on his crossed legs. "To thank you."

"Thank me? For what?"

"For whatever your involvement was in my brother's arrest."

"Your brother. As in…" My eyes twitched wide. "You're Alexi's brother?"

"The one and only. Though, I wish I wasn't. There's a reason I took my mother's name and stayed the hell clear of my father's. My brother has dragged it through the mud. Used our father's legacy for his own personal gain for years when he became head of the family. My father built his companies from the ground up as an immigrant. Well, when he died, my brother took creative license to turn the Marvelli name into the one it is today. It's become one of fear, and I hate that. It goes against everything I stood for in my previous line of work."

Shocked, I sat back.

Leo sighed. "Well, now that my brother is behind bars and I'm next in line, I'm making changes. I have my family to think about, both close and extended. I plan to get us out of the game and the messes my brother has dragged us into."

"What about Alexi?"

"I love my brother. I do, but I'll honestly be surprised if, after he's tried and charged, he'll even make it out of prison. He's made a lot of enemies *everywhere*, and most of them are behind bars. He'll most likely befall his fate there. I hate it, but that's probably what's going to happen."

"You still good, Lance?" I heard in my ear, and since I thought I was, I smiled.

"Yeah, you hearing this," I said to the detective.

"Every word." A smile in the man's voice.

The same one faced right back at me, Leo. He nodded. "I guess I just wanted to say thanks and give my personal apologies for any issues you've had with my brother. You or the authorities will see no retaliation from the Marvelli family. I'm not entirely sure of your involvement in my brother's case, but since I heard your name around, I wanted to meet with you personally, give you some peace of mind, I guess."

I appreciated that, and when his hand came out, I shook it. "Thank you."

"You're welcome. Let the authorities know that too."

"We heard," came into my ear, and I laughed. I smiled. "They heard."

Another nod from Leo. "Well, I guess this is good day then. I hope it's a good one."

I had a feeling it would be, and after letting Leo go, I went about my own. I made it to the electricity van across the street, and though I got a good scolding for going rogue, I got a pat on the back too.

"We appreciate all your help with this, Lance," the detective said, smiling when he shook my hand. "Maybe you should consider a job in law enforcement."

Nah, didn't think that would be happening, but I was glad I'd been able to help. After shaking the detective's hand, it turned out he hadn't been the only one who wanted to shake.

Billie's dad had shown up, the prosecutor himself. He obviously didn't have to be there, but came through anyway. He also shook my hand, commended me on how brave I was.

"Well, these guys had my back," I said, referring to the detective and his team. They were all wrapping things up. I eased hands into my pockets.

"And I feel like he wasn't the only one."

The man personally had fought to make sure I'd been looked out for, my family too, and I more than appreciated that.

Billie's dad appeared modest at the acknowledgment, scratching the side of his neck. I never saw him in anything less than a business suit, and something told me usually DAs didn't make it off the golf course, let alone hung around criminal investigations. They definitely didn't pick up guys from crime scenes such as myself, yet here he was. He shrugged. "It was the least I could do. You're obviously my daughter's friend."

I was more than that, but I had a feeling he knew that. Things were definitely complicated with him and his daughter, and I was on her side always but could give credit where credit was due. This guy had gone to bat for me, and I appreciated that.

"Thanks for all you did." I put my hand out again, shaking his hand hard. "My family's everything to me, and Niko's is to him too. I think I can say on his and my behalf that we appreciate you making calls to get police details for our families too."

Another shrug before he released my hand, then a nod. "I'm just glad everything turned out all right. Sounds like it did."

These men around us were headed off to far more important issues now and I was grateful for that. Fuck, I was happy for all this to finally be behind me.

Billie's dad rocked on his shoes. "I suppose you're going to go see my daughter now?"

"I am. She's been giving me an earful about not being there."

"Well, I guess you can let her know everything's okay now. That she's safe. *I'd* appreciate that." His smile didn't quite reach his eyes, but he shook it off, and all that red hair reminded me so much of his kid. He clasped my arm. "And you, uh… you just take care of her, okay? Be good to her?"

He didn't have to ask, always in Billie's corner as long as she'd have me. I'd been stupid before when it came to her, but I wouldn't be now. I refused.

I loved her.

"I will," I said. "Sir."

I had respect for the man, and when his smile stretched, I felt I had the same on his end. I was happy for that.

He backed off to talk to the detective and his team more when my phone buzzed. Seeing it was a certain red head, I grinned too wide. Crazy, how she affected me.

I swiped my thumb across the device, then put it to my ear. "Hey, beauty queen. I just got done and—"

"What are you *doing*, Sinclair?"

I twitched. Sinclair? Her ex-boyfriend motherfucker? What the hell?

My lips moved to speak.

"Why have you taken me?" she questioned, my gut twisting right away. She panted. "I'm scared. Let me go."

My heart racing immediately, I started to speak but didn't know if I should or she could. This fucker had taken her?

"Shut the fuck up, Billie!" Sinclair seethed but not directly into the line. He was somewhere wherever she was at, and the sudden charge of an engine accelerating grappled my insides. He had her in a car. He was driving her someplace.

"*Please*," she pleaded. "Why are we in this white van? Where are you even taking me? Why did you grab me off Henderson trail and drag me in here? Stop. You might hit someone jogging on the paths. The roads are too narrow for big vehicles up here."

I listened to every word, taking in every detail as I got my keys.

"*Baby, just keep telling me where you are,*" I thought, trying to keep it all straight and not let my mind wander. I had to stay calm.

If I didn't I might be too late.

Chapter Twenty-Eight

Billie

I widened my legs a little, my phone tucked beneath them. I still had it in my hand when Sinclair grabbed me and managed to keep it concealed even when I climbed between the front two seats to sit beside him.

A glance down and the screen was black, but I hoped to God the call to LJ had gone through.

Sinclair had been navigating the road when I hit my recent contacts. LJ had been the last person I'd spoken to so it'd been easy. I'd touched the screen, then shoved the thing between my legs. I couldn't hear anything on the other end with all the bumps in the woods, but the moment Sinclair got us away from the wooded trail to the dirt paths, there'd been nothing but silence. LJ could be on the line still as we sat, but I had no way of knowing it.

I swallowed, a sticky knot in my throat. Sinclair was horrifying with his appearance, a shell of himself. A shadow darkened beneath each eye, and showers seemed to have been a thing of the past. My lips parted. "Sinclair…"

"I told you to shut the fuck up, Billie," he gritted, and his hands working the wheel, I'd definitely seen this inside him. He'd snapped at me quite a few times in our relationship. But even *this* I hadn't guessed. Even with the signs of his stalking. He'd been mad, yes, but not crazy mad. His jaw worked. "Haven't you done enough? I've lost everything because of you."

"What do you mean?"

He actually laughed, the dark tone shooting a

chill directly down my spine. My hands curled at my sides as I attempted to keep my panic inside and my legs completely apart for my phone. He grunted. "You and fucking Lance Johnson." His gaze dragged down my body. "He's obviously obsessed with you."

Him obsessed with me? What the hell? "Sinclair, I have no idea—"

"Of course, you don't. You're daft as a fucking doorknob. Meanwhile, you rip through people's lives without any fucks given. You *ruin* everything. Everything…"

He rounded a turn too fast, and up here, there was little to no traction.

I gripped the door. "Stop! You're going to tip us over. The turn is too tight on this road."

I shouted everything I saw, tried at least. Even still, I had no idea if what I was doing or saying was falling on deaf ears.

Meanwhile, Sinclair was shooting down the dirt hills of the Grey Woods at top speeds when they maybe allowed for fifteen miles per hour. We'd only seen one car up here, but the way he was moving, he'd have us out of the woods and on the main roads.

God only knew where else after that.

I didn't know where we'd go then, so scared as I closed my eyes, and Sinclair merely laughed in my direction.

"You're scared of me?" A dry chuckle. He hit his chest so hard I thought he'd stop his heart. "I'm the victim here. *Me*. My dad has put me on leave. I've lost everything."

"Why would he do that?" I gripped my chair, trying to sound calm. Trying to sound *soothing* so he'd keep talking and not do something even crazier than he already was.

"Because of that guy at the party." Sinclair shook his head, his knuckles white on the wheel. "I ghosted that guy, and he got pissed and put a video up on social media. A video of him and me together."

My mouth parted.

"The whole fucking office saw it!" Sinclair slammed his hand on the wheel, the sound blasting into my heart. "My dad saw it, and he told me he wanted nothing to do with me. He put me on leave for show, but it's over. It's over. I'm dead to him."

My swallow hard, I sat up. "If your dad is like that, that's on him, Sinclair. It's okay—"

"It's not okay! No!" He shoved his hand into his hair. "I wouldn't even have met that guy if it wasn't for you. You and that fucking asshole Lance Johnson."

He was taking no responsibility for his own actions, things he'd done like cheat on me. I sympathized for him, yes, but I couldn't give him any more than that. He'd acted on his own. He'd chosen to go behind my back.

Even still, I was dealing with a new Sinclair. One who wasn't thinking straight at all.

After all, he had snatched me.

I wiggled in my seat, trying to keep the phone from being obstructed. "Your dad's the problem. Not you."

"No, you're the problem." A dry laugh fell from his lips, his tone so cold. "I loved you, but you threw it all away. You threw me away. I could have made you happy. I loved you!"

"Sinclair—"

"I wanted you, Billie!" He took my hand,

placing it on his chest. A shake of his head, and his tears finally fell. "I could have made you happy. Not that piece of shit Johnson. You know he's a drug dealer? Some of the shit he's into and who he works for?" He hit his head back against the seat, then snarled. "You know, you were in hiding because he's a piece of shit, right? He put you in danger."

I blinked. "How did you know that? How did you even find me?"

"I'm a lawyer, Billie. I have friends at the DA's office." He threw my hand, almost disgusted. He faced the road. "People talk over beers. They were going on about this girl in hiding and her association with this Lance Johnson. Lance goddamn Johnson."

A growl and his foot accelerated on the gas.

I screamed, and he wheeled us off the dirt path and onto the main road. So quick he darted toward a semitruck on the other side.

I grabbed the wheel, jerking us back.

The semi passed us with a honk, and once clear, Sinclair shoved me off the wheel so hard my head hit the window.

Groaning, I dragged my head off the glass and when I faced Sinclair, his eyes were no longer on me.

Wild, they darted toward the floor of the van, my phone there.

In seconds, he reached for me, seeking the device, and I clawed at him, digging my nails into his skin.

A roar and he punched me in the face, my jaw searing. He worked around my legs for the phone, and I forced my head up, seeing the crosswalk. I angled down. "We're coming up on the intersection of Ivy Lane and Robin Road. Hurry—"

A fist to my jaw again, my teeth lodging into my tongue so hard I tasted blood.

I moaned, and finally getting the phone, Sinclair opened the window. I had just enough time to see the screen flash with LJ's name before Sinclair threw it outside.

"You're going to pay for that, you stupid bitch," he seethed, claw marks on the side of his face. I guessed I'd gotten him a little, the welts deep. He wet his lips. "You're going to fucking pay for that. You could have had me, and you called him!"

His foot accelerated the van again, toward a tree this time, and I screamed, reaching for him, but he held me back.

He had a full hand around my neck, cutting off my air supply, and I closed my eyes, not sure if it was from his hold or fear.

I braced myself for impact and went flying when it hit.

Sinclair's hand left my neck with a jolt, and strapped in, I hit the side of the door.

The wind instantly knocked out of me, my right impacted but not my front. The airbag exploded in my face, my screams radiating through the air as the van scraped off the road and came to a stop in a shallow ditch.

No sounds then, my head heavy and weighted. Dragging it up, I glanced over to the left side. Sinclair's airbag had also gone off, but he was pinned between that and his door. The windshield had exploded and he had a piece of glass shoved so far into his skull blood seeped over his closed eyes.

My stomach rolled, and I clawed at the seat belt until I got it off. I fought around the airbag to get out of the door, and the moment I did, I fell into a hard chest.

"Billie, oh my God!"

Shaking, LJ grappled me to his chest, so hard I thought he'd fuse me to him.

The tears filled my eyes instantly, gasping for him. "You're here."

"Yeah. Holy fuck." He kissed my hair; over and over, he kissed me. Hands framing my face, he studied me. "Are you okay? God, baby. I didn't know what to do. I saw him going for that tree, and I panicked."

To the side, Sinclair wasn't moving, but behind him a familiar car sat on the other side. It'd crashed into us. LJ had *crashed* into us and managed to stop him.

LJ spoke wildly in front of me, and I missed most of it until he hunkered down, running his fingers through my hair. "Thank God for your dad."

"My dad?"

He nodded. "He knew these woods. Told me where to go. He was right beside me the whole time. We drove here together."

Something in my heart stopped just then, something made me look for my dad who *wasn't* with him. LJ said he'd been with him, but he wasn't now.

Until he was.

Right behind LJ, he stood, so much fear and raw terror in his eyes I felt it myself. His bright hair was swept, his fists clenching like he wanted to do something but couldn't. Like he wanted to come over, but felt he couldn't. His mouth opened. "Billie…"

That word broke me, my tears overflowing a dam, and LJ let go and allowed me to go to my dad.

I *ran* to him, literally in his arms, and he gathered me up like I was his little girl. I was his little girl, a familiar home in his arms.

"Billie…" He felt that too, had to have. Emotion lined his voice as he grappled me back and lifted me off the ground. He covered my head. "I was so scared, sweetheart. I was so scared."

"It's okay, Daddy. I'm okay."

I was okay, okay because of him and LJ.

LJ stood off to the side, smiling at us as the streets suddenly filled with flashing lights and sirens. Squad cars came from everywhere, the road a cluster and out of one came, Niko.

"Queenie!" He ran in my direction, ran for me, but LJ held him back. My guy brought his buddy under his arm, staring at me and my dad, and I closed my eyes.

"I'm okay, Dad," I said, my dad's tears sounding in my own ears. "We're okay."

"We are, Billie," he gasped. "We are."

I finally felt we were, at least we would be. He returned me to the ground, but I wouldn't let him go.

I found LJ's hand then, and he let me have it as I hugged my dad again. I kept them both with me, needed them both in that moment. They'd saved me.

"Everything's going to be all right now," Daddy said, over and over in my ear. "You're okay now."

I hugged him, squeezing LJ's hand. Truth be told, I didn't know what would happen after this moment. I didn't know where my dad and I would go from here, but I did know I needed him right then. I needed to be my daddy's little girl for just a second, and it felt so good being in his arms again. I couldn't let go of that feeling once I had it, I didn't want to. It mended my soul.

And made me finally feel whole again.

Epilogue

LJ

I stared at my girlfriend from across the dance floor, smiling as I lounged against a high-top table. Her dad took her hand. But even donned in a fancy tuxedo, he couldn't steal the show away from his daughter.

The shimmering black of Billie's evening gown glistened across the dance floor as Mr. Coventry tugged his daughter over to him. The material flared off those full hips, hugged her perfect breasts, but the kicker was what she wore around her neck.

My Court ring sat right there between the swell of her breasts, reflecting in the light of the ballroom, and I think it really all hit me then. Not that I'd given it to her, a symbol of my past, but that she was with me. That I'd managed to keep her.

That's what got me.

I released her for this dance with her father, the father-daughter dance. It'd been her dad's idea to do this at his wedding tonight instead of the mother-son dance. He'd run it past Billie, of course, before he added it to the list of the reception dances, and Billie, she'd been more than willing to oblige.

My girl had been connecting so much with her dad lately, letting him in. She'd actually been a part of the wedding a bit when Mr. Coventry exchanged vows with his new spouse, Clarise, who also stood across the dance floor.

The woman in a cream-colored ballgown, she stared on, nothing but pride and smiles upon watching her new husband and stepdaughter. I wasn't too much in the knowledge of how Billie was dealing with that, a woman half her dad's age marrying her dad. Especially considering the circumstances in which the union had happened, but I did know my girlfriend was at peace with her dad's decisions. Billie had even flown down early with me for the wedding, the reception and ceremony in a beach house off the shores of Miami. The whole thing had been lit, and Billie'd had the time of her life. She'd *enjoyed* herself and let herself be a part of all this.

Currently, she beamed up at her father, the two of them in their own conversation as they danced in front of everyone.

I couldn't seem to steal her away from her dad these days back home in the Midwest. She spent a lot of time with him this summer. I think something about that day when her douche ex snatched her triggered something within her. Things weren't so simple for her anymore, her priorities changing, and I think everyone saw it that day. She'd burst into tears upon seeing her dad, like she needed him.

I think she really had.

I set my drink down as I thought about that day. It'd been a day of ruin, and it'd taken me basically all goddamn summer not to be leaping for joy that her asswipe of an ex was behind bars and couldn't darken my girl's life anymore.

Yeah, he'd made it out of the crash and he must have had angels on his side. He'd suffered some pretty good trauma to the head, but he'd made it out okay. He'd been swiftly arrested after his recovery for kidnapping and attempted murder and if I never saw that guy again, it'd be too soon. Billie's dad had taken care of that part, put Sinclair behind bars himself.

It was better that than what I'd do to him if he was out in the streets.

It took Billie to ease me back from relishing in her ex's lock up, not to celebrate the fact but empathize. The guy'd seemed plagued with some heavy shit, and in the end, I accepted that was what his madness had been about. I was still grateful he wasn't around to hurt Billie anymore, behind bars and unable to hurt anyone else, but I no longer celebrated what ended up happening to him.

I guessed I was at peace too.

A lot of that was going around these days, Billie and her dad. Billie and *her mom*. The dress Billie wore tonight ended up being made by her, something I guessed the woman used to do on the side before she'd gotten married to Billie's dad. These days, Genevieve was taking it up again, and Billie said her mom was actually designing a gown now for a princess in Greece to wear at her wedding.

It seemed a lot of good things were happening for Billie and her family, and for Billie, I knew her therapy had been helping. After all that shit with Sinclair, she'd started seeing someone again. Even had a few sessions with her mom. I think that had been helping the both of them tremendously, and from what I gathered, Billie and her dad were considering some sessions as well after school started back up. What's crazy was *he'd* been pushing for it. At least, that was what she told me.

It made me tremendously happy her family was coming together. I was proof it didn't always work out that way, and though I wished I'd had my perfect family unit, I wouldn't change what my mom, my sisters and I had. We were our own family unit, our own slice of chaos and love, and I couldn't get enough.

It'd been all I could do to convince my mom to even let me finish school after I did break down and tell her what happened with the Marvellis. Not to mention, how fucking livid she'd been when I told her how I'd earned the cash I'd sent her and my sisters.

Yeah, I'd had to spill all that too. Mom told me I never had to do such things to help them, and though I let her think that, I'd do whatever I had to again. They were my family. They were my everything.

An extension of that out there on the dance floor now, I braced myself to move in and relieve Billie from her dad once the father-daughter song stopped. Her dad had his time, and now, it was mine.

My gaze cut away from the floor to the exit doors when they opened, and seeing who arrived, my smile rerouted for a second. The fucker actually made it, my buddy Jax.

Better late than never.

His ass had been invited to attend since he told me the wedding coincided with his arrival to the state. He was moving down here for school. Fresh off the plane actually. I told him he could get himself settled. I'd only be here for a weekend, but since he was coming down anyway, he'd said he wanted to catch me. Because he had, I'd made sure he got an invitation.

After all, I knew the daughter of the groom.

His gait heavy, Jax traveled across the room in a dark suit, his head full of hair, which was different for him. In high school, he used to buzz it, but no more. With some length, his brown hair feathered with a wave. In fact, if he grew that shit out the way mine had been in high school, I bet it'd be curly. Currently, he had his styled back a little, and catching me, he lifted a hand.

I returned, waving him to join me by my high-top. I wore a gray suit tonight, easy to find because I had started growing out my hair again. I wore it over my shoulders, slapping my buddy's hand when he joined me at the high top.

"Took you long enough. Shit," I jostled, bringing him into a hug. I slapped his back. "Your flight okay?"

I pegged him crazy for transferring from the Midwest for college his senior year, but from how it sounded, the whole thing had been his dad's idea. The guy had been bugging him to hell, I guess, to reconnect with him, something he'd managed to convince him of now.

Upon sliding away, Jax pounded my fist, then snapped his fingers with me. "All good. And I'm fucking here. Ain't that good enough?"

Bumping laughter, I smirked. I started to give him hell for missing the entire ceremony, but the music changed.

The dance floor opened up, the tempo changing. The father-daughter dance concluded, everyone else gathered on the floor. I looked for Billie in the shuffle, and catching her, I smiled.

She'd moved into another dance with her father, the pair shimmying, and I laughed, making Jax smile in that direction.

"I see your girl's out there," he stated, having met her already. I'd brought Billie home a few times this summer, mostly to officially meet my mom and the rest of my sisters. She'd, of course, met my boys too, but her wearing my ring around her neck was a new development. Jax's lips parted. "And she's wearing your ring."

Not surprised he noticed that, I waggled my eyebrows. Our buddy Royal had actually started the tradition. He'd given his fiance December his ring. She wore it around her neck, and Knight's girlfriend, Greer, the same when he gave it to her last semester. It was just something I guess our little circle did.

Nodding, I tapped Jax's arm. "Wanna get a drink? Looks like my girl'll be a little bit."

And that was completely fine with me, totally happy for her and this openness she was experiencing. I wanted nothing but the best for her and would give her anything she wanted if she'd only ask.

How I'd become this person I didn't know, but I had to say, I liked this side of myself. It felt more free, more complete.

Jax and I got a couple beers at the open bar, and after, we stood at another high-top table. This was still well within view of the dance floor, well within view of my girl and that shimmering gown hugging her full ass. Upon basically seeing me drooling in her direction, my buddy nudged me.

He chuckled. "Never thought it'd happen to you."

"What?"

"Being in *love*," he jostled, his elbow in my side. "Hope that shit's not catching. I really don't have time for that lovey-dovey bullshit."

"Well, I got news for you, bro. It's not really a

choice once it happens." I clinked our bottles. "Just kinda does."

He rolled his eyes, the first to lay into me when I'd first texted I had a girlfriend.

I'd gotten *reamed* in that entire group text, and a whole lot of "I told you sos" from Knight and Royal, the fuckers. Jax had given his fair bit of jostling too, and I couldn't wait for the day he'd be eating his fucking words. That shit just happened, and once it did, good luck getting away from it.

"Won't happen to me. At least, not now." He drew off his beer, a curled smile on his lips when he lowered it. "Got other priorities these days."

"I'll bet. You excited to start classes? Meet your new roommates?" I knew he'd chosen to live on campus instead of getting his own apartment. He was going to Bay Cove University in the fall.

"Quite." His brow jumped before he drank more of his beer. "It's sure to be a good-ass time."

"For sure, and hey, you'll get to meet your step-family. Your stepmom and stepsister?" I stated, knowing he had those and for a while now. I mean, *a while.*

After Jax's dad had left the picture when he'd been a kid, the guy had gotten remarried within months. This marriage ultimately resulted in a kid and new mom, a step-family that Jax had managed to never meet either of until now.

He'd literally had zero relationship with his dad, which was why we'd all been surprised to hear him *want* to come down here for school. In fact, the decision had been so sudden it'd been almost alarming, dizzying even.

At the mention of his steps, Jax's smile

widened. "I sure will. Dad and stepmom are out of town, but they're supposed to be back tomorrow. Dear old stepsister should be at home, though. Plan on stopping by after this."

"You excited?"

"Ecstatic." He panned, something dark glinting his green eyes I didn't understand. "I got some plans for her. Plans for my dad. It's going to be a riot."

A chuckle as he picked up his beer again and with a sigh, I scrubbed my hand into my hair. "I thought you were coming down here to connect with your dad, man. Not work some 'plans' or some shit."

His eye twitched like I'd said something blasphemous.

I shook my head. "Seriously, bro. I'd use this opportunity to fix the bullshit with your dad. Not make it worse."

"Because you'd know so much about reconnecting with asshole fathers?" he cut, but couldn't phase me. I'd long gotten over the woes of my own asshole father. He'd left when I was so young I barely remembered his ass, and all this aggression with Jax now obviously came from somewhere.

Being one of his best friends, I knew this attitude stemmed from basically years of hurt. His dad could pretty much win the award for absent father. The guy literally hadn't tried to connect with Jax until he'd turned eighteen, and even then, the attempts had been few and far between since. Even still, if the guy was trying to reach out now, be better and get to know him…

Jax was right at the end of the day, though. I

didn't know much about this shit; it was his own journey. It may not be how I'd deal if it was the other way around, but I had no right to tell him what to do, not my place.

I raised my hand. "I'm not saying you have to forgive your dad. Fuck. You know what? Fuck him. But I am saying try to find some peace. And you do that for you, buddy. Not him."

I'd like to say I saw some consideration behind his eyes, but that'd be a bald-faced lie. Whatever he was doing, he'd obviously made up his mind, and I could only hope he'd make the right decisions about his life in the end.

Jax was generally a pretty happy-go-lucky guy, but this dude standing in front of me now looked seriously fucking plagued. I'd hate to see some of that ease and love for life bleed away from a situation that wasn't his fault. It was on his dad for leaving his family, leaving him.

We chatted for a few more moments before the air changed, and I was clouded with honeysuckle, my sexy-as-fuck girlfriend pushing her soft curves up on me. She'd surprised me from the back, her arms looping around my waist.

Turning within them, I brought her in, caging her face and sealing our lips.

She moaned beneath my mouth, melting underneath me as my tongue flicked out to taste hers.

A throat cleared beside us.

I rolled my eyes but did let go of Billie enough for Jax to say hi to her. Being the welcoming girlfriend she was, she embraced him, the girl fitting right into my world. My buddies weren't just my friends but brothers, family.

"Nice to see you again," she said.

He extended her out. "Same. And you look…" A whistle. "Damn gorgeous—"

"All right, buddy." I dropped an arm across *my* girl's shoulders. "You got a bridesmaid to find or…"

"Sure." A chuckle from him and a shake to Billie's head. Jax bumped my fist. "Get at you later."

"You better."

A two-fingered salute and he disappeared into the crowd. He'd probably be leaving with a couple women tonight, knowing him, or maybe he'd call it a night since he said he was going to meet his stepsister.

Wishing him luck with that and the situation, I asked my girl for a dance. She joined me on the dance floor, and I tucked her into me.

We danced close, this girl my air and every breath. She hugged her pillow-soft body against me, and I drank her in.

"You guys were talking for a long time," she said, lifting her head. Obviously, her attention had been on me and what I'd been doing as much as I'd had mine on her earlier.

I spun her before dancing her back to me. "He's just dealing with some shit. Stuff with his dad. His left him too when he was young. Jax is here now to try and reconnect with him." I'd told Billie Jax was moving down here but hadn't told her why. I frowned. "I hope he can be at peace with him. Take advantage of it like you did with your dad."

Her cheek pressed against my chest in that moment, looking at her dad and new stepmom across the dance floor. The pair looked at us too in their dance, her dad waving at her. He winked, and Billie smiled.

Billie faced me. "I'm glad I did. We're far from there, but at least, we're making strides."

She'd made heavy ones, one of the strongest people I knew, male or female.

Her arms fell down around my neck. "How's Dasha doing? She all moved in or…"

Dasha was starting at Woodcreek, and though she was all moved in to the dorms, I grumbled a little at the reference. "Yeah, she is, but she's been seeing a whole lot of Niko. Not really liking that."

They'd actually been… *shudders*… dating, and I couldn't be more livid. She'd come to stay with me for a few weeks over the summer, and I thought I'd lose my shit when I found out they'd been "hanging out" without my knowledge. My buddy had said he'd kept that close to the cuff because he wasn't sure it was going to be a thing.

I grunted. "They've been dating, and I seriously want to rip off his balls and feed them to him. He's too old for her."

"She's nineteen, babe."

"Yeah, and your point? Still too old."

Laughing a little, Billie laced our fingers together. "Niko is a good guy. Your sister is lucky to have him, and you know that."

I did know that as much as I didn't want to admit it.

Niko had done the right thing in the end regarding the Marvellis, protected Billie when I couldn't. He was ride or die, a rare find, and with things working out so well with his mom's treatments lately, he actually did have the time to fully invest in a relationship with my sister.

I supposed she could do worse, and like Billie could see my thoughts, she grinned, kissing me.

Her full, fuckable lips took me to my perfect place, a place with only her and me and no one else.

My arms fell around her, and when I hugged her to me, I felt impulsive. "We should move in together."

She stopped the dance, her eyes curious. I had to say, I wasn't surprised. She'd already moved into her new apartment for the new year, and though she'd spent more time at my place with me than there, the subject of moving in together hadn't really been discussed.

Her lashes fluttered. "Are you serious?"

I pinched her chin. "Why not? Niko has been talking about wanting to move out." I drew next to her ear. "He's tired of *hearing* us."

We literally did it everywhere, no surface untouched, and that was bothering my buddy more and more these days. He'd actually walked in on us once in the shower, said it "scarred him for life."

We'd ignored his ass and finished as he'd slammed the door. When I was with Billie, no one else was in the goddamn room.

Billie's cheeks shot up 195 degrees in color. She braced my arms. "Can I redecorate? No offense, babe. But your house looks like a dude's."

She could do whatever she wanted as long as she kept calling me hers.

Swinging her around, I cemented the decision with a kiss. A move-in was only the beginning for us, and if the next wedding we attended could be ours, I wouldn't mind that. She kept me whole, made me free, and I'd never be able to thank her enough for that. I loved her down to my fucking toes. She was mine…

And I was so happy to be hers.

Printed in Great Britain
by Amazon